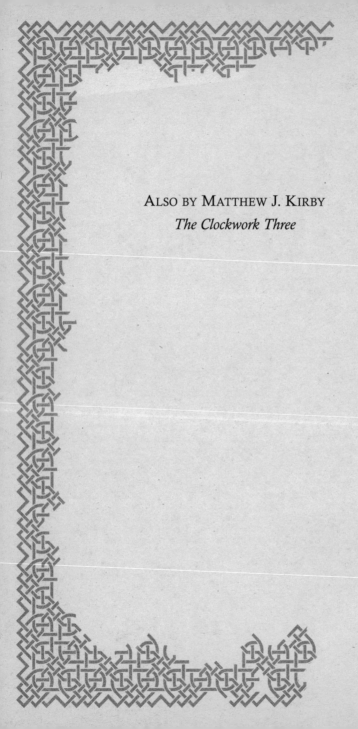

ALSO BY MATTHEW J. KIRBY
The Clockwork Three

MATTHEW J. KIRBY

SCHOLASTIC INC.

This book was originally published in hardcover by Scholastic Press in 2011.

ISBN 978-0-545-27425-8

12 11 10 9 8 7   16 17 18/0

The text type was set in Calisto MT Regular.
The display type was set in BubbaLove Bold.
Book design by Kristina Iulo
and Elizabeth Parisi

Printed in the U.S.A. 40
This edition first printing, February 2013

FOR AZURE

TABLE OF CONTENTS

Listen to me. For I have many stories to tell. . . .

ICE

The fjord is freezing over. I watch it from the edge of the cliff near our hall, and each day the ice claims more of the narrow winding of ocean. It squeezes out the waves and the blue-black water, while it squeezes us in. Just as Father intended it to. Winter is here to wall us up, to bury us in snow and keep us safe.

Today, there is a cold wind that bears no other smell but the ghostly scent of frost. I feel it through my furs and woolen dress, down to my skin. My younger brother, Harald, stands beside me, watching the cloud of his own breath.

"Do you think they will come today, Solveig?" he asks me.

"They will arrive soon," I say. "Father said they would."

"I hope so." He turns to walk off. "The larder is nearly empty." And he whistles.

Harald is a stubborn, willful child, full of confidence and mischief. He reaches the earthen walls that surround our hall, and the warriors who guard the entrance bow to him. He stops to talk with them, and I can see in their affectionate smiles that they love him even now, their future lord. He will make a strong warrior, and a fine king one day, so long as Father still has a kingdom to pass on.

All of the sky looks like a burnt log in the morning hearth, cold, spent, and ashen. Harald is right. I have noticed our helpings at the supper bench getting smaller, how Bera does not cook so great a quantity as she always did at home in Father's hall. We didn't bring enough provisions with us to last a whole winter here. But there was so little time for preparation before Father sent us away and went to war. He promised a boatload of food, clothing, and blankets, but we have seen no ship.

And none today.

And the fjord is freezing over.

I leave the cliff, pass through the gate, and nod to the guards. Inside, the hall is dim and smoky. Asa, my older sister, sits shivering near the fire in the center of the room. She looks up for a moment when I enter, her eyes and cheeks red, and looks away again as though she did not see me. She does not eat much, and does not sleep much, and never comes outside with me or Harald anymore. I miss the way it used to be between us. I do not know where her joy has gone, but her beauty remains, her skin like new cream, her golden hair.

I wish that I had her grace, but I am plain, and Father's eyes do not shine with pride when he looks on me. I would gladly go to war, bearing spear and shield beside my king, were I to have the strength I see in Harald. But Father does not laugh and boast of me the way he does his son and heir.

I am only Solveig.

We have been here for several weeks, having left our home at the end of harvest-time just as the farmers were bringing in the last of the barley and wheat and butchering the livestock too weak to survive the winter. We will miss the celebration for Winter Nights, something Harald has complained about loudly, so I told him stories of the Wild Hunt as we sat by the fire and ate our cheese curd drizzled with honey.

But in the span of these last few weeks, we've fallen into a kind of rhythm, whether we want to or not, and I have taken to helping out around the steading, including the milking of Hilda, our one goat.

Harald leans against the cowshed's doorpost, rolling a bit of straw between his teeth as he watches me. Hilda casts me a defeated glance as I wring what milk I can from her droopy teat. She is the only livestock we managed to bring with us, and she is drying up. We did not bring enough food for her, either. During the day, she wanders the yard or lies in the shed we use as a byre, but at night she sleeps in the hall near the hearth, as we have no other animals to keep her warm.

Sometimes, when Asa's sleep is restless, I leave the bedcloset and lie next to Hilda, my cheek against her winter coat.

"Why are you doing servants' work?" Harald asks.

A strand of hair crosses my face, and I blow it away. "Bera and her son have enough to do. Besides, it does me good." I tug a little too hard on Hilda, and she shies away from me. "You could stand to take on a share of the chores as well."

Harald laughs his easy laugh. "Have you not seen me practicing with the guards every day?"

"Will your wooden sword feed us, then?"

"No." He holds the needle of straw before him like a blade. "But if father's enemies find us, you'll all be glad I learned to fight."

He slashes the air, and I shake my head, grinning. "Perhaps we will."

Harald parries and stabs a few more times, and then chuckles at himself. Then he is silent a moment. "Perhaps I should help out more with the chores. Maybe go fishing with Ole. Things are different here."

I give up on Hilda's udder and stand with the nearly empty bucket. I don't know what we'll do without milk for sour skyr, curd, and cheese. We rely on those to see us through the winter. The nanny goat shakes her head, relieved, and I turn away from the thought that we may have to slaughter her for meat.

"Things are very different here," I say. "I'm going to take this to Bera."

He steps aside and lets me pass through the door. The milk rolls around the bottom of the bucket as I cross the yard. Our hall is situated in the wedge at the end of the fjord, flanked by tall mountains to the north and south. The hills to the south are covered in soft pine, while the rocky crags to the north march above us like a procession of trolls, a party out hunting for human daughters to carry away in the night as stolen brides.

I find Bera in the hall, at the hearth, stirring a stew. Her hips are broad, her gray hair braided and gathered in a thick knot at the base of her neck. She has served my father since I was a child, and raised me after my mother died giving birth to Harald.

She hears me approach. "Hilda still giving us anything?"

"Not for much longer," I say.

I hand her the bucket and she peers at its contents. "Hmph. But at least the old goat tries." She glances at Asa, who lies on a bench against the wall, staring at the ceiling.

"Is there anything else I can help with?" I ask.

"Raudi's trying to dig the last of the carrots out of the ground."

"I can help with that."

"Ground is near frozen."

"I know," I say, and leave Bera cooking in the hall. Asa doesn't move, and in a moment of frustration with her, I shut the hall doors a little too hard behind me.

The feel of coming snow waits in the air like the inhale before a sigh. I walk around to the vegetable patches in back, the remnants left from the harvest ruined with frost. Raudi kneels on the hard ground, hacking with a pick. A few frozen carrots, lumpy and misshapen from too much time in the ground, lie in a basket by his side. They're the same rusty color as his hair.

I drop down beside him. "Can I help?"

He keeps digging.

"Raudi?"

"I suppose."

I grab another pick and choose a spot farther down the row of browned tufts. We work in silence, and within a few minutes, I feel a rim of sweat on my brow in spite of the cold. Raudi and I used to be friends, though he is a winter older than me. We often swam and ran and played together, but then his older brother died in battle, and Raudi decided that he needed to spend his time with boys and men. I tried to understand. It is the way of things. And even though he started walking taller and talking louder, we still smiled at each other as we passed in the yard.

But ever since we came here, he has grown aloof and curt with me. Never openly disrespectful, but never friendly. I feel his absence like a dull ache, even though he's right here, working only a few feet away from me.

My carrots come out of the earth looking like half people, with legs and arms and other appendages. After we've pulled up the last of them, we rise to our feet and take them to the larder, a shed with a turf roof, built mostly underground. We set the carrots in the darkness next to the few turnips and onions, and return to the hall for the night meal.

Harald is already there, waiting with his wooden bowl and bone spoon. Old Ole sits next to him, mending a fishing net. Bera sings a song over the kettle as Raudi and I take our places. Moments later, our three warriors march into the hall. Two of them, Egill and Gunnarr, I do not know well, but I know the kindest and handsomest. His name is Per. The three of them sit down at a slight distance the way they always do, outside the circle of family and servants. Harald would like to sit with them, I am sure, but chooses to remain with us. Raudi takes a bench between the warriors and the rest of us, not really sitting with either group. Asa rises and drifts across the room to her seat near me, and we're all gathered. All the members of our household.

We eat the stew of fish and pork, with golden pearls of fat glistening over the surface, and it is delicious because Bera made it. But there isn't much of it, and we're all wiping out our bowls with stale bread before long. After that, the men drink some ale, and we sit together in the descending night.

A banging at the door draws Gunnarr, the gray-haired oldest soldier, from his bench. "Blasted goat," he mutters. When he opens the door, Hilda prances into the hall. She shakes her horns, bleats, and then settles down in the straw on the floor. But then she looks at me, and gets up and comes over to lie down at my feet. I like that she has come to prefer me, and I smile.

Per clears his throat. "The fjord will be closed off before long." He looks around the room, his blond hair and dark blue eyes soaking up some of the firelight.

No one says anything at first.

"What is your point?" Ole asks without looking up from his net. He is a thrall, a slave captured in war many years before I was born. He has seen much of the world, or claims to, and has come to love my father as his king.

"Ships won't be able to reach us," Per says.

"They'll come before it closes," Ole says. He has been with us for so long, he can say things that other thralls can't.

Per glances toward Asa, and she looks back at him, and something passes between them. Some silent communication, and I wonder what it means. I have always liked Per. As the second daughter, and the plain one, most of the time I feel like people only notice me and bow because they have to. But not with Per. When he bows to me, and smiles his broad smile, I feel that he really sees me, and that he means it.

Raudi leans toward Per. "How soon until it freezes over, do you think?"

"Hard to know," he says. "A week. Two, maybe."

"They'll come," Ole says again.

Raudi looks at his lap and mumbles, "We shouldn't even be here."

"Silence," Bera says to her son.

And then it occurs to me, the reason for Raudi's ill temper. He blames my family. If it wasn't for us, he and his mother would be safe at home. But because of us, they are both imprisoned in this forgotten place, threatened with starvation or worse if we're found by my father's enemies. So he broods over the hot coals in the hearth as if they are the embers of his anger, and they are glowing red. I want back the boy I knew.

"I'm sorry, Raudi," I say, but he only stares.

A week passes, and the fjord is still open, barely. From the vantage of the cliff, the way inward from the sea is but a stray black thread fallen from a loom. So long as it stays that way, Ole can fish without having to break through the ice.

He wants to slaughter Hilda, but I won't let him, even though she eats our food without giving a single drop of milk in return. I have grown fond of her, and only when we are starving, and when there are no fish left in the sea, will I let Ole take his knife to her throat. I know that is foolish and wrong of me.

But a boat *will* come.

Harald and Per are sparring in the yard, and Harald holds a wooden shield. The day is overcast and dim, our hours with the sun diminishing with the season. Snow drifts through the air like dust, landing cold on my cheeks and refusing to settle to the ground, which is still bare and frozen. Harald shifts from foot to foot as Per waves a blade.

"Don't try to stop the blow directly," the warrior says. "That'll shatter the shield and take your arm."

"Then what should I do?" Harald asks.

"You need to move with the strike, use the shield to glance it away from you."

He brings the sword down slowly enough for Harald to get his shield under it.

"Which way am I striking?" Per asks.

Harald grunts. "To the left."

"Then sweep my blade to the left."

Harald heaves the shield to the side, and with it Per's sword point.

"Good." Per steps back. "Again. Faster, my little prince."

"I'm not little."

Per laughs, and when he laughs it's from his belly. He is tall and strong, his hair pulled back with a bit of yarn, his leather armor oiled and well kept. In spite of his reputation for prowess in war, there is a mirth about him when he is at home. Not like some warriors. Some men never really leave the battlefield, and if they do, they bring the ghosts of the dead back with them. Like Father when he falls into one of his black moods.

I notice Asa peering from the doorway. Her face is half-shadowed, but she seems to be following Per with her eyes. She sees me watching her, and ducks back into the hall.

"Good, little prince. Again." A crack and a ringing as Per strikes Harald's shield.

"I'm not little!"

I smile and look up, above and beyond our steading, where a winding ravine joins the north and south mountains like a ragged battle scar poorly stitched. And up high in the clouds, deep in the crook of that scar, there is a glacier. A massive floe of ice bearing down on us at all times, groaning and cracking under its own weight as though it readies for a charge that will grind us underfoot. This time of year, a little stream of meltwater trickles past our steading on its way to the sea, as cold as water can be without turning to ice. Come summer, the runoff will swell to a torrent, forming a waterfall up among the troll mountains like a long white beard.

Beyond the glacier, there is a pass, frozen and impenetrable until winter's thaw.

"A boat!"

I look to the gate and see Ole hobbling in, waving his arms.

"There's a boat!" he calls.

We all look at one another. Then we rush outside the walls to the cliff. And we see it, a ship sailing the slight crack still open in the ice. Everyone begins to cheer.

Per claps Ole on the back. "You were right, old man."

Ole winks. "Old men usually are."

The ship comes up the fjord, at first a bug skimming the water, its oars moving like legs. But as it draws nearer, and its features become clearer, I turn to Ole in confusion. He and

Per are both scowling, shifting on their feet and casting hesitant glances at each other and the sea. The boat is not a *knarr*, not the cargo ship we expected. It is a *drekar*, a dragon-headed longship. A ship of war.

"Everyone inside the walls," Per says. "Now."

It was on a summer's day when I ran off barefoot into the fields of tall grain. I chased you, Raudi, as the sun set and bronzed the swaying oats. You were much quicker than I. We ran down the rows, ducking and weaving, laughing and teasing, until you decided to play a little prank and went back in without telling me. And I, small and alone, became lost in the field. I wandered, and as the shadows between the rows of grain deepened, I began to cry.

It was then that you, Asa, came looking for me.

"Solveig!" you called. "Where are you hiding?"

"I am not hiding!" I cried. "I am lost!"

You laughed. "You are not lost. Follow my voice. I shall stay where I am until you reach me." And so you said my name, "Solveig, Solveig, Solveig," until I found you.

And I realized that I had not been lost, after all. I had been very near the edge of the field the whole time, within sight of Father's hall, and I realized I could smell the smoke of the hearthfire. But I had felt lost. And it was my sister's voice that had led me back.

Then, Asa, you took my hand. "Come, let's go inside."

CHAPTER 2

THE SKALD

We hurry from the cliff. Per's face has lost all traces of his smile, and I now see the man that others see on the battle-field. His brow rides low, and his jaw and lips tighten. A determined, capable man, and the sight of him awes me and chills me through my furs. He moves with speed and effi-ciency, closing and barring the gate, giving orders to the other two warriors. They climb the wall to stand watch.

"Ole," Per calls. "Get them to the cave."

"Cave?" I ask, afraid, my voice quavering.

"I want to stay," Harald says. "I can fight."

"Nay, young prince," Ole says, wrapping an arm around my brother's shoulder. "You're to stay safe and alive, the way your father intended."

"What cave?" I ask again.

Per turns to Raudi. "Are you better trained with a sword or a spear?"

Raudi stands up tall, and I notice how much he has grown. He stares at Per. He doesn't blink, and he doesn't answer, and I know he is afraid. He is too young to fight, but too old to admit it. My heart falls at the thought of anything happening to him.

"Spear," he finally says.

Per nods, but then Bera comes out of the hall shaking her head. "Asa won't come."

Ole curses, and Bera takes my arm. "Solveig, you need to go in and get your sister."

I shake my head. "I don't think she'll listen to me."

"You must bring her," Ole says.

But I know Asa. I believe she does have some love for me in her heart. She used to show it, and I miss her affection, the bond we shared. But she grew distant in the months before coming here, and now she doesn't speak to me at all. Yet I nod to Bera and agree to try to talk with her.

"Good girl," Bera says. "We'll wait for you, but be quick."

Ole points up into the mountains. "The cave's a place where we can hide you. It's up the ravine, at the base of the glacier."

"I'll hurry," I say, and run inside the hall.

Asa sits on the ground near the hearth, her legs bent, head resting on her knees. I approach her with as much gentleness in my voice as I can, but the urgency in my arms and my legs makes it difficult.

"Sister," I say. "We must go."

She says nothing.

"Asa, please. They are waiting."

"Leave without me," she says.

She must know how ridiculous that sounds. "You know we can't do that. I won't do that." I sit down on the ground next to her.

She turns on me. "Leave!"

Her eyes are wide with anger, more emotion than I have seen from her in weeks, and it surprises me into a moment of silence. Then I whisper, "No. We all go together."

She looks away.

"Why will you not come?"

"It doesn't matter."

I hear pain in her voice, something she is carrying inside, and it hurts me that she hasn't felt able to share it. "It matters to me. It matters to Harald. He needs you."

She looks into my eyes. Hers are cold, watery, and empty, like an ice cave in the spring.

I stand and offer my hand. "I need you. Please come, Asa."

She stares at my hand for a moment, and then she takes it.

I sigh in relief, then lift her to her feet, and we walk from the hall leaning against each other. Out in the yard, the mood has changed. No one is running about, and everyone watches the gate.

16

"We can leave now," I say to Ole.

"It's too late," he says.

I hear voices outside the safety of the steading, and heavy marching. Per stands on the wall, and a moment later he looks down at Asa. In his face, in the creases around his eyes, there are signs of fear, the first I have ever seen in him. And that causes a different kind of chill. He leaps down from the wall.

"Who is out there?" I ask Ole, but the old man ignores me.

The noises grow louder and closer. I hear coughing, deep rumbling voices.

Per positions himself before the gate. He stands tall, hands behind his back. "Open," he commands.

Egill and Gunnarr look at each other, and then follow the order. They lift the bar and pull the doors wide. I hold my breath for a moment, craning my neck to see what waits on the other side.

A moment later, an army of bears and wolves marches through the open gate. *Berserkers*. The sight of them hollows out my stomach with dread and weakens my legs. They are Odin's men. Warriors who refuse armor and go to battle wearing animal skins. Men who fight in a rage with the strength of wild boars, feeling neither fire nor blade. They are all of them giants, the shortest standing almost a head taller than Per. They are my father's personal guard, and they terrify me. They are too untamed and unpredictable. Their presence here is almost as frightening to me as the thought of my father's enemies.

They come forward into the yard as a wall of pelts and beards, axes and shields, but Per stands his ground before them.

"Halt," he says, and they do.

One of them steps forward. He wears the fur of an enormous brown bear, the snarling maw over the warrior's head like a helmet. His chest is broad and covered with gray hair, and there is a scar down one of his arms. Across his back is a heavy war hammer I doubt I could even lift. He speaks, and his words tumble like falling boulders.

"Greetings to you, Per."

"Greetings, Hake," Per says.

The mountain nods. "The king has sent us to guard his heir."

Everyone turns to look at Harald.

Per clears his throat. "We do not have enough provisions for you and your men. We were not expecting —"

"We have brought food. And supplies," the berserker says.

Per is silent. He does not blink, and then he swallows. "The hall is not large enough —"

"It will do."

"We do not need you to protect the king's son."

"You refuse us?" Hake takes another step forward. "Who are you?" He looks over Per's head at all of us standing back. "We are staying. By my king's order."

"So you say," Per says, "but I am the one who —"

"If I may," someone says from behind the berserkers. The

giants look down as Alric, my father's skald, slides out from among them. Per appears surprised, as am I, to see Alric with them. The skald is the poet of the living past, bearer of our ancestors' history, their tales of sacrifice and valor. He approaches the two men, and Hake narrows his eyes.

"I believe, Captain," Alric says, "that Per would simply like some assurance that the presence of your warriors will not disrupt this steading. And, Per, it would be wise to acknowledge the authority of your king's war chief."

Alric looks back and forth between them, the expression on his face mild and unconcerned. He is a small man, with a sharp black beard and hair cropped short. Light snow floats around and between the three of them.

"What are you doing here, Alric?" Per asks.

"The king ordered me here."

Hake grunts. "Liar. Coward. You asked to come, even though your place is at your king's side. It is where we all should be, fighting the warlord, Gunnlaug."

Beside me, Raudi swallows.

Alric shrugs. "Can your sword grant immortality? Because my voice can. You would defend the king's body, an honorable endeavor, but I would defend his legend. Which do you think will outlast the other, Captain?"

Hake stares and says nothing.

"What I do," Alric says, "I do best when my body still has breath."

Per regards the skald and then turns to Hake. "Welcome, Captain. I'm sure the king's heir will feel much safer knowing your warriors are here to protect him."

And what about protecting Asa? And me? Do we not matter to these men? Are we not also in danger?

Hake nods. "We will not be a strain or burden. The king sent enough food with us to last this steading through the winter and beyond."

"Let us hope we will not be here beyond winter," Ole says to me.

But now I chew my lip and worry over new thoughts. Why would Father send unnecessary provisions when he needs every resource for his war? And why would he send his most feared and trusted warriors here to protect Harald when he needs them on the battlefield?

It seems there is something my father fears even more. A danger coming our way, though no one has yet spoken of it. Instead of reassuring me, the presence of these berserkers has brought on an even greater apprehension of what's to come.

The evening is spent unloading the ship. Bera stands with her hands on her hips, pointing and ordering, empress of her larder. When the ship's hold is empty, we all retire to the hall for a feast. And unlike meals during the past several weeks, there is plenty of food. The berserkers brought with them pork, salted and smoked; dried stockfish; and a few chickens for fresh eggs. The grain and flour sacks are free of weevils, and there are several pots of amber honey, which might as well be gold for the way Harald's eyes widen when he sees them. But most important, they brought two cows and plenty of hay, so we'll have milk for cheese and skyr, and beef if it becomes necessary to slaughter them.

The crowded hall is filled with smoke, the sour smells of sweat and wet fur, the flicker and shadow of firelight. The berserkers laugh and curse and brag and challenge one another with tongues drowned in mead.

Per, Egill, and Gunnarr do not join them, but stay with the rest of us in a corner of the room. Asa and I huddle together like rabbits, wary of these wolfish invaders. Even Harald is quiet.

Alric moves among the newcomers. He pats their backs and tries to jest with them, but gets scowls in return, and through it all he smiles. Then he moves toward us. Ole slides down his bench to make room, and Alric gives him a grateful nod and sits next to him.

The skald leans forward, hands on his knees. "The price of an army, I suppose, is living with it when you're not at war."

"But we *are* at war," Bera says.

"Not here," Alric says. "The war cannot reach you here, which is why the king chose it."

"If it cannot reach us here, then why send Hake with his men?" Bera asks.

I listen for the answer.

Alric rubs his chin. "An abundance of caution."

I raise an eyebrow at that. My father is not given to anxiety or fears that have no basis. He often seems without emotion at all. When he acts, it is with deliberation and purpose.

"How fares the king?" Ole asks.

"Very well, the last I saw him. Towering as a tree, strong as a rushing river, with eyes of the raven from which no man can hide." Alric pauses. "But the outcome is far from certain."

"Far be it from me to complain," Bera says, "but I notice the king didn't send along another cook. Who is it that'll be feeding all these men?"

Alric nods. "They do eat prodigiously." He leans toward Bera with a conspiratorial hand in front of his mouth. "But I doubt they would notice if you were to simply serve them their food raw."

A crash causes me to jump. Nearby, one of the berserkers has fallen from his bench. The men around him laugh and point at him, and as he gets to his feet, he swings his fist at one of them, which knocks him off balance and to the floor again. This time, he stays there.

Alric laughs out loud, but none of us do.

The skald notices and drops his gaze to the floor. "I have been too long with these men, I think."

But I think it would not matter how long he spent with any-one. The skald seems able to reshape himself into whatever form he wishes. A flattering tongue and a storyteller's flair

22

might mold him to his audience's desires, but I wonder what is there when the audience has left? Does he have a true form underneath all his layers?

Alric is looking at me. I smile and nod, and he lifts his cup toward me.

I want to go to bed, but the berserkers do not. And the night is long.

I wake in the dark to the sound of bleating and a man cursing. I leave the bedcloset and peer out into the hall, where lumps of sleeping warriors cluster around the hearth in the middle of the room. I squint in the dim ember-light and see two glowing eyes peering back at me.

"What's that goat doing in here?" one of the lumps asks.

Hilda bleats again.

"Shh," I say to her, and she comes toward me. Even though she has the two cows for company in the shed now, she has grown used to sleeping in the hall with us. But these new men are strange to her, and since she cannot sleep inside the bedcloset with Asa and me, I settle her down near my door where she will be out of the way. "Good night," I say to her and climb back into bed. I pull the door closed and fall asleep to the sound of the glacier groaning above us.

There are men everywhere.

A week ago, in the span of a single day, our steading went from a household to a garrison. It doesn't help that the fjord has finally frozen over, and we are sealed in with them. There are twenty. Twelve wolves and eight bears, and all of them rough and wild. I do not care to learn their names, and they barely look at me. Perhaps, like Raudi, they resent being sent to a prison when they have done nothing wrong. Well, I resent them, too.

No matter where I go, they are there. Standing at the cliff. Snoring in the hall. Laughing in the yard. They cease speaking with one another when they see me and resume when I move on. I feel unwelcome in a place that is already unwelcoming enough.

I decide to go down to the shore to see if I can find a moment of solitude there, and leave through the gates. The path descends a steep hill through a grove of tall pines. The sweet spice of their fragrance clears my head. We have had our first snowfall, and the trees look black against the fresh white. The snow crunches and creaks under my feet.

The *drekar* has been dragged up on the shore, a feat I can believe of the berserkers. If it had been left in the water, the movement of the ice over the course of winter would have crushed it. The dragon head at the tall prow snarls down at me, and I look away from it.

"An impressive ship, yes?"

I turn, and Alric is sitting on a rock behind me. I can't help but feel nervous around him. He speaks too carefully, his words too well-chosen, and so I never know what he's really thinking.

24

"Yes, it is impressive," I say. "Now I think I know what the Irish feel when they see our people on the horizon, come to invade."

Alric has his mouth open to say something, but doesn't for a moment. "Indeed."

I won't find peace down here with Alric around, so I start for the path.

"Wait, Solveig," Alric says. "Can we talk?"

I have nowhere I truly want to go and can think of no reason to offer for leaving. "I suppose." I sit next to him on a log polished smooth by the sand and the waves, and stare out over the fjord turned still and white between the steep mountains on either side.

"Have you noticed that ice is the only thing that can tame the sea?" Alric asks.

"Perhaps. But is it truly tamed if you can't see what's going on under the surface?"

Alric has his mouth open again, the same speechless expression. "Indeed."

It is an odd thing to be by the water, and yet hear nothing. An occasional crackle, the wind, and that is all.

"I watch you, you know," Alric says. "As you watch others."

I keep my eyes on the ice and squirm a little at the thought of his eyes on me when I wasn't aware of it.

"You are very observant, Solveig. And you are intelligent. You would make a fine skald."

That turns my head. "What?"

Alric holds up two fingers. "Memory and sight are all that is required. Memory and sight. Everything beyond that, a pretty voice and commanding visage, is honey for the curd."

"Sight?" I ask.

"Yes. A skald must watch people. You must recognize the changes in their mood before they become of aware of it themselves. Your father is angry for a day before he ever raises his voice."

"How can you know?" I ask.

"He walks around with his right hand in a fist, as if he holds his sword."

I think about that for a moment, and then I widen my eyes in surprise. "You're right."

"When you know what to look for in your audience, you know what is required. The moment may call for you to entertain, to flatter, to reverence, to encourage, or to soothe. So long as you have learned and can recall the appropriate story, song, or poem, you can deliver it." Again he holds up two fingers. "Memory and sight."

"And you think I have them?"

He nods. "I do."

I swell a little at his praise, though it is tempered by the fact of who it comes from. But I realize I have always liked telling stories. To Harald mostly, and I used to tell stories to Raudi when we were younger. But I never thought of it as being like a skald. My stories have always been light and silly things, a way to fill the cold, long spaces of winter. "Are there many women skalds?"

"Not many, but there are some."

"My father would never allow it."

"Why not? What other purpose does he have for you?"

I snap my gaze back out over the fjord. So still, on the surface.

"I don't know," I say.

In the weeks before slaughtering season, when the whole kingdom took stock of grain and counted flocks and heads of cattle, my uncle, whom I had never met, came to stay.

It was a time of reunion, with feasting and drinking, a time to make men laugh and render Alric's voice raw. My father brought us forth, his children, to boast and proclaim his good fortune. But I held back among the shadows and watched.

"Here is my son, Harald," said Father. "You'll not find a more spirited boy in any hall."

You were but three winters old, Harald. You bent and pulled on the tail of one of the hunting dogs. The hound got up to move away, and you, giggling, tumbled after it. Father and his brother both laughed.

"And this," said Father, "is my daughter Asa."

"She is beautiful," said our uncle. "Much like her mother."

"Very much like," said Father. "It is a source of comfort to me in my grief to see my wife live on through her."

He sat back down then, having forgotten me.

My uncle looked around. "Do you not have another daughter?"

"Oh. Yes, I do," said Father. "Solveig. The quiet one. Where is she?" And he searched the room until he found me hiding. He pulled me forward and placed me before my uncle. "Say hello, Solveig."

"Hello, Uncle," I said.

He nodded to me, and smiled on me with pity. Then he turned to Father. "Well, at least when she speaks, she has a pleasant voice."

My father sighed. "At least she has that."

CHAPTER 3

HILDA

lric was wrong. The berserkers do not like their food raw, and I am the one who has been helping Bera cook these last weeks, while Raudi splits the hearth-logs. And even though there is little time and so much work, Bera still insists on making the meals we prepare respectable.

"Your father knows my cooking," she says to me. "I have a reputation to uphold."

Most days since the warriors came, Asa has rarely left her bedcloset, let alone the hall. She peeks out for meals, and to wash her face, but otherwise hides herself away. Without even knowing what it is, her secret pain has become my pain, and I find I am more patient with her. I only wish that I could reach into that bedcloset to pull her out and help her.

Tonight we've made a thick gravy with turnips and peas and glistening pork fat to pour over dry barley bread. The smells set my stomach talking.

When it is suppertime, the men pile in from wherever they've been. There is a restlessness about them, growing by the day. They do not like being penned in. Arguments break out between them more readily, and they complain about everything. Hake controls it when he is present, but when he is elsewhere, I fear what the berserkers might do. Back home, some berserkers have been known to sack their own villages if they go too long without raiding or war. And I have heard stories of the *berserkergang*, the battle fury, coming upon them without warning, and when it does, neither friend nor foe is safe.

Even Hilda seems to know they are not to be readily trusted. She stays close to me most of the time, and when she gets nervous, she rubs her horns up against my leg, asking me to scratch her ears and reassure her.

We serve the berserkers from the steaming cauldron. They grunt their thank-yous and belch their approval as they dig into their bowls. Bera nods to me, then toward them, satisfied. Per is next in line, and I give him an extra large helping, for which I get a smile and a compliment, the same one every evening that causes me to blush.

"You bring grace to this place, Solveig."

"Thank you, Per."

"Move along now," Bera says. "There's mouths waiting."

"Solveig?"

I jump. Asa has appeared behind me.

"Oh, sister. I didn't hear you." But I am pleased to see her out of the bedcloset.

"I am sorry," she says.

"Would you like some supper tonight?"

She nods, and I serve her. She then takes a seat by herself in a corner, and the men nearby stare at her. Openly. It grits my teeth with anger. Were my father here, they would not dare lift an eye in her direction. But in this frozen place, so far from their king, with ale so strong and walls so close, they forget themselves.

One of them says something to her — I can't hear what — and Asa's gaze drops to her lap. Her neck flushes, and I set my ladle down.

"What is it?" Raudi asks.

"Trouble," Bera says.

The man says something else, and I hear the leer in his tone, but Asa doesn't look up. I know that I should do something to help my sister, but in fear of the berserkers I look away. Then I hear Per's voice.

"You will apologize to the king's daughter," he says. He stands between Asa and the berserker, and his voice is iron-cold. "Now."

The berserker gets to his feet. His hair and beard are long and braided. "I take no orders from you."

Per strikes him, a full blow on the mouth that knocks the berserker backward over the bench and sprawls him on the floor. He feels his lip and then looks at the blood on his hand.

The berserker gets to his feet and is about to draw his sword.

"Halt!" comes a shout that causes me to flinch. Hake steps out of the crowd now gathered around the two men. "Leave that sword where it rests, or I'll take the arm that pulls it free."

The berserker bows his head and drops his arms to his side.

Per stands defiant. "He owes Asa an apology."

Hake looks at Asa. "She deserves one from me. I am sorry, daughter of my king, that I have allowed my men to become so familiar with you. It shall not happen again."

Asa gives a bare nod of her head. "Thank you, Captain."

"You." Hake turns to the berserker. "Outside. I will deliver your punishment personally."

The warrior bows and retreats, followed by Hake. Over the heads of the other berserkers, I see the hall doors open and shut.

Per turns to Asa. "I am sorry as well. I will never leave you alone —"

"I'm all right, Per. They are only words."

"They are words you should never have to hear." He looks at me. "Nor you, Solveig. If any of these men ever show you disrespect, tell me or Hake."

I'm comforted by his desire to protect me. He is different from the others. "Thank you, Per."

I return to the cauldron and pick up my ladle. The gravy is beginning to form a skin.

The next day, the warrior with the braids has a gashed lip, a bruised cheek and eye, and he walks with a slight limp. I should be angry at him and see it as his due, but I feel a little sorry for his pain.

As I watch him cross the yard, Harald comes up beside me.

"I'm bored, Solveig."

"Have you practiced with your sword?"

He shakes his head. "I'm already good with it."

"You could watch the berserkers sparring."

"No. I don't like them very much."

"Well, I don't know what to suggest to you, Harald. Perhaps some chores?"

He kicks the ground. "I knew you were going to say that."

I laugh at him and rustle his hair. "Have you seen the *drekar*?"

"Of course I have."

I put my hand on his back. "Well, let's go look at it again."

We move toward the gate, and I notice someone following us. It is Hake.

"We're just going down to look at your ship," I say.

He nods and continues to follow us.

Harald looks back. "He's always there, everywhere I look."

"He's protecting you."

"I don't need protection."

We drop through the pine trees to the rocky shore, and there is the ship. A layer of frost has formed over the wood, turning the boat into a pale ghost. The dragon prow snarls down at us, and Harald smiles up at it in admiration. I lead him over to the log, and we sit. Hake stands a distance off. I could no more forget he is there than if a giant were standing over my shoulder.

I remember what Alric said to me down here by the water, about being a skald. "Shall I tell you of Sigurd's battle with the dragon Fafnir?" I say to Harald.

"Oh, yes," he says.

So I begin. "Once, Sigurd went to the swordsmith Regin and asked him to fashion a blade. Sigurd needed a sword of legend to carry into battle. Regin made a sword, but Sigurd decided to test it."

Harald sighs and settles against my side.

"Sigurd set a shield on an anvil and struck it with the new sword. The blade shattered in his hands, and he told Regin to make him another and to make it stronger. Regin made another sword, and this time as he worked the forge, he whispered runes into the metal to strengthen it. During this time, Sigurd dreamt of the dragon Fafnir sleeping under the mountain."

"Tell me about Fafnir," Harald says.

"Fafnir crawled through his cave, his scales glittering like mail, his body as long as a company of men marching to war."

Harald tugs on my sleeve. "And his treasure. Tell me about his treasure."

"It was a great hoard of gold and silver and all manner of gems. It was treasure enough to turn a man into a god, and Sigurd dreamt of it piled under the dragon's body and scorching breath, and he coveted its wealth. So Sigurd returned for the second sword, and this time when he smote the shield, the shield broke in two, but the sword bent when it struck the anvil. When Sigurd saw this, he went to his mother and told her of his design."

"What did she do?"

"She gave to him the pieces of Gram, the sword that Odin had given to Sigurd's father, and which had broken in battle upon his father's death. Sigurd took the pieces of Gram to Regin and bade him make a third sword out of them. Regin labored for days at his forge, until the sword was complete. It gleamed brightly, and when Sigurd held it, a flame ran along its edge."

"Then he tested it," Harald said.

"He did," I say. "And what happened next?"

"He smote the shield, and it broke in half, and it cut through the anvil as well."

"It did. And Sigurd took the sword to the lair of the dragon Fafnir. The heath was black and blasted all about the entrance to the great worm's cave. Sigurd entered with his sword, and he battled with Fafnir. The dragon struck with his talons and his teeth and his venom. But the sword forged from Gram cut through the dragon's scales to his heart and killed him."

"And the treasure belonged to Sigurd." Harald strikes the air with his fist.

"Well, that is another story."

"Tell me another."

"Shall I tell you the story of when Sigurd avenged his father's death?"

The eagerness fades from Harald's face. His wide eyes dim, and his shoulders sag a little. "Not that one."

"It's a good story."

"I don't want to hear it," he says, and stands. "And now I've seen the ship. I'm going back up to the hall."

"What is the matter?" I ask.

But he leaves me sitting on the log and starts up the path. Hake looks at me and then follows after Harald.

When I think about it, I should have known that story would upset my brother. He wants to be Sigurd fighting the dragon, not Sigurd grieving the death of his father on the field of battle. Not when our real father is at war. I think Alric was wrong about me. I would not make a good skald, after all.

I stay down by the *drekar* for a while to be alone. On my way back up to the steading, I find a miraculous, frozen stalk of yarrow poking out of the snow. It's one of Hilda's favorite things to eat, so I dig it out of the snow and bring it up to the steading for her. But I can't find her. I ask a few of the berserk-ers, Ole, and the others, but no one has seen her. I am concerned, and later that night when she does not come into the hall to sleep, I begin to panic. I call for her out in the yard, the yellow light spilling over my shoulder from the hall. I spend a long time doing this, until I have no choice but to go back inside. But I don't sleep well, and first thing the next morning, I go looking for her.

I search every shed and outbuilding and find no sign of her. I worry that she wandered out of the steading during the day, and tears come to my eyes when I think that she may have been lost in the forest, frozen or devoured by wolves during the night.

But the guards at the gate swear they never saw her leave. And they would have noticed a goat, they say.

The only place remaining to check is the larder, but I don't see how she could have gotten in there. We keep the door locked and secured to protect against scavengers, even wolves or bears who might find their way into the steading if hungry enough. Bera gives me the key hanging from her brooch, and I go to the storehouse.

At first, everything inside is dark and indistinct. But then my eyes adjust, and I jump when I see a figure in front of me. Then I realize it isn't a man, but something hanging from the ceiling. I reach out my hand to touch it. The thing feels cold and slightly sticky. An animal skinned and hung to age before Bera carves it. But the berserkers brought none with them but cuts of pork, and it is too small to be a deer. Then I see the face and the horns.

"No," I whisper and cover my mouth.

I fly from the larder into the center of the yard. I look around at all these men, these berserkers. I want to scream. Who did it? Who butchered her? But I am helpless. My chest aches. I remember Hilda looking to me from across the darkened hall as she searched for a safe place to settle among these strangers. I remember her bleating.

I slide to the ground and sob, and then I start to pound the frozen earth around me. I tear at the ice and pummel it. I feel nothing inside. I am only my anger and my fists.

There are several people gathered around me now. A moment later, I hear Bera's voice, but not what she says.

Then one of the berserkers clears his throat. "She just started having a fit."

"Something must have happened," Bera says.

I look up at her. "They killed her!"

She drops to my side and puts an arm over my shoulders. "Killed who?"

"Hilda!" I say, and start weeping again.

Bera whips her head up at the berserkers. "You killed the goat?"

Uncertain glances pass among them. "I thought she was dried up," one of them says.

"The girl had grown fond of it," Bera says. "The only piece of home she had here."

No. She was not a piece of home. She was my friend, and I was hers.

"Go on, all of you," Bera says. "Give us some privacy." And I hear feet shuffling away.

"I hate them," I say.

"Solveig, child, they didn't know."

I look up at Bera, sputtering. "You didn't stop them!"

"I didn't know of it, or I would have." She shakes her head. "She was a fine goat."

"She was . . . ," I start, but in my mind I see that red thing hanging in the larder, that carcass, and a gag doubles me over.

"Come now," Bera says, and pats my back.

I cough a bit until the nausea subsides. Then I sit up and look around. Everyone in the yard is staring at me. I glare at them all, each and every one. Hake is the only one who doesn't meet my gaze.

"Here, dry your eyes," Bera says, and lifts the hem of her apron. She wipes my face and makes a sh-sh-sh sound. "Enough of this, now."

She doesn't understand. "Where is Per?" I ask.

"Per?"

Per. He told me to come to him if the warriors ever showed me disrespect or hurt me.

"He's out back, splitting wood with Raudi," Bera says.

I pull away from her and stumble down the side of the hall. Per will make it right. I don't know how, but he will. I round the corner and he and Raudi are there, halved logs spread out around them. Per looks up, sees me, and drops his axe.

"Solveig?"

I rush to him and throw my arms around him, and then I'm sobbing all over again.

He puts one of his hands against my head, the other on my back, and holds me.

"What is it, girl?"

"Hilda," I start, but I stammer and can't get it out. Raudi stands nearby, looking confused.

Per sighs. "Oh. That."

It takes a moment for me to understand the meaning of what he has said. When I do, I shake his hands off and pull away. "You knew?"

He looks away from me, at the ground. "Not before it was done."

"But afterward? And you didn't tell me?"

"Solveig, I didn't want to upset you."

I whisper, "I thought you . . ."

"You thought I what?"

But I don't know what I thought. I can only stare at him, the cold anchor of disappointment in him dragging me even lower into my grief.

"Solveig?" he says, and when I don't respond, he throws up his hands. "For pity's sake, it was just a goat."

When he says this, Raudi steps forward, and my stomach

freezes over. Per doesn't understand at all. Hilda was mine to care for, and she needed me. Without her . . . "You aren't any different from *them*," I say, and then I run, a sparrow's flight.

I don't know where I'm going, I just race away from the hall, across the field, into the ravine, up the mountains. I have to get away from everyone, even from Bera, Asa, and Harald. From the berserkers, those foul, violent, cruel men. And from Per.

The snow is deep but I press on, higher and farther, and the steading grows small behind me. When I finally stop, I am standing under the glacier. It rises up white and blue, as if it has frozen some of the sky within it, and from somewhere deep inside, it groans. Water runs out over the rocks underneath, and I stoop to drink from the stream. It is so cold it hurts my teeth, and then I splash some on my face to wash away the tears.

I sit down. I don't want to cry anymore, so I keep my thoughts away from Hilda and listen to the ice. It speaks to me of scouring winds, of cloudless nights, of endless cold. It measures its loneliness by the weight of its layers, the years and years of snow falling unobserved. I've been told its lament is loudest at the beginning of winter and the coming of summer, as if it knows that is the closest it will ever come to warmth and thaw. As if it yearns for its own demise. But it can and will only be what it is, bleak and alone, until the breaking of the world.

In the depth of winter, when the frost giants gathered and the storms raged outside the hall, Father's men sat drinking. The ale and mead flowed freely, and stronger than usual. More than one fight had broken out, and had threatened to mount into brawls if not for the control Father exerted over them.

I had fallen asleep outside my bedcloset, on a bench among them, unnoticed.

When a loud curse woke me, I startled from the bench and fell to the ground. All the men around me saw it, and they stifled their laughter. My cheeks flushed red as I knelt there, embarrassed and scared. I didn't want to get up.

But then you were beside me, Per. You bent and offered me your hand.

"There, there," you said. "Nothing to be afraid of."

You smiled at me, but not like the others did. There was no mockery in your eyes. And I let you help me to my feet.

"Are you all right?" you asked.

I could only nod.

"Good," you said, and then you turned your face away from me, toward the mealfire, and called to Bera.

Bera, then you came and brushed the straw from my woolen skirt, and picked it from my hair. "Why aren't you in bed?" you asked. "Let's get you to sleep, eh? Asa is already there."

"Good night, Solveig," I heard you say, Per, as Bera led me away.

"Good night," I said, so grateful to you.

CHAPTER 4

THE CAVE

I remember that Ole spoke of a cave up here, near the base of the glacier. A place of safety where we could hide. I need a place of safety right now, so I begin to search for it. It must be a secret cave, or else it wouldn't make a very secure place of hiding. I scramble up the sides of the ravine, looking under outcroppings and studying the rocky ledges. And then I feel a warmth on the breeze and smell the tang of sulfur. I turn to find its source and see a billow of steam rising from the stones, the breath of the earth, or perhaps of a dragon sleeping deep underground. The steam marks an opening in the troll mountains. The cave.

I cross over and pause at the mouth before climbing through, imagining sharp fangs and glowing, serpent eyes waiting for me. I inhale some clean air and then enter, my shadow sliding ahead of me. Once inside, I wait a moment for my eyes to adjust. I am in an empty room with rough walls. A few empty sacks are piled in one corner, and there is an unlit torch close at hand. The air is warm, like a hall with a full fire in the long pit and cauldrons steaming over the hearth. The smell is unpleasant, but bearable.

Farther in, the walls narrow and fall into the mouth of a shadow, then down the mountain's dark gullet. I could light the torch with the flint I carry at my brooch, but I have no desire to go any farther. I am no Sigurd, and I have no Gram. And with the warmth in here, I need no fire.

I sit down against one of the walls and lean my head back. I think of Hilda and feel like crying again, but no tears come. It is odd that she came to mean so much to me in so little time. I know I took to Hilda in an unusual way, but I'll miss looking after her. I won't ever milk her again. She won't ever rub up against my skirts, letting me know she wants her ears scratched. And I won't help her settle down to sleep outside my bedcloset anymore. I feel empty.

I close my eyes, and now the tears do come. I squeeze them out and they roll down my cheeks. I sniff and cover my face with my hands. I am nothing.

I discover that I have fallen asleep when I wake and see it is dark outside. I know I should go back to the steading, but I don't want to. I don't want to face any of them, even though I feel bad for what I said to Per. He is nothing like the berserkers. But why can't I stay here? It is warm, and small, and safe, and it doesn't matter that I am only Solveig the plain, second daughter, friend of goats.

I close my eyes and slip back down the dreamroads.

I am standing at the cliff watching enemy ships sail up the fjord below, *drekars* with leering mastheads and shields down their lengths. They bristle with spears and swords; the warriors on deck rattle their weapons and scream battle cries. The wind carries their vulgar threats up to my ears, and my body recoils.

I flee to the safety of the steading walls, but find the gate broken wide. The yard is littered with the pale bodies of the berserkers. Their mouths hang open, their tongues loll, and their eyes dry in the air for raven food. None show any sign of hurt or wound, as though they simply fell where they stood by some witchcraft. In the sky above the steading, a cloud leers in the shape of a wolf's head, a maw opening over us with dagger-teeth.

The enemy's cries are closer. Somehow I know their ships have landed; they are climbing up to the steading. I dart into the hall, close and bar the doors. I struggle to catch my breath, my eyes darting around the room. Asa clutches Harald in a far corner, her eyes wild with the panic of a wounded deer. Harald cries for the mother he never knew and I barely remember. He is no warrior now. He is a frightened boy.

At the cold hearth, Bera stirs a wooden paddle inside an empty kettle, her face blank. "Your father knows my cooking," she says. "I have a reputation to uphold."

Raudi sits on the ground next to her, staring at me with eyes like the burning timbers of a funeral pyre. "This is your fault," he says. "We are all dead because of you."

"No," I say. "Where is Per? Per will save us."

Asa pulls Harald closer. "Per is gone," she says.

And it feels as though the ground has collapsed beneath me, and the fire is not in Raudi's eyes, but everywhere. The walls burn around us, the pillars blacken, the carvings of vines and animals twist in the blaze. The heat scorches my cheeks, and the smoke chokes the air from my lungs. Then I hear a deafening crack and the sound of a thousand waves crashing on the shore. The glacier has finally heaved its bulk down the mountain. I feel the ground shake with its rush toward our steading. In a moment it will fall on us and smother the flames, smash the hall, crush our bodies, and drive the splinters into the sea.

Yellow light flickers off the cave walls. I blink away the dream and realize the cave is not on fire. Torches move outside, then voices. One of them is close, and I recognize it to be Ole. The others are more distant, their words sounding as if they range across the ravine. I think about calling out to Ole to let him know I am here, but before I do, he sticks the torch into the cave and pokes his head in after it.

"There you are," he says, grunting as he climbs into the chamber.

"You found me," I say.

He nods once, a quick jerk, and crosses the room toward me. I think he is going to help me up, but he doesn't. He stands over me, and I notice he is holding his bone knife.

I climb to my feet. "I hope I haven't caused too much trouble."

He says nothing, just stares at me. His eyes are cold, like the eyes of the berserkers in my dream, and his mouth is a hairline crack across his stony face.

"Ole?" I say.

And then Per climbs into the chamber. "Solveig!" he says. "Are you all right?"

"I'm fine," I say.

"I found her," Ole says. He gives me a narrowed glance, and he leaves. I watch him climb out of the cave, and then I become aware that I am alone with Per. We are both quiet for a few moments.

"I should have told you," Per finally says. "Hilda was not just a goat. I should have told you."

Hearing him say it makes me feel a little better. "I'm sorry I said those things to you. You're nothing like Hake and his men."

He shakes his head. "My king's daughter has no need to apologize to me."

"But I do apologize."

"Does this mean we are friends again?"

"We are," I say. I think about sharing my dream with him, but I hold my tongue. He would only think me more foolish than I'm sure he already does. "We should return to the steading."

"Yes," he says. "Everyone will be relieved to see you."

He leads me from the cave, out into the night. The glacier looks like a wedge of fallen moon, and thin silver clouds race across the black sky. Torches float over the hills around me, across the ravine, flickering specks of bobbing light. Everyone has come out looking for me, and suddenly my cheeks are not red from the cold. I hang my head in embarrassment.

"I've caused so much trouble," I whisper.

"Do not worry yourself."

Per calls to the others, announcing that he has found me, and the lights all pause a moment before moving as one back down the ravine. "Watch your step on these rocks," Per says, and takes my arm. His kind and reassuring touch warms me.

A short while later, we walk into the steading. Bera paces the yard and rushes me into a hard hug when she sees me.

"Oh, you reckless thing," she says. "Don't you go running off ever again."

"I won't," I say. But it feels good to know she cares about me.

"She did find the cave," Per says. "She looked like she'd been sleeping."

"Oh, by the gods." Bera rolls her eyes. "Sleeping? While the rest of us have been stewing and pacing, thinking you were going to freeze to death out there. You wicked child."

"I'm sorry, Bera."

Asa and Harald come out of the hall, and Harald runs at me. He throws his arms around my waist and buries his face in my dress. Asa looks at me with an expression I can't read.

"I'm fine, Harald," I say.

Harald pushes away. "I knew you were. I told Asa." He looks at our sister. "Didn't I tell you?"

Asa nods, and I wonder if she was worried about me, too.

"Now let's all go inside where it's warm," Bera says.

We allow her to usher us into the hall, and then I sit down on one of the benches. Alric is seated nearby, and he nods to me. Asa comes over and places a bowl of fresh skyr in my lap.

"You must be hungry," she says.

I am, and I eat the sour milk quickly.

Gradually, the warriors come in, ruddy-cheeked and stamping their feet. I feel ashamed and only steal furtive glances at them. They look at me with scowls of confusion, anger, and open hostility.

Alric clears his throat. "Would anyone care for a tale?"

No one answers. He turns to me. "What about the second daughter of our king? What does she fancy?"

"Please," I say. "Lift the mood."

Alric bows his head, but does not raise it. He lets it hang on his chest for several moments as if asleep or contemplating his lap. Then he stands, and a hush spreads like hearth-glow over the audience. He looks out across the hall, meeting the eyes of all who watch him. He opens his mouth and he speaks.

"High up the cloud-paths, you will find Asgard, the realm of the gods, where one day Thor, Thunderer, master of lightning and all that is in the heavens, awoke to find his mighty hammer, Mjollnir, missing."

Alric's voice has the warmth of a hot spring, and I try to settle into it. This is a familiar story, a humorous tale of gods.

"Without Mjollnir, the mountain-crusher, Thor could not defend his realm. He and all the gods were vulnerable until the hammer could be found. And so he called upon the god Loki, who took a feathered cloak and flew whistling across the land in search of what was lost. Loki traveled far and wide, until he came upon a giant sitting on a barrow. The giant laughed at Loki and said, 'I see that something is amiss in Asgard.' And Loki told him of the missing hammer.

"The giant then confessed to stealing Mjollnir and said he had hidden the weapon eight leagues beneath the earth. He would restore the hammer to Thor, but only if he could have Freyja, the goddess of love and beauty, for his wife.

"Loki flew back to Asgard and reported what he had learned. Thor thundered and raged, and split the earth open with lightning. He carved fjords and leveled mountains, but could not find the hammer's hiding place.

"And so he went to Freyja, and told her that she must put on her bridal headdress. And Freyja . . . objected to the marriage."

Here, Alric pauses and lets a smirk crawl across his mouth.

"Her indignation and her anger shook the very halls of Asgard, and Thor was forced to flee from her. Without her, he knew not what to do, until Loki suggested that Thor wear the bridal headdress himself. And so the thunder god put on a dress, and jewelry, and all the trappings of a bride, and went down to the thieving giant."

I laugh at the image Alric has conjured, at the giant so easily fooled.

"And so began the wedding celebration, attended by many of the giant's kind, and at which Thor forgot himself and ate two whole oxen. When the giant remarked on his bride's appetite, Loki said, 'She is hungry, for in her anticipation, she has not eaten for eight days.' When the giant wanted a kiss from his bride, but saw the fire burning in her eyes, Loki said, 'She is tired, for in her eagerness, she has not slept for eight days.' The giant, flattered, accepted both these explanations."

Again I laugh.

"Then the giant called for Mjollnir to be brought forth. 'My wedding gift,' he said, and laid the weapon in Thor's lap. The Thunderer looked down upon it. And he smiled. He grasped the hammer, threw off his disguise, and leapt into battle, the sound of which shook the earth. With Mjollnir in his hand, Thor destroyed the wedding party, and slew the giant who had stolen his hammer from him."

This is where the story normally ends, and I am about to clap, but Alric holds up his hand.

"Having obtained his weapon and his victory," he says, "Thor rode back up to Asgard in his chariot, which was pulled by his two powerful goats, Teeth-Barer and Teeth-Grinder."

I swallow at the mention of goats. The beginning of the story had helped me to forget about Hilda, but now it reminds me of her, bringing back the pang of loss.

"In their flight across the sky, they stirred up the winds and trampled the clouds, and as Thor coursed over a lonely fjord, he spied a single nanny goat below. Though old, he could see she was a noble beast, and had given her long life in service to her masters. And as her reward, berserker men were about to slaughter her for meat.

"Thor descended in his chariot, but did not reach the warriors in time to save her. So the Thunderer waited until after she was butchered and then gathered up the nanny goat's skin. With it, he flew to his father Odin's great hall. And there he laid the skin upon the ground, and with Mjollnir restored to him, he used the hammer's power to fill the skin with flesh and bone and bring her back to life.

"And as soon as the nanny goat leapt to her feet, she

pranced right up to one of Odin's enormous hall doors and butted it with her head, asking to be let in."

At that image of my Hilda, I laugh, this time with tears.

"And behold," Alric says. "The great doors opened, the goat was welcomed, and in she walked to find a place to sleep among our fallen heroes who wait in Odin's hall."

Now Alric smiles and bows his head, his tale finished. The berserkers around me are silent, perhaps guilt-stricken, for they are Odin's men, and in placing Hilda in their god's hall, Alric has inspired a new respect and admiration for my goat. And I am comforted by the thought of Hilda honored and nestled among friends.

After the last voice-echo has died, Alric walks over to me.

"Thank you," I say to him.

"You are most welcome," he says.

I look around the room and see that the expressions on the berserkers' faces have changed. When they look at me, they nod and smile, and I can see they have softened toward me. I turn back to Alric, grateful and awed.

"You weave a spell, sir."

He shakes his head. "Memory and sight." Then he walks away.

After he has left, Raudi comes over and sits down near me, though not near enough that I think he's come to talk to me.

But then he clears his throat. "I'm sorry."

His words surprise me. "It wasn't your fault."

"I mean earlier. By the woodpile."

I don't know what he's talking about, and I turn to him. He is gazing at me with more kindness than I have seen from him since coming here.

He looks down at his boots. "I should have stood up for you when Per said she was just a goat."

"She *was* just a goat." I shake my head. "I know I am being foolish, but I cared for her." Now I drop my gaze to my lap. "I am embarrassed."

He frowns. "I don't think you're being foolish. Anyone with eyes could see she liked you, and she looked to you to take care of her. And I could tell you liked taking care of her. Like you both sort of took care of each other."

And I realize he's right. Hilda and I did take care of each other, needed each other, and I have never felt that before. Asa and Harald have obvious purposes, roles to play in my father's plans, but not I. Father has never spoken of my virtues, and I don't even know what they might be. Alric said I have memory and sight, but of what use are they? No, I would gladly trade either for beauty or strength. Or to have Hilda back. To be needed again.

Raudi stands up, his cheeks red, and sticks out his chest just a little. "I would have stopped them. If I'd known."

"Thank you, Raudi." I want to hug him. But he nods awkwardly and walks away before I can figure out if I should.

Later that night, I lie with Asa in the darkness of our bed-closet. Her breathing is deep and slow, and I think she is asleep, but my thoughts keep me awake. What Alric does is as necessary to us as eating or drinking, but he feeds something else. We need and value what he is. I want to feel that way, to give something important to others. Perhaps with practice, I *could* be a skald. That is, if Father would allow it.

The glacier is moaning. I feel that I understand it better, having stood at its feet and slept in the cave nearby, underneath the troll mountains. We are on familiar terms, the ice and I.

Even with Asa next to me, I feel alone. My sister has shut herself off from me, from everyone, and has become a stranger. For a single moment, I imagine that Hilda is sleeping right outside the door, if I only peek my head out to look. But the moment is short-lived.

"Solveig?" Asa says, and I startle.

"I thought you were asleep," I say.

"No." Her slow breathing has not changed. "I'm glad you're with me."

I pause. "You are?"

"Yes. I need you."

Her voice is so weak in the darkness, so insubstantial, I would swear there is nothing in the bedcloset with me but a ghost. I begin to shake a little in fear and reach out to touch her, to find an anchor. Her skin is cool, and I leave my hand on her arm to keep hold of her.

"I'm here for you," I say. "But I don't think you need me. You bring honor to Father. You're beautiful, Asa. You will join powerful allies to his kingdom in marriage."

She does not answer for several long moments. "That is why I need you. . . ." Her voice trails off.

I wait, listen, and it seems that now she has fallen asleep. I snuggle up to her, breathing her lavender-scented hair, still holding her arm. It is as though the trolls have already come down from the mountains for a bride, broken into the hall, and stolen my sister away. My beautiful, vibrant, light-filled sister. But they left an empty changeling here to remind me of what they took.

I remember the way you used to comb my hair, Asa. My brown hair that is neither curly nor straight. Bera, do you remember the time you tried to dye it, to make it the color of gold, like Asa's? Not even your strongest lye could bleach away its dullness, but left me instead with hair the color of a dried leaf.

But that did not stop you, sister, from plaiting and braiding and weaving flowers through it. We used to sit by the fire, and Bera, you were there, too, with your sewing. We would sit and gossip in whispered laughter about the goings-on in the hall.

And the whole time I would fret about my hair.

My brown hair.

Do you remember what you said to me, Asa? Do you remember how you consoled me?

"You have the softest hair I've ever felt."

That is what you said.

CHAPTER 5

STONE

The next day I wander down to the icy shore, then off into the woods to be alone and to think. I miss Hilda terribly, her prancing presence about the steading, but something in what my sister said to me last night has lessened the ache I feel inside. Asa needs me. And the way Harald hugged me when I returned tells me that he needs me, too. I'm not sure what either of them needs me for, but it feels good to be needed for something.

And after the way Raudi spoke with me, I wonder if perhaps we can be friends again. It would make me so happy to have him back, especially here and now, when everything is so uncertain.

The woods around me are completely still. I enjoy the silence as I walk deeper into them.

And then I come upon a runestone.

It rises tall and narrow from the snow, like one of the black tree trunks that surround it. I did not know it was here. No one has ever spoken of it before. The inscription has long since weathered to a whisper. I run my hands over the faint tracks and dimples that remain, wondering what king or chieftain the stone once might have honored.

Runestones usually mark a grave or barrow. I shift my feet and look around for a swell under the snow, a mound of earth or piled stones. Something tingles at the nape of my neck, a cold breath, and I turn to look behind me. I am still alone. But I do not feel alone.

I know that death is not the end of the body. The person can live on . . . no, not live. The body can *persist* in the grave, a *haugbui*, the undead. I've heard stories of corpse-black figures, warriors of dark magic and infernal strength. They guard their resting places jealously against any who would defile them. By simply standing here, I could wake something. My heart beats faster.

I imagine a dead king shifting in the earth below my feet, flesh corrupted, and the tall runestone takes on a sinister cast, a darker hue and sharper edges. The gaze of an unseen observer crawls over my skin, leaving a trail of ice. I tell myself I am imagining it. It is just this moment and this place. But then a twig snaps off in the trees. I hold my breath and listen.

Nothing.

Nothing but the trees overhead and the unquiet ground beneath my feet. I back away slowly from the runestone. Only when I am several yards away do I turn and run from the woods, to the shore near where the berserkers have secured their ship, chased by a blinding fear back up the path to the steading.

It takes several hours to feel at ease again, and then around midday I look for Alric. Of anyone here, he may know who is buried down in the woods. I find him in the hall, dozing on one of the benches, an arm draped over his eyes. I sit down near him and he rouses.

"Hello, Solveig."

I greet him, tell him about the runestone, and then ask, "Do you know whose it might be?"

"Possibly." He rubs his eyes. "I'd like to see it. Will you show me?"

The sensation I felt around the grave returns, a chill, and I hesitate in answering him.

He nods and chuckles. "I think we're safe from a *haugbui* during the day," he says, and I wonder what kind of sight he has that he can know my thoughts.

He rises and extends his hand. "Come."

I allow him to help me up, and we leave the hall together.

Out in the yard, Hake walks up alongside us. "Where are you off to?"

"Solveig has found a forgotten runestone, and she's going to show it to me. Care to join us?"

No. I do not want him to c... to me since my outburst in the y... my poor Hilda. I am still hearts... Hake who killed her. I want to stay a... as I can.

"Yes, I'd like to join you," Hake says w...

"Wonderful," Alric says. "Solveig? Shall...

I can't see any way out of it, so I nod w... looking at Hake, and lead them through the gate. We walk down to the frozen waterside, and I take them into the woods. Before long, I catch glimpses of the runestone, like a slice of shadow, waiting off in the trees. I point to it, Alric and Hake peer ahead, and soon we're standing under it. Alric walks right up and traces with his finger the few lines still visible. Hake stands back, rubbing his beard.

"Well?" the berserker asks.

Alric doesn't answer.

Hake chuckles. "It seems the monument has outlived the legend, eh, skald? Your weapon of choice in preserving your king seems to have failed this one."

"Not quite." Alric frowns. He steps back, looking askance at the runestone. "This is very, very old. Older than almost every story I know."

"But do you know whose it is?" I ask.

He turns to me and nods. "But I shall need time to remember the details of his life."

an recite it for us," Hake says. He turns and

into the trees. "I'm going to have a look around."

he stalks away, a giant among the branches, and he doesn't make a sound. When he is at a safe distance, I let out a relieved breath, and Alric raises an eyebrow at me. He looks in Hake's direction, then back at me, but doesn't say a word.

He circles the runestone several times, looking it up and down. His boots tear a seam in the snow, an opening in the white above the grave.

"Do you really think there might be a *haugbui* dwelling here?" I ask him.

He stops and looks at the ground beneath his feet. "I don't know. I've never seen one before. I doubt they truly exist."

"But you tell stories about them."

"I do." He lays a flat hand on the runestone. "But if stories were told for their facts, I'd be hard-pressed to find an audience willing to listen to them."

"So you don't believe your own stories? They aren't true?"

"Forgive my boldness, but you're asking the wrong question. A story is not a thing. A story is an act. It only exists in the brief moment of its telling. The question you must ask is what a story has the power to do. The truth of something you do is very different from the truth of something you know." He leaves the runestone and comes to stand over me, looking down. "My tale last night. Did it comfort you?"

"Yes."

"And was the comfort real? Was it true?"

"I thought it was."

"Then the story was true. And that is what is most important in the telling, whether Thor's chariot is really pulled by two bucks, or not."

I look up into his eyes. At first I see mischief in them, but I realize it is something else. Alric sees the world differently than we do, and I think he simply takes pleasure and pride in carrying a secret that no one else knows.

Hake emerges from the trees.

"Did you see anyone down here before?" he asks me.

"No. But I thought I heard someone. Thought I felt someone watching me."

"I found tracks," Hake says.

"That's not so unusual," Alric says. "Surely one of your men —"

"My men have not been down here." Hake's voice is low.

"How can you be so certain?" Alric asks. "Perhaps one of your men came down without telling you."

"If that's true, then one of my men hid his presence from the king's daughter. And none of my men would do that." He turns to me. "I assure you."

But I remember how one of his men treated Asa that night in the hall. I was right. I was not alone before. Perhaps not a *haugbui*, but a man. That thought causes a very different unease.

"Let us return to the steading," Hake says. He marches several yards before turning back. "Please come, Solveig."

I do not like it when he says my name. But Alric and I follow after him.

Later that afternoon, when the sun has set and the winter twilight has poured in like an icy river, I go to fetch some firewood from behind the hall. As I approach the corner, I overhear a hushed conversation.

"I have questioned all my men." That is Hake's voice. "None were down there."

"I checked with Egill and Gunnarr as well." That voice is Per's. "And the servants."

I peer around the corner. The two of them are standing near the woodpile, an axe buried in the stump between them. They speak quietly, but their low voices carry to where I stand and listen.

"What about the old man?" Hake asks. "The thrall."

"Ole?"

Hake folds his arms.

"No," Per says. "He is loyal."

"He served another king before his capture."

"He is loyal," Per says more firmly.

"Then we are left with only one possibility. A spy has somehow reached us."

I am holding my breath, hugging the wall. A spy? How? The sea and mountain pass are frozen shut. Are we not safe here after all? Was I in danger before? The same prickling feeling returns, the sense that I am being watched.

"We need to double the watch at night," Per says. "Possibly even during the day."

"Agreed. I will see to it."

"And the king's first daughter must not leave the steading without a guard."

Hake tips his head to one side. "And the king's heir?"

Per stammers. "Right. Of course. He must be protected as well."

Hake waits.

And me? Has Per forgotten me? I bow my head against the sting of tears and the pain of not mattering.

"And Solveig," Hake says. "She must be protected, too."

"Of course," Per says without stammering.

Hake grunts a farewell and turns to leave. I scurry back down the side of the hall and reach the end before either Hake or Per round the corner. I pretend as though I have just come from the front of the building and walk toward them. Hake doesn't say a word as he passes me, but Per stops.

"What brings you out in the cold?" he asks.

"Firewood," I mumble. He did not think of me. He failed me a second time. But Hake didn't.

"I'll fetch the wood for you," Per says. "You go back inside."

I nod and return to the warmth of the hall, where Bera sees my empty arms.

"The firewood?" she asks.

"Per is bringing it."

Bera sighs. "I don't know what we'd do without him."

I nod a weak agreement. I used to feel that way, but I don't know if I do anymore. I thought he was my friend.

I am watching the doors when he enters the hall with an armload of logs. He sets them on the ground near the hearth and bends to stack them. His features are so handsome in the firelight. His hair glints like bronze. He looks up, notices me, and smiles. That same smile he has always given me.

I offer a smile in return, then quickly look away. I thought his smile meant something. I thought it set him apart from everyone else. But now I don't know what it means, even though it still warms a part of me. I am so confused.

I cannot sleep. My thoughts are like a winter gale trapped in a barrel, tossing and tumbling me in my bedcloset. The steading was supposed to keep us safe, a refuge from the dangers of war. But if what Hake and Per said is true, and an enemy has found us, then the steading has become a prison. The icy fjord may keep enemies out, but it will just as surely keep us in. And something dangerous may have been sealed in with us.

I have lost all privacy.

Everywhere I go, I am accompanied by a guard, either one of Per's men or one of the berserkers. They hang back and try

not to intrude, but they are there, smelly bears and wolves loping after me. I prefer Per's men to Hake's, but I would prefer
Per most of all. He spends all his time watching Asa, and
sometimes Harald. Usually, it is Hake who follows Harald
around, and my brother has become quite fond of the berserker
captain. Harald hangs about him like a cub at the heels, eyes
up, admiring.

"When I am king," he says one night, "I will have you as
my captain, Hake. Just like my father."

Hake bows his head. "May I live so long, little prince."

"I'm not little," Harald says.

"You will be big and strong soon enough."

"And I will be a berserker like you."

"A berserker king?" I ask.

"Why not?" Harald shrugs. "I can be whatever I want."

I open my mouth to protest, but I close it. Harald *can* be
what he wants.

"The life of a berserker would not suit the duties of a king,"
Hake says.

"What do you mean?" Harald asks.

"For one thing, a king must have a queen and an heir. A
berserker can have no family to divide his loyalties. How could
I die for my king if I had a family to live for?"

As Hake speaks, I notice that the lines around his eyes have
the slightest pinch, like a wince he almost hides. For the first
time, I see the man under that great bear pelt.

Hake is lonely. He is vulnerable to pain, like me, and trapped by that pelt as surely as I am trapped by the order of my birth. And then I realize that same birth order traps Harald. And Asa, too, sitting silent across the room. Bera and Raudi are trapped by their servitude. We are all prisoners, bound with shackles at birth that only tighten as we live and grow. Only Alric seems free, laughing at the rest of us.

Harald leans back with his arms folded. "It's not fair."

"And neither are the seas," Hake says. "But what mortal man can change their course?"

On the darkest night of winter, when Odin's Hunt was at its wildest, Asa, Harald, and I left out sugar and oats for Odin's steed as he charged across the sky. And in return, Odin left us each a gift. A new belt of fine leather for Harald, with a golden buckle. A silver brooch for Asa, bejeweled and adorned with the clever shapes of birds and animals. Do either of you remember what was left for me?

A new knife and spoon.

And did you hear what Father said to me as he patted me on the head? "Perhaps these will help you put some meat on those skinny bones."

I took my gifts into a corner, and I watched Harald strap on his belt. I watched Bera pin Asa's brooch to her apron. I held my knife and spoon in my lap and I cried.

But then, Ole, you called me over to your corner where you sat mending your nets. With a wry smile, you took your bone knife and sliced away some pieces of rope. And then your fingers went to work twisting, and knotting, and tying. And when you were done, you handed me a doll you'd made before my eyes.

I took it and I hugged it to my chest. It smelled of the sea, and I slept with it in my bedcloset. I carried it around Father's hall until it was so tattered it couldn't hold together any longer.

CHAPTER 6

RAVEN

A few days later, Hake comes to me in the yard with something large and square in his arms, wrapped in a sack. Everyone watches him, and he shifts back and forth on the heels of his boots in front of me. He is so rough, and yet it was he who thought to protect me when Per did not.

"I have something for you, Solveig," he says. "It is a gift."

I manage a nod.

"Can we go inside?"

I nod again. We turn and approach the hall. There is an awkward moment standing before the door when Hake clearly wants to open it for me, but he looks at the bundle in his arms.

"Let me," I say, and open it.

He steps through, sheepish, and looks around as if to make sure we are alone. It seems we are. Bera and Raudi are out milking the cows in the shed. Asa may be hidden away in our bedcloset, but I'm not sure.

Hake sets the bundle on the ground, and I hear a flutter inside. "First, I must confess something to you."

I wait.

He clears his throat. "It was I who killed your goat."

I know that, or had guessed it, but his integrity touches me. His voice becomes quieter. "I am sorry for that. I had no idea you had become so fond of the animal. So in recompense for what I did, I wanted to give you something. Something else you might be fond of." He looks at me as though waiting for me to reply, and when I don't, he kneels on the ground. "Here is your gift," he says, and whips off the sack.

It is a cage made of sticks and fastened with leather cords. A young raven sits inside the cage, flicking its black-jewel eyes at me. Its feathers are glossy as pitch, almost blue. The bird makes a few halfhearted caws and hops around the cage. Its head is plucked bald in patches, as though someone had started preparing it to eat, and I can see its pink, wrinkled skin. Its wings are short, the flight feathers clipped, and one of them is bent at an odd angle.

Hake notices me looking at it. "That wing made it easy to catch him, as he can't truly fly. It looks like it got broken some time ago, and you can see where the other birds have pecked him. I'm surprised he's survived."

"Poor thing," I say. He's an outsider, which is how I often feel.

"Ravens are smart. I once saw a man who had trained his raven to fetch things about the steading for him. They can even learn to talk. This one is young, and after he's bonded to you, he'll ride your shoulder."

I am nervous about having this bird for a pet, but out of politeness I thank him.

"He'll eat anything," Hake says. "Your table and kitchen scraps. They're scavengers."

"Thank you," I say again, wishing I could think of something more.

He hovers, hands behind his back, looking back and forth between the bird and me. "Do you like him?" he asks.

The bird hops toward me in the cage, looks up at me, and makes a clicking sound. I imitate the sound back at him, and the raven cocks his head and makes the clicking sound again, as if we're talking to each other.

"I do like him," I say. "Thank you, Hake."

"You're welcome. Will you name him?"

"Yes, but I don't know what." And then I remember that the god Odin has two ravens that whisper to him what they see in their flights across the land. Their names are Huginn and Muninn. Thought and Memory. "I think I'll name him Muninn."

Hake's smile says he is pleased. "A good name."

I crouch down near the cage, and Hake lingers a moment longer.

"Well," he says. "Good afternoon."

"Good afternoon, Hake."

He marches out the door, a different sort of man to me now than he was but minutes before. As brutal and violent as berserkers can be, Hake can also be thoughtful. And caring.

I look into the eyes of my bird, my new friend, and he looks back at me. "Hello, Muninn," I whisper. Now that I have memory, all I need is sight.

After the night meal, Harald tries poking Muninn with a stick through the bars of his cage. Muninn flaps his bent wing, trying to get away, and I snatch the stick from Harald's hands. "Leave him alone."

"Look at that ugly bird." Harald laughs. "Why's it bald?"

"He's not ugly," I say. "He's picked on and bullied. His feathers will grow back."

Harald laughs again, and Per comes over.

"Leave the bird alone, lad," he says. "It was a gift from Hake."

Harald wrinkles his nose. "I'd give it right back."

Per smiles at me with a slight shrug, and I give my eyes a little roll.

Other than Harald, everyone admires Muninn. Raudi continues to smile at me. The berserkers worship Odin and they nod to the cage in respect and appreciation. Ravens mean something different to them. The berserkers call ravens swans of blood, because they feed on the bodies after a fierce battle. Hake probably thought it was a noble gift, but my Muninn doesn't look very noble half-bald, and I don't like to think of him eating anything but bugs and berries.

I try to feed him from my hand. At first he is wary, and jabs his beak at me as if he wants me to just drop the food on the ground for him. But I am stubborn. And patient. He must learn to take the food from me, so he will trust me. As the evening passes, he begins to come closer to my fingers, and his beak becomes gentler. Before long, he is feeding right out of my palm.

Hake comes over and watches me pass Muninn bits of food. "He's already taken to you."

"I hope so," I say. "But I don't think he's ready to ride my shoulder."

"No. But he will be." Hake smiles and moves off to be with his men.

Asa joins me after he has left, and we sit together, word-lessly. I pass her a bit of bread, and she holds it just inside the bars of the cage. Muninn makes a grab, and Asa flinches, drop-ping the crumbs. The raven snatches them with a caw that sounds like a laugh, as though he has won some victory. Asa laughs, too, a sound I haven't heard from her in a long while.

"Your bird reminds me of Gunnlaug," she says. "You remem-ber what he was like when he came to our hall? Before the war?" Asa sits up. "Gunnlaug's head is just as bald and pink."

I remember him at Father's table, after he'd drunk too much mead. "And he laughs like Muninn, too."

Asa nods, but the smile falls from her lips. She reaches for another bread crumb and doesn't bother to hand it to my bird. She just tosses it inside the cage.

"He wanted to marry me," she says.

I stare at her. "I didn't know that." Then I think about Asa leaving our hall to be Gunnlaug's wife and I don't know what to say.

"Father refused him," she says. "That's why we are at war. Because of me."

No. That's not right. "It isn't your fault," I say. "Nor Father's. Gunnlaug is the one who declared war." And I begin to feel the burden that Asa has been carrying. This is what has driven her into silence and sadness.

She stares at something across the room, and I follow her gaze. She is watching Per, as he laughs with Hake. Asa's eyebrows are sloped in worry, and she stays that way for some time without moving.

At last she rises. "I'm tired. I think I'll go to bed."

"Good night, then."

"I envy you, Solveig," she says over her shoulder as she walks away.

I am stunned. What is there in me to envy? Asa is everything to our father, and I am nothing.

Muninn flutters and draws my attention. I give him a bite

of turnip and watch him swallow it down. The more I think about it, the more I realize he does resemble Gunnlaug. Wrinkled skin, sparse black hair. I stare at him, seeing not my bird but that old chieftain in my cage.

I know I've told myself that I would gladly marry for Father, but I've never considered that such a pledge might mean marriage to an old man who resembles a scraggly raven. I feel foolish for never having thought of it. I am sad for Asa, and for the first time see her beauty as a burden instead of a blessing. And I feel the guilt-weight she has been carrying this whole time.

She is asleep when I climb into the bedcloset later that night. I nestle down next to her, trying to think of how I can help, but my thoughts are like snowflakes drifting away from me, or melting on my skin as soon as I catch them.

The next several weeks bring the fullness of winter's cold weight. The pale sun is too weak to warm us for the few hours that we have its light, and the nights seem to swell, filling the world with stars and endlessness. The glacier has slowly settled into its season-sleep and fallen silent, and the fjord is a narrow white road to the sea.

We spend more of our time indoors, and the fires in the long hearth are never allowed to burn out. The berserkers have stopped complaining, but that frightens me even more than when they bluster and fight. If they're pacing the hall like chained dogs, I at least know how they feel. Silence makes them even more unpredictable.

Ole sits with his bone knife in the corner, showing Harald how to repair the frayed ropes and holes in one of his fishing nets. His movements are practiced and almost loving, like an old woman braiding a granddaughter's hair. Harald yawns and gets his fingers tangled.

Muninn hops around his cage, cawing at me, his head feathers still a little sparse. But his flight feathers have lengthened. I have never let him out since Hake gave him to me. I felt that I had to shrink his world before I could trust him to not fly off. But perhaps it has been long enough, and I can let the walls loose just a little.

"Raudi," I say. "Will you watch the doors for me?"

Raudi gets to his feet. "Watch the doors?"

"I'm going to let Muninn out of his cage."

Raudi looks at my bird, nods, and walks over to the doors. He stands in front of them, arms crossed. Those in the hall with us, including several berserkers, are watching me now.

I take a deep breath and look right into my raven's eye. "I'm going to let you around the hall for a bit. But only for a short while. And I'd like it if you perched on my shoulder for at least a moment."

Muninn shakes, ruffling his neck feathers.

I pull one of the cage sticks free, and then another, and then a whole side falls open. Muninn cocks his head and hops right out. He looks back at the outside of his cage for the first time. Then he launches himself into wobbly flight, hampered by his bent wing. But he manages to flutter up to one of the rafters, where he caws in delight and proceeds to preen.

I go and sit under him, my head bowed, a bit of food in my hand. At first I hold the food in my lap, then up at my neck. I tap my shoulder.

"Patience, miss," one of the berserkers says. "He's looking right at you."

I call to him. "Come to me, bird of Odin."

"He's cocking his head," Harald whispers. "He's got one eye on you."

I whistle. "Come, Muninn, my memory."

His talons click on the wooden rafter.

I smile and look up. He shuffles his little rear end out over the beam. And he squats. His droppings fall right in my hair. I let out a little yelp; everyone laughs. Raudi looks like he's trying not to laugh, and covers his mouth with his hands. He is distracted when the hall doors open. A blast of frozen wind pushes into the room and sends Muninn flapping and cawing. He staggers into the air and flies straight for the opening, that strip of free sky.

"Raudi!" I shout.

He slams the doors just as Muninn reaches them, and my bird thumps against the wood. Then he turns in the air to find a new perch, frantic wings beating, unable to keep him aloft.

He slowly descends to the floor, where I'm able to scoop him up and drop him back into his cage. I close the side and slide the sticks back in place. Muninn hops and screeches, as if I'm trapping him for the first time.

"I'm so sorry," Raudi says.

He's still holding the doors shut, but now lets them go. In walks Per. He glares at Raudi, confused. Then he sees me at the cage.

"You had him out?" he asks me.

I nod. "I think he almost came to my shoulder."

Harald laughs. "And then he pooped on her head!"

I grimace and raise my hand to hide my hair. I'll have to brush the droppings out later, after they've dried.

Per grins. "He must still be trying to figure if he can trust you."

"That's not it," Ole says. The old man is still sitting in his corner, the net spread over his lap and around his feet. He looks up at me. "You're the one trying to figure if you can trust *him*. It's you that needs the cage, not that bird."

"What do you mean?" I ask.

"Once you've trapped a wild animal, he'll always want out. So you always have to keep him locked up, or else wonder every time you open those bars if this'll be the day he turns on you and flies away."

"He'll come to me," I say. "I trust him." But even as I say it, I know I won't let Muninn go flying around again anytime soon. Perhaps in the hall, but not outside.

Ole looks at the cage, and then goes back to the rope in his hands.

The rest of the afternoon and evening pass uneventfully. We eat our night meal. Alric recites a few stories to make us feel something bigger than the hall we're trapped in, and then it is time for bed.

I am standing at the cliff, and it all happens as before. The *drekars*, bearing evil. The berserker corpses, open-eyed and pale. The wolf-cloud, snarling destruction. The burning hall and our doom under the glacier's heel. There is nothing I can do to stop it. I wake with a gasp and lie panting in the darkness. I have had the dream twice now, which means it must be a portent. And then I think of Hake's suspicions about a spy, watching me from the woods.

Something is coming. The enemy will find us, and maybe already has. I hug myself, feel my own heart beating in my chest, and find it hard to fall back asleep.

It was only last Midsummer, Asa, when you tried on one of Mother's finest dresses for the first time. Father said you were a woman now, and so it was time. I remember you standing there before the fire and how amazed I was at the deep colors in the fabric, the softness of its weave.

"Oh, Asa, you look so beautiful," I said.

You smiled. For a moment. And then you began to cry. You fell to your knees and wept into your hands, and I looked around confused, not knowing what I had said or done.

"It's all right," I said, and tried to hug you, but you pushed me away.

But then you came over, Bera.

"There, there," you said, and rubbed your hand across Asa's back. "She'd be happy to see you wearing it."

And, Asa, through your tears you said, "I miss her." And then I realized that you were talking about our mother. The mother you remembered, but I could not. But now I know it wasn't only that.

"I wish I could say it gets easier," Bera said to you. "But I have to be honest with you, child. You'll cry on your wedding day, and you'll

cry at the birth of your first child, and each child thereafter, because your mother won't be there. But she'd be proud of the woman you've become."

Asa, you looked up at her then, tear-streaked. "You think so?"

"I know it," Bera said.

Then you said, "You'll be there, won't you, Bera?"

And Bera said, "Always."

CHAPTER 7

THE WOLF

It takes me a few weeks more to tell anyone about my dream. When I finally decide to, I go to Alric. We sit in a corner of the hall away from the others, and I whisper my fears to him. As I say it, I sound foolish even to myself, and I expect Alric to dismiss it all as a childish nightmare. But he doesn't. He nods his head gravely and leans toward me, listening.

"So who is the wolf?" he asks when I'm finished.

"I don't know."

"And how deep was the snow in your dream?"

"The snow?" I ask. Why would that matter?

"Yes, in your dream, how deep was the snow?"

I stop to think. I remember the bodies of the berserkers lying on the ground. "Not as deep as it is now. The snow was melting."

"So it was near the end of winter. Months from now."

"I suppose it was. Why? Do you think it will come true?"

Alric shrugs. "I don't know. But it's best to be aware, isn't it? We have some time, at any rate, before the ground begins to thaw and we meet our doom."

He gets up and walks away, leaving me alone, counting days. Months from now seems no time at all before the coming of the wolf when the berserkers fall dead and the hall burns to the ground.

Raudi comes around one of the columns and stands next to me. Then he sits on his hands and looks at the ground near my feet.

"I heard what you told Alric," he says.

I don't mind that he was listening. It's hard to avoid overhearing things in the winter-hall.

"Why would I think it's your fault that we're here?" he asks.

"I don't really think that, Raudi. It was just a dream."

"But I don't feel that way, and I would never say it." He looks up at me. "So I don't think your dream can come true. You see?"

"At least not that part of it," I say.

He nods once, as if satisfied that he has said what he meant to say, and rises to his feet.

"Wait," I say.

He pauses.

"If you don't feel that way," I say, "why have you been so angry with me?"

"I'm not angry with you."

"Raudi."

He rubs his chin as though he wears a beard, like a man would do, even though his face is still smooth. "I'm just frustrated that we're here. All of us. I'm supposed to be fighting alongside the other men. But they didn't think I was ready."

I don't like to think about the fighting back home, and I'm glad that Raudi is here instead of there. But I don't tell him that. "Just because you're here doesn't mean you're not ready."

"How so?"

"Well, the berserkers are here. It seems my father has only sent those whom he trusts the most. That includes you."

"I guess that's true."

I lean forward and punch him lightly on the arm.

"What was that for?"

"For being so cross with me this whole time."

He smiles, but it doesn't reach his eyes, and I can tell there is something he has left unsaid. "I better go help Mum."

"All right."

He walks away, and after he is gone, I turn my attention to Muninn in his cage near my bedcloset. I wish, like Odin, I could send him flying back to my father's hall, or to the battlefield. I wish Muninn could return and tell me what he has seen.

⊠　⊠　⊠

The next morning, I help dish up skyr for Harald's day meal. Our two cows can't keep the whole steading in fresh milk, but they produce enough that we don't feel so far away from home. I'll miss the skyr and curd when we have to butcher the cows for meat, and judging by our stores of pork and dried fish, that isn't too far off.

After I've served Harald, I dish some up from the crock for Asa and myself, and I sit to eat it. But before I've taken my first bite, I look up at those sitting around me, those eating something other than skyr.

Bera always insists the sour milk and curds go to Harald, Asa, or me before she offers what's left to any of the men. And there's an order there as well. Per is first to receive a portion, then Hake, then Per's men, then the berserkers. Poor Ole is last because he is a thrall, so he never gets any. Bera doesn't take any for herself, but I am sure she lets Raudi eat some occasionally. I hope she does.

Harald scoops his into his mouth until his bowl is empty. Everyone watches him and he grins.

I pause before eating mine, and stare into the bowl. Then I get up from my bench and cross the room to where Ole and Raudi are sitting next to each other.

"Would you two like to share this?" I ask.

They look up at me and then at each other.

"Thank you," Raudi says, and takes the bowl from my hands.

Ole sucks on one of his cheeks like he's puzzling something over. "That's yours," he says.

"I want you to have some. We should all have a share." I look at Raudi. "Eat."

But he has refrained. He looks back and forth between us as if Ole's words have made him unsure of what he should do.

Ole looks at the bowl in Raudi's lap. "If you insist."

"I do," I say. Before he can summon any further protest, I turn and walk away.

This place has done strange things to the people I know. Before coming here, Ole was always a friend to me, but he seems to resent me now. And he is not the only one who has changed. Bera no longer hums while she cooks at the hearth. Harald seems even more impatient and impulsive than he usually is. Asa's beauty used to have a rich glow, like a golden summer evening when the setting sun seems to light the fields on fire as it touches them. Now her beauty has become a winter wood, stark and frosted and still. It makes me wonder how I have changed.

I catch Bera's eye as I return to my bench, and she seems pleased at what I have done. From across the room I watch Ole and Raudi enjoy the skyr. Moments later, Ole licks his lips and lifts the empty bowl in salute to me.

After the day meal, Bera sends me to milk the cows. I do so, missing Hilda, but as I haul the sloshing bucket across the yard, there is a sudden break in the gray sky above, as though a giant has pulled away a fistful of clouds, and I am awash in sunshine. True sunshine. Not warm, but bright, and I smile.

After handing the milk off to Bera, I pick up Muninn's cage and carry it outside. I set it on a snowbank and sit down next to it, my arm draped over the top. Muninn grows still, looking around, the sun threading his feathers with glints of silver shine. I close my eyes and tilt my face up toward the light, and we sit together enjoying it for some time.

Then a shadow falls across me, and at first I think it's a cloud, but when I open my eyes I see Hake standing over me.

"May I sit next to you?" he asks.

His request startles me, but I am not as uneasy in his presence as I used to be. "Of course."

He lowers himself onto the snowbank beside me, emitting a low grunt. He looks around me at Muninn, smiles, and squints up at the sun. Moments pass. The silence between us feels awkward to me, but I don't think it bothers him at all.

"Thank you again for my raven," I say.

"You're welcome."

More silence, and thoughts from his conversation with Harald come to my mind.

"Hake?" I say, feeling bold.

"Yes?"

"Do you ever wish you had a family?"

He doesn't answer, and I fear I may have angered him. But then he sighs. "If I had a daughter, I think she would be about your age."

He says it plainly, but I think I hear the same hint of pain and regret underneath it. I mourn for him, though it's for the loss of something he never had.

That evening, Alric pulls me aside. We sit on two stools facing each other. He doesn't say anything at first. He just stares at me, sometimes tipping his head as if trying to see me from every angle, and I feel exposed and uncomfortable beneath his scrutiny.

"I'm convinced," he finally says.

"Of what?" I ask.

"You could be a skald. If you wanted to."

"Whether I want to doesn't matter. I doubt my father would allow it."

He waves that off with his hand, like clearing smoke. "Don't worry about that yet." He leans forward. "First, suppose your father did allow it. Is that something you would want?"

I pause before answering. "I think so."

"Then let's give it a try, shall we?"

"Give what a try?"

"I am going to teach you. Perhaps if you learn well, we could demonstrate your skill for your father when we return to his hall. To help convince him."

"I would hate to waste your time," I say.

"It's not a waste."

"And I doubt I have the skill," I say.

"That remains to be seen."

I say nothing.

"Good." Alric slaps his thigh. "We'll begin tomorrow."

I open my mouth before I've found any words to say and close it. Then the hall doors open, and a flurry of snow rushes in ahead of a wide-eyed warrior. He scans the hall and then hurries to Hake. They speak with each other in low voices, heads leaned together, and then Hake rises. He motions for Per, and the two of them follow the warrior outside.

Everyone has noticed their departure, and when they're gone, the conversation in the room begins to boil like a kettle over the coals. Alric and I are still sitting together, and my expression must appear to be asking a question because the skald shrugs as though he doesn't know the answer. We wait for several minutes. Long minutes.

Then Hake returns and stands in the doorway. "There is nothing to worry about," he says. He turns to my brother. "Harald, come and see."

My brother jumps up and follows the berserker out of the hall. My curiosity lures me to my feet and out into the night after them. I hear Alric following me. We cross the yard, large flakes of snow floating all around us, the moon a silver brooch peering out between folds in the velvet clouds. Several guards stand at the top of the earthen wall with torches, looking into the woods. We climb up to join them.

Hake points Harald's gaze into the forest, and I lean forward.

At first I see nothing. Just the black trees and the dark spaces between them. Then I catch movement. Something gray, low to the ground, and fast. A blur. A ghost. I see another, and another, and I hear a panted breath. They are everywhere, flying through the forest.

"A large pack," Alric says beside me.

Wolves. Odin's bane, shadow made flesh.

"They're just passing through," Hake says. "South to find prey."

For a moment, I imagine myself out there in the woods, cold and defenseless. A shiver takes me, and I turn to go inside. But then I notice two glowing eyes, two pinpricks of reflected torchlight. I stare back at them, and a wolf emerges from the trees.

He is the most magnificent creature I have ever seen, enormous, of a bearing I have only met in the powerful chieftains that come to my father's hall. The wolf's coat shimmers with frost, his neck is thick, and his long legs plant him in the snow like a monument to all that is free and untamed in the world. He is not afraid of us at all.

At the sight of him, the berserkers go quiet.

"Now there's a trophy," one of them whispers.

But I doubt that he or any man would have the strength to bring down this wolf-king.

"We're not here to hunt," Hake says, with a note of regret in his voice. "Everyone stays inside these walls."

"Perhaps," Alric says, "this will be an opportunity for your men to learn that there are other ways of appreciating an impressive creature than killing it."

"Or perhaps a time for you to be of use," Hake says. "When we go back inside, why don't you tell us of Fenrir? Satisfy our thirst in other ways."

"I'd be honored," Alric says.

I haven't taken my eyes from the wolf. And he doesn't seem to have taken his eyes from me. His gaze is intense, full of confidence, without any hostility. He is not the wolf of my dream. He *knows* his place in the world and where he belongs. I wish I could know the same.

Eventually, and for no other reason than his own, the wolf turns away from us and vanishes into the woods.

After that, no one speaks. We file down from the wall and back into the hall. There is some discussion between the men who saw the wolf-king and those who didn't. Boasting by those who claim to have killed one larger. I am cold from being outside and take a place near the fire, rubbing my hands together over the coals.

Before long, Alric rises up, extinguishing the noises of the hall. He looks up into the rafters and begins.

"Far to the east, deep in the Ironwood, a giantess bore children by the god Loki. One of them was the giant wolf, Fenrir, who prowled astride the mountains, chasing the moon, feared even by the gods. For they knew that when he was fully grown, he would be too powerful for them to defeat. So they devised a plan, and had a fetter fashioned by the dwarves in their underground realm, a chain as soft as silk but strong enough to muzzle Fenrir until the breaking of the world."

Alric pauses. He looks around the room, and we wait. His eyes find me, and he motions with his hand for me to stand. I do so, confused, my eyes darting in embarrassment.

"Solveig," Alric says. "Will you tell us what the dwarves made the chain out of?"

Every head turns silently in my direction. I swallow. I know the story. Every child grows up hearing it. But I'm unsure of the rhythm necessary to tell it, the devices and techniques. All eyes are on me, bringing heat to my cheeks. And then I see Harald on a bench nearby. I have told him this story many times before, and he looks at me as if wondering what I'm waiting for. Then I look at Raudi, and he offers an encouraging smile. I realize that if I am to be a skald, I will need to get used to people watching me. And if I am to be a skald, I will need to speak. So I begin.

"The dwarves made the chain from the sound of a cat's footfall." My voice is quiet at first. And I feel silly, just a girl telling a story. "The strands of a woman's beard, the roots of a mountain, the sinew from a bear."

But as I speak, I find the story emerges from my memory, and the words come easier. I gain a little confidence, and so I attempt to embellish the lines. "The breath of a silver fish swimming in the pool. And the spittle from the beak of a blackbird soaring in the sky. And because the dwarves used each of these, now none of them are found upon the earth."

Several of the berserkers gently applaud. Harald is smiling, and Alric nods, seeming pleased. At their demonstrations of approval, I feel a surge of heat in my veins, a rush of flame and excitement that lifts my chest.

Alric rolls his hand toward me, asking me to continue with the story. But I shake my head. I am afraid I will ruin this small moment. It is enough for now.

Alric nods and finishes the tale of Fenrir. I sit down and listen to him intently, watching how he does what he does with a new awareness. I notice when he raises and lowers his voice, and the effect that has on the audience. He makes eye contact and looks away, to mark certain moments in the story. And each of his words seems like a perfect piece of fruit, plucked from the tree at the exact moment of its ripeness.

He tells of how the gods taunted the giant wolf, dared him to try his strength against the chain. How Fenrir did not trust them, and so the god Tyr inserted his hand into Fenrir's mouth as a gesture of the gods' sincerity. A hand that Tyr lost to Fenrir's teeth once the chain was around the wolf's neck, and he realized he had been tricked.

Later that night, in the bedcloset, I lie on my back with my hands behind my head. I sigh and relish the lingering warmth from my skaldic moment. I am startled when Asa reaches out and takes my hand. Then she squeezes it.

"You did well tonight," she whispers.

Normally, I would want to say, *No, I didn't*. I'd try to diminish it. But tonight I want to simply accept what she has offered. I want to believe it is true, and that my sister, the one who is loved by all, has seen something in me she admires.

"Thank you," I say.

At the far edge of winter, when the ground was black and sodden with melted snow, you, Raudi, must have decided that my hair looked much too clean. For without any preamble, and apparently without any thought, you scooped up a handful of mud and flung it at me. The cold muck caught me right at the base of my neck.

But I could throw almost as well as you back then, if not as far, at least as accurately, and I took aim with the same armament. Before long, we were both of us laughing, smeared and brown as dwarves.

It was then that you, Asa, came upon us.

"Solveig!" you shouted. "What do you think you're doing?"

I held up my fist. "A mud war! Join my army, Asa!"

"I'm not a child anymore," you said. "And you should not behave so, either."

I folded my arms then. "Why?"

"Because Father will be angry."

"No, he won't," I said. "He doesn't care what I do."

"You are still a young lady."

Then you spoke, Raudi, and said, "I'm not a young lady. Does that mean I can throw mud?"

I laughed at that, and then I started to think that Asa's hair looked much too clean.

"I care not what you do, Raudi," Asa said. "But my sister knows better."

But, Raudi, my friend, you stood up for me. "Don't be angry with her. It was my fault for starting it."

Asa shook her head at me. "Such a disappointment."

CHAPTER 8

HUNGER

The next morning, Raudi is sent to milk the cows. He leaves the hall and is only gone a few moments before returning with an empty bucket. He stands in the doorway, looks back over his shoulder toward the shed, and wrinkles his brow.

"Well?" Bera asks. "What is it?"

Raudi looks over his shoulder again. "The cows are gone."

"What do you mean?" Bera asks.

"They're not in the shed."

Per stands and moves toward Raudi.

Bera still looks confused. "Well, where else would they be?"

"I'll go and see what this is about," Per says.

But we all follow him out into the yard and across to the cowshed. The door is open, and the shed is empty, just as Raudi said.

"Where could they have got to?" Bera asks.

A quick search of the steading tells us that the cows are not anywhere within the walls. Cows can't really hide, and can't really be hidden. Which only leaves the possibility that they somehow got outside the walls. A heavy snow fell most of the night, and would have covered any tracks the cows left behind.

"We'll organize parties to go into the woods," Per says. "We'll need everyone."

Per doesn't say it, but we're all thinking the same thing. If the cows managed to slip out into the woods last night, they're dead and frozen. The search is not for the cows but for their meat. Meat we can't afford to lose.

I am assigned to a group with Ole, Egill, and Gunnarr. Harald goes with Hake and several berserkers. Even Asa has come out to help, in a group with Per, Bera, and Raudi. We strap on our snowshoes, leave the steading walls, and each group takes a different direction.

"Spread out," Per says as we separate. "But stay within sight of those next to you."

My party widens the distance between us to ten yards or so, and we march into the trees. The snow is soft and deep. Even with snowshoes, my legs begin to burn and the cloud of my breath is a drift of its own in front of me. I look to both sides now and again, to check for Egill on my left and Ole on my right. The woods are silent as we pass through them, any noise swallowed by the snow. I focus my eyes on the ground, searching for a sign of the cows, but I don't see anything. Not even the tracks of smaller, wild things.

"I must thank you," Ole says, coming closer to me.

"For what?" I ask.

"For sharing your skyr. I hadn't eaten any for a while, and it tasted good."

"You're welcome," I say.

He nods and we continue walking. "I worry that the wolves may have found the cows last night," he says.

"I hope not."

"If they did, they won't have left any meat for us. And now they've found some food here, they may not be so ready to move on."

"How do you think the cows got out?" I ask.

Ole looks up into the branches overhead. "The only way I can figure it, someone put them out."

I stop walking. "What? You mean, on purpose?"

He nods.

"But why? Why would someone do that?"

"To weaken us. You've heard these rumors about a stranger out here in the woods. If anyone wants to take this steading and capture you children, they'll need to get through the berserkers, which is no easy thing. Unless you weaken them first."

I remember my dream, the berserkers dead on the ground. From starvation? Is there a traitor in the steading, some enemy sleeping at our own hearth who deliberately put the cows out in the wolf-wood? I shudder. If so, if that person wishes us harm, then what is to stop their knife in the dark of the bed-closet? I worry for Harald, who sleeps with the men.

"But don't worry," Ole says. "Per and Hake won't let any harm come to you." He starts to walk away. "I better get back over there so we don't miss anything."

"Ole," I call, and he turns back. I hesitate. "Have I offended you?"

He looks away. "I took you for a royal fool. And a selfish one to go running off like you did that night. Who knows what could have happened to you, or to those of us searching for you. There's worse than wolves in these mountains." He looks at me and smiles. "But you proved me wrong yesterday morning. You may still be a fool, but you're not selfish."

Then he walks away.

We continue our search, but in stopping and talking with Ole, I've lost sight of Egill, and I assume he of me. I grow nervous at the thought of an enemy lurking out here somewhere. Perhaps watching us even now. But I can still see Ole among the trees, and I turn my attention back to the forest and our purpose for being there. I'm looking for a carcass now, for blood in the snow, not the bulk of a frozen cow.

We keep searching for an hour or more, and I find nothing. I am getting cold, snow clinging to the fur of my leggings and boots in clumps. My woolen skirt is pale and stiff with ice. I come to a shallow wash, a frozen creek bed I need to cross. I climb down into it, and as I do, Ole disappears from my view. It takes me a few moments to scramble back up on the other side, and when I do, he is gone. I try not to panic. I keep to my course, pressing through the winter-wood alone. I'm sure to catch up with him if I hurry.

But I don't catch up with him, and my fear rises in spite of my attempts to calm it. Then a figure moves in the trees ahead of me. It isn't Ole, and at first I think it may be Egill. But as I draw closer, I realize it isn't him, either, and there are two of them.

It is Per and Asa.

They are facing each other, standing close enough to embrace. Asa's hands are clasped at her stomach, and Per's are behind his back as though he is restraining himself. Per says something I can't hear. Asa looks down at the ground and wipes her cheeks. She is crying. Per reaches out and lifts her chin so that they are looking in each other's eyes, and he whispers to her. They stay that way for several moments, close enough that I can't tell their breath-clouds apart. Then, gently, Per lowers his hand and steps away from her. They turn as one and I watch their backs, the way they lean toward each other as they walk. And for the first time, I see it. My heart and chest are colder than my legs or my hands, ice cracking at the core of me.

Per and Asa are in love.

Ole was right. I am a fool.

How could I have not known? I roll back against a tree and look up at its bony branches, a hundred fingers wagging at me. And I remember things. Things I should have seen from the beginning, ever since we came here. How Per treated Asa, and Asa watched Per. Things I took no note of at the time.

Per, so kind and handsome, and my beautiful sister, with whom I share a bed. I stamp my foot in the snow, furious at myself, embarrassed. Tears come to my eyes and blur the sky, the woods around me. I don't know why I'm crying; I don't know why it hurts to see them together.

I want to be angry at the two of them, but I can't bring myself to that. They haven't done anything wrong, not really. I'm angry at myself for not seeing it, for being such a child.

A sudden call breaks my thoughts apart. Someone has found the cows.

Ole was right about something else. There isn't much left of them. The wolves ate or carried away all but the largest bones and some shreds of tough hide. The carcasses are opened up and spread out over the slushy red snow, and I only hope the poor cows had already frozen to death before the wolves started in with their teeth. Several of us stand in a silent circle, studying what's left.

Asa and Per are on opposite sides of the bodies. I watch the two of them for a moment and then force my eyes away. I don't want to see them look at each other.

"Gather all of this up," Hake says to his men. "There's still a little meat on some of those bones, and there's the cartilage and marrow. Some fat still hangs on the skin as well."

His men comply, and the rest of us head back toward the steading. We make a somber procession through the forest, and I know the question on each of our minds, the question I asked earlier. Who is the enemy in our midst?

I have other questions, too. Without the cows, can we survive? We'll have to cut back on rations, but even then, will there be enough? We're deep in winter as it is, with deeper yet to slide. I have seen no sign of real game to hunt. Will Ole be able to drill the ice and catch any fish? One thing is certain. We will all be hungry, and the thought of hungry berserkers worries me.

As soon as we reach the steading, Bera goes to take stock of the larder, to refigure how she'll feed us all for the rest of winter. Per wanders off in discussion with Hake, and Asa goes back into the hall. She doesn't even glance toward him. But I saw their meeting in the woods. That was the truth. This is a lie.

Alric walks up to me, shaking his head. "Do you regret sharing your skyr now that you know it may have been your last taste of it for a while?"

"No. I don't regret it." I say this as emphatically as I can. I would do it again, or at least I hope I would. But the question has annoyed me, and I move to leave him.

"I think I would regret it." Alric follows me into the hall. "But I admire your generosity. As I admired your portion of the story last night."

That stops me. "It was only a few lines."

"You did quite well, as I thought you would."

"I was scared."

"Have you seen children afraid of water? All the patience in the world won't get them wet. You just have to throw them in where it's shallow enough that they won't drown."

He guessed one thing right about me. I would never have willingly stood to recite for the hall. But in the end, I managed to stay afloat.

"Would you like to have your first formal instruction?" Alric asks.

I'm about to say yes, when it occurs to me that Alric could be the one who sent our cows out to be slaughtered. I don't have any reason to suspect him, except that he's here in the steading, and right now anyone in the steading could be the enemy. It could be Alric. It could be Hake, or any of the berserkers, or Ole, although it was he who started me thinking such things. And Per? No, not when he's in love with Asa, and I don't think it could be Bera, either. She's known me and my siblings from the time we were nursing. But there is someone among us who means us harm, and that thought unnerves me.

So what am I to do? Hide away from everyone in my bed-closet the way Asa does? No, I won't do that. That would just be a prison within a prison. But it would be prudent to keep myself to the busier places, with others around, and not go off alone with anyone.

"Can you teach me by the fire?" I ask. "I'm quite cold."

"Well, that's often crowded, but I don't want you to be uncomfortable."

We cross to the hearth and sit facing each other, straddling a bench. There are a few berserkers here, and Bera is close by. If I can't trust Alric, at least I have them around me for safety.

"One thing I noticed," Alric says, "was your repetition of sound. 'The breath of a silver fish swimming in the pool.' A fine line and a fine use of alliteration. How did you know to do it?"

"It just sounded right, how it was supposed to be."

"That's good. It means you have already perceived the patterns, even if you weren't aware of them. How could the line have been improved?"

I stop and think about it, and then I say, "The breath of a silver fish swimming in the *sea*."

"Yes, excellent."

"It's difficult to think of it in the moment, though, isn't it? When everyone is staring at you."

"But you'll remember that line now. And you'll get better at improvisation as well, with practice."

I don't like to think of practice, because that means I'll have to perform in front of others again and again, while making mistakes.

"Now, let's talk about some of your other lines. . . ."

But I don't hear the rest. Per has walked into the hall. He stops just inside the doors and looks around the room. Before today, I would have thought he was looking for one of his men, or perhaps just seeing who was present. Now I can't help but think he's looking for Asa, a thought that makes me feel a little jealous of his attention.

He sees me, smiles, and walks over to us.

"I'm sorry about the cows, Solveig," he says. "I'm sorry you had to see it."

He's worried that I was attached to the cows as I was to Hilda. "Thank you," I say, feeling embarrassed. "But I'm fine."

"Hake and I will address the steading this evening," Per says. "It will be a dark speech. I hope you will cheer us with another of your wonderful stories."

"I'd be honored," I say, just as Alric did.

"She'll be ready," Alric says.

Per takes his leave, and Alric and I spend the rest of the afternoon and evening practicing, rehearsing lines and tone of voice. Alric has chosen the tale of how the earth was formed, and how the first god came into it. It began with Audumbla, the ancient ice cow, and Alric spends some time making sure that I remember the details of the story.

"Before the earth, there was only fire and ice," Alric says. "And from the rime frost rose Audumbla, the cow. She licked the salt from the ice, and as the ice melted away, it revealed the first god and father of Odin."

"You choose this tale because of our cows," I say.

"Yes, as I did with your goat. And so the audience will see that life comes from ice, and though we are frozen into this fjord, we shall emerge when spring, like the tongue of Audumbla, brings the thaw." He sits back, obviously pleased with himself.

Perhaps he has forgotten about my dream, and what may come with the end of winter. But his thinking makes sense to me, and I trust him to know what the steading needs. Still, I am nervous when I imagine myself standing before the audience again.

"You will do fine," Alric says. "Try to relax, and accept that you will make mistakes. You are just beginning, and that is inevitable. Remember what I said about stories? They only exist in the moment of their telling. Let whatever story you are telling be what it is, mistakes and all, for its moment will soon be at an end."

This does not reassure me.

"And keep your breathing deep and even," Alric says.

◫　◫　◫

That night, Hake and Per stand before us. But while Per appears stern and calm, Hake appears furious. His beard twitches with the gritting of his jaw, and he glares at everyone, awl-eyed, as if trying to pierce their secrets by sight. I swallow and avoid his gaze. He makes me feel guilty for things I haven't done.

Per speaks in a voice that carries through the hall. "You all know of our circumstances by now. We have lost our two cows, and we were counting on them for milk and meat to last the winter. Rations will be cut back, and we expect all to sacrifice. We will be hungry. Bera assures me that we will not starve."

We do not need to starve to be weakened.

"But that is not what concerns me most over the loss of the cattle." Per stops and looks at Hake.

The berserker captain nods. "Last night, while Alric and Solveig were telling their tale, the guards at the gate left their post to stand in the hall and hear the story." He pauses. "Those warriors have been . . . appropriately punished for their negligence of duty."

The way he says it chills me.

Hake raises his voice. "During the absence of the guards, someone led the two cows from their shed out into the woods. It may be that an enemy entered the unguarded gate and stole the cows away." He pauses. "Or, it may be that an enemy within this steading put the cows out."

Murmurs and whispers begin to slip through the hall.

"Know this!" Hake holds up one of his massive arms and everyone stills. "If there is a traitor within the sound of my voice, I will find you. I will execute you. There will be no hesitation. There will be no mercy unless you confess. If you come forward, you will be spared until we have returned home. Then, you will stand trial at the Thing, with judgment meted out by your people. Perhaps you will only be banished." His voice descends into a growl. "But if you do not confess, I will kill you on the spot whenever and wherever I find you."

He lowers his arm, and I relax as though he had been holding me up, pulling me toward him by a cord around my neck.

"You have until dawn to act," Hake says.

After Asa's chiding, I did not feel like fighting any longer, and Raudi and I laid down our arms, ending the mud war. I trudged back to Father's hall, encrusted, leaving a trail of dirt-crumbles behind me. When I entered the yard, I saw Father talking with you, Per. I did not want you to see me so filthy, so I tried to hurry past. But my father sees everything. He called to me and I stopped, trying not to look at you. Father said nothing, at first. He simply stared in a way that took in every inch of me, and my stomach churned with humiliation.

"Solveig," Father finally said. "Go clean yourself."

"I'm sorry, Father," I said.

He sighed. "One cannot apologize for one's nature."

Then you spoke, Per. "But as a child grows," you said, "her nature changes, does it not?"

I did not like to hear you call me a child, but I was grateful to you for defending me.

"Perhaps, my lord, it is only a matter of time," you said, "until you see that Solveig can bring you as much honor as her sister."

"Let us hope," Father said.

CHAPTER 9

STORY

The hall is silent and no one moves, except for the suspicious glances cast at one another. I can imagine the emotions racking the members of our steading. Fear. Anger. Dread. And I sense the coming hunger, a fearsome traveler skulking toward us with his belt of special knives.

Per clears his throat and continues. "Alric and Solveig have agreed to tell another tale. Something to lift the weight off our shoulders."

He looks at me, and I wonder if I have the strength to do it. After Hake's speech, I don't know if I believe anyone would, even Alric.

The skald nods at me to begin. We agreed previously that I should speak first, as the apprentice. Alric will finish the tale as it should be finished, because endings, as he says, are the most important element of a story, for that is where you discover the story's purpose and meaning. But I can't seem to work my legs, and my tongue feels as dry as a strip of stockfish. I take a deep breath, as Alric instructed, and manage the rise to my feet.

The time spent rehearsing was wasted. I stand here, a hall full of faces watching me, expecting me to make things right, and I can't remember a thing. What story was I supposed to tell? What tale? It had to do with the cows we lost, I think. Yes, the cows. Why would we tell a story about the cows? Why would we want to be reminded of that?

I look into the eyes of my audience. The safety and future of the steading is so uncertain now, with dwindling food supplies, enemies outside our walls and possibly within. They need something they know, something predictable, something comfortable and safe. But what?

I see Harald, and something about him has changed. He isn't smiling. His face bears the pain and shock of a child struck by his father for the first time. The reality of our situation here has finally penetrated his youthful shield of confident ignorance. He sits alone, vulnerable and afraid. I want to go to him, to comfort him, but I can't. Not until I finish my tale.

So I will tell my story for him, one of his favorites, the story of the god Loki's wager with the dwarves. He is my only audience. My mouth no longer feels dry, and I am no longer afraid.

"Loki, the Wolf-Father, god of dark mischief and murder, once saw the metal craftsmanship of the clever dwarves, and thinking himself clever, too, he offered them a wager."

The eyes on me are impassive. Except for Harald, who leans forward, and Raudi, whose lips curl into a frown that fights a grin.

"Loki spoke with the dwarves and said, 'The gods have been given many gifts. I'll wager you my head that you can't fashion any that are better.' The dwarves, being proud, accepted Loki's bet and began to labor at the forge, making three gifts for the gods. First, they made a golden boar for Freyja, whose bristles shine throughout the long nights, lighting the hall and the path before him."

The men around me seem to have settled into the story, some reclining, hands behind their heads. Perhaps they are enjoying it.

"Second, they made a golden ring for Odin, a ring that multiplies itself on every ninth night so that eight new gold rings fall from it."

And here comes Harald's favorite part, a part that perhaps the berserkers will also appreciate.

"And finally, the dwarves made Mjollnir, mountain-breaker and bone-crusher, the war hammer of Thor. Never would it fail its wielder, whether swung or thrown; a fearsome weapon to sway the tide of any battle. Now, when the gods received these gifts, they deemed them worthy, and more than that, the finest they had ever received. And so it seemed at first that Loki had lost his wager, and . . ." I pause.

Some in the audience lean forward.

". . . almost lost his head. But clever Loki had planned this all along and said, 'My neck was not included in the wager. You may have my head if you can take it without harming the place where it rests.' And the dwarves realized they had been tricked, and in their vanity, they had freely given to the gods the three greatest treasures in all the world."

I bow my head, and after an endless moment of silence, I hear applause. I look up, right at Harald. He is smiling, bright again, my little warrior once more. Everyone else is grinning, too, and nodding. It seems my story, short and simple, did what it was meant to do and lightened the mood.

I don't want to look at Alric. He will be furious with me. I changed the story and finished it without leaving anything for him. But I can't avoid him, and when I see him, he is clapping, too.

I hold up my hand to silence the hall and everyone grows quiet. "Thank you," I say. "But now, Alric has a story to tell."

"Nay," Alric says. "I would not want to sully the air after you've just cleared it so thoroughly."

It humbles me that he would leave my tale as the last for the evening. Before long, the warriors are settling down on the floor and benches to sleep. I get up, yawn, and move toward my bedcloset. Before I reach it, I feel a tap on my shoulder.

"I must have a word," Alric says.

"I'm sorry I switched —" But he silences me with a finger to his lips.

"I am not angry," he says. "You saw what the steading truly needed. Tomorrow, you must tell me *how* you saw it."

"I don't know that I can explain it."

"Tomorrow, you will try. Good night, Solveig."

"Good night," I say. Alric leaves, and I look down at Muninn in his cage by the bedcloset. I check his food and find he still has some cabbage and barley grains he hasn't eaten. I whisper a good night to him and climb into bed.

Asa is already there. As soon as I see her, the image of her and Per in the forest enters my mind. The memory drains away the excitement of the evening as a cold bed draws out a body's heat. I lie there, not knowing how to act toward her.

"I enjoyed your story," she says, as if nothing has changed between us when everything has. I wonder how she can't see it, even as I know there's no way she could.

"Thank you," I whisper.

Should I tell her that I know about her feelings for Per? That I saw them together? What would she say? How would she feel?

"I haven't heard that story in years," she says. "It brought back good memories."

"I'm glad."

"Of when we were children."

"Yes."

"It was better then, wasn't it?"

"When we were children?"

"Mm. No one expects anything from a child, not really. Respect or even fear, and that is all anyone requires of them. Not like the demands of womanhood."

At first I am angry, and find it hard to summon any of my earlier sympathy for her. It sounds as though she's complaining about being beautiful, the demands of being desirable. Does she not realize how I envy her? But she may have to marry one man when she is in love with another. Father would never wed her to one of his warriors, even one so highly regarded as Per. Per would bring nothing to the union, no advantage for my father's coffers, lands, or armies.

How must it be to love someone and know that you can never be with them? Perhaps her guilt over this war is not the only reason for the sadness that has so consumed her. Now I do pity her, but still can't think of a way to tell her that I know about Per. Not without shaming her. Not without risking the ruin of my friendship with Per, such as it is.

"You're right," I say. "It was better then."

No one confesses to putting the cows out. But I doubt that anyone expected the enemy to actually step forward. Hake's offer last night was not an act of compassion. It was meant to satisfy honor, and to justify him should the enemy be found out.

I do not want to be there to see it when Hake finds the traitor.

Winter continues to gather our steading in its arms, closer to its frigid chest. Storms rush up the fjord in their tumble from sea to land. Snowbanks rise almost to the roofline of the hall and threaten to bury the smaller outbuildings. The berserkers find themselves tasked with keeping the doorways and yard clear.

Muninn has grown quite calm in his cage. He doesn't flinch from me at all anymore. In fact, when I come near the cage, he hops as close to me as he can, right up to the bars. So I decide to let him out. Only this time, I shout an announcement in the yard to let everyone know, and I bar the doors to the hall.

Once again, there is an audience encouraging me as I open the cage and step back. My raven is not so quick coming out this time, as though he has come to mistrust what is not his prison. And he doesn't stray far from the cage once he's free.

I keep still and wait near him, my chin up, following him with my eyes.

"His wing is still crooked," I hear Harald whisper from nearby. "But at least his feathers grew back!"

"Shh, lad," one of the berserkers says.

"Come to me," I whisper. "Come, my memory, bird of Odin."

Muninn cocks his head to one side, his eye pointed right at me. Then he hops over to my feet and climbs up on the toe of my boot. He shifts a bit, side to side, and settles there.

"That's not your shoulder," Harald says.

I ignore him, and slowly offer Muninn my finger. He regards it from his inch-high perch. I bring my finger closer, sliding it right under his belly. His feathers are so soft I can't say that I truly feel them, but I feel the heat off his little black coal of a body.

When I've almost reached his legs, he raises one foot up and grips my finger. Then he raises the other, and I feel his weight on my hand, heavier than I would have thought. His long twig-toes are cool against my skin. I almost giggle at this success, but keep it in so I don't startle him away. Then I lift him up near my neck. Muninn requires no coaxing to climb onto my shoulder, and once there, he flaps his wings twice and begins to pick at my braid. Now I do laugh, because I can't contain it, and so do others around me.

Muninn perches there for the rest of the day, and for much of the days that follow. Whenever I am in the hall, I try to have him on my shoulder. Sometimes he flutters about up in the rafters, and sometimes he hops among the benches, rooting in the straw that lines the floor for crumbs and food scraps. He stays close to me even when they open the hall doors, although I still don't trust him enough to take him outside. He is with me when I sew, or cook, or eat, and I feed him from my own plate. Even though he eats but little, I don't want to give anyone cause to complain. So I don't ask for any extra food for him, and instead share with him from my ration.

I am often hungry, as are we all.

Telling stories hasn't become any easier for me in the past weeks. I expected it to after that night when I told the story of Loki and the dwarves, but nothing like that has happened since. I keep making mistakes. I forget important parts of the story and Alric has to go back and add it later. I think it is frustrating to him, and I know it is to me. I've tried doing what I did that night, picking one person in the audience to tell the story to, but that hasn't helped.

I've come to regret starting down this path, because I don't think it's going to take me anywhere after all. I dread standing up there most nights, as I do tonight. I'm hiding in a corner of the room, Muninn on my shoulder, hoping Alric doesn't feel like entertaining, and if he does, that he wants all the attention for himself.

But he calls on me soon enough.

I sigh and move into the light of the hearth where everyone can see me. Before I begin, I search out Raudi, and Bera, and Harald in the crowd. That way, I know where to look if I start to do poorly. Which I surely will.

But I raise my voice anyway. "Tonight we will share with you the story of —"

But everyone is looking at me with odd expressions of

amusement. They smile and elbow each other. I turn to Alric, and he gives a nod and flicks his eyes to my shoulder. Oh. I had forgotten that I still had Muninn there with me.

I laugh a little. "I've been forgetting some of the stories lately," I say. "So I brought my memory with me."

Now the audience laughs, too, easing my nervousness.

"Will you help me?" I say to Muninn. "Will you whisper the stories in my ear as you whisper in Odin's?"

The raven responds by gently pecking at my earlobe.

I never hear Muninn's voice, but for some reason the story goes well that night with him beside me, better than it has in weeks. Not as good as that night after the cows, but almost, and I feel a deeper kind of love for my raven.

"And I never would have thought of it," Alric says to me afterward.

"Thought of what?" I ask.

"Having your raven with you. It was brilliant!"

"I didn't mean to. I forgot he was there."

"But it gave you an air of magic, or legend. Like a skald of ancient times. And the way you suggested that the bird whispered to you only confirmed the image in the audience's mind. It was magnificent, Solveig."

"I'm glad it went well." All the praise has started to make me feel a little uncomfortable.

"You should have Muninn with you from now on. Never perform without him."

"Really?" That is a comforting thought, actually.

"You can build a reputation on this kind of thing."

After Alric goes to find a place to sleep, I put Muninn away in his cage. I lean close and whisper a thank-you to him, and as I do, I catch a glimpse of something dark in the straw beneath his feet.

"What is that?" I ask, and reach in.

He flutters out of the way, and I pull out an iron key. The larder key that Bera normally keeps at her brooch.

"Where did you get this?" I ask, but he says nothing as I steal back his treasure.

Bera is surprised when I return it to her.

"But how did he . . . ?"

"I don't know," I say. "It was just there in his cage."

"What a mischievous little fellow," she says. "You'll have to keep an eye on him. Things go missing around the steading, I'll know right where to look." She winks at me, and we say good night.

I climb into bed, burrow into the blankets, and feel contented. I am so grateful to Hake for his gift to me, for my mischievous little fellow, my story-whisperer, my key-stealer, my courage-giver, my friend.

I have grown up with war. It seems at times that my life has been made up entirely of two feelings: fear and relief. They are like two opposing elements of nature, the ocean and the rocky shore, and I dwell in the breach, dashed back and forth between them. Fear that I will lose someone I love in battle; relief when my father and his army return home safely.

I remember when you learned of your brother's death, Raudi, and I cried for you. I hope it does not cause you pain for me to speak of it. You stood before my father and accepted a gold ring in your brother's stead, an honor bestowed for his valor before he fell.

"And with this ring," my father said, "I charge you to honor your brother's memory, and to one day serve me as did he."

You bowed low, and though I grieved with you, I was proud of you, too.

Per, you were there when Raudi's brother died. And you stood beside my father as he laid that burden on my friend. You stood in your armor, your hair pulled back, your beard trimmed, and I could see that you meant to look after Raudi. That comforted me.

Did it comfort you, Bera? I think that it must have, mourning the loss of one son even as you took the first step toward the loss of the next.

CHAPTER 10

DOUBTS

When all the pork is gone, they eat Hilda. Bera warns me, and I look away from the meat steaming on plates all around me. Some of the others refrain from eating out of respect for me. Bera, Raudi, Ole, my brother and sister, and Per. Alric, too, and I am surprised to see Hake sitting quietly, fingering his empty bowl. I know he must be hungry, how he must crave the taste of meat, and a feeling of gratitude toward the berserker captain swells in me. Before long, I have to leave the hall. I can't bear the smell, and I wait outside in the cold night alone.

Ole hasn't been able to catch any fish through the ice. After Hilda is gone, there will be no more meat.

※　※　※

Another day passes, and I begin to regret giving Raudi and Ole my skyr. All I want is a taste of its deliciously sour flavor, the feel of its creaminess on my tongue. If I had the only bowl of it left in the world, I don't think I would share a single bite with anyone. But the last of the milk and butter are long gone from the steading.

The hunger is making everyone more irritable, and an irritated berserker is a frightening thing. Fights break out more frequently and are met with harsher punishments. There have already been two today: one this morning in the hall that then spilled out into a second fight in the yard. So far, no one has been seriously hurt, for the drawing of weapons within the steading walls has been expressly forbidden. I hope we can at least enjoy the night meal in peace.

I sit next to Alric, Muninn on my shoulder, as we discuss which story we will tell tonight.

"You choose," Alric says.

"I wouldn't know which one."

"Yes, you do."

"I don't."

"But you did before. Better than I did."

"That was different. And I'm not sure I want to tell stories anymore."

Alric frowns. "When will you learn to trust yourself? You keep yourself captive, Solveig. You could throw off the fetters at any time, for you hold both ends."

I am speechless. And angry. I did not choose my birth order. I did not choose to be plain. I did not choose to be born without any qualities of worth. And this skald sits here and taunts me. Throw off my fetters? What would he have me do, wash away my face? Does he think I've been hiding my charm and beauty, strength and bravery? I want to shove him away from me.

But instead, I speak in a low and even tone. "I am who I am, sir." Muninn stirs on my shoulder. Perhaps he can feel my anger through his feet.

"If that is what you believe, then that is the problem."

"What is?"

"You don't really know yourself." He rubs his thighs and then stands. "I will tell the tale tonight. You needn't worry."

I am still glowering long after he has walked away. And I am not worrying about any tale. I am poking at his words, stirring embers, raising sparks. Who could I know better than myself? If I don't know myself, then I don't know anyone.

A shout and clamor rouses me back to the room. Two angry men face each other, Egill and one of the berserkers, their noses almost touching. The berserker bares his teeth. In that instant, Egill strikes a blow to the berserker's mouth, and he goes down.

The room erupts.

Curses, shouts, and fists tear free, the sounds of splintered wood and shattered crockery. Enraged berserkers battle Egill and Gunnarr, and battle with one another, as if they don't care whose jaw they crack or whose face they bloody. And then, above it all, I hear the metallic ring of a sword pulled free of its scabbard, its whisper through the air, and then a grunt. I want to run and hide.

"Stop!" I barely hear Hake above the roar. "Stop!" he shouts again, but the room doesn't slow. So he charges into the middle of it.

He isn't armed. But he doesn't need any weapon. He swings his war-hammer fists, a giant crashing through a wood, breaking trees. One blow and men fall before him. And as the brawlers become aware of him, they scatter out of the way like gulls.

And then, for no reason I can tell, Hake halts. His eyes roll back and his face turns an angry red. He begins to shiver and tremble, his teeth chatter. Something is happening to him. There is a moment of pause in which everyone notices the berserker captain, and then his men shout alarms. They rush to him, calling his name as though trying to reach him across a great distance.

Alric hurries up to me and pulls me back. "You must come away."

"What is happening?" I ask, stumbling.

"The *berserkergang* is coming upon him."

My eyes widen. I look back at Hake. He is breathing hard, his head and shoulders heaving above the chanting wall his men have formed around him. I have never seen the battle fury take a berserker, and I am both curious and terrified.

"Come away, Solveig," Alric whispers. "He won't know you. Please."

I let him guide me to a far corner, where Bera and Raudi shield Harald. I crane my neck, watch, and wait. Across the room, a low growl rumbles from the midst of the berserkers. They raise their voices and press in tighter.

"What's wrong with Hake?" Harald asks.

"He isn't himself," Bera says, stroking my brother's hair.

I listen to the berserkers chant. They pray to Odin, calling on him to draw the fury out of Hake, to calm the bear.

"He could kill us all," Raudi says.

Harald's eyes dart up, and Bera slaps her son.

"Quiet," she hisses.

I add my own silent plea to the chanting, which has begun to swell. The berserkers are in their own kind of trance around Hake, rising, rising like a rushing wave. The rhythm of their chant thunders through my chest, terrible and consuming. And then at the moment when I fear it will overwhelm me, it breaks and begins a slow retreat. The beating of my heart seems to fall in step with it, calming me. Hake's shoulders sag, his breath comes easier. And when the other berserkers are silent, he lifts his head. He looks around, blinking, and when we make eye contact, I see that he recognizes me. The wall of berserkers tumbles away from him.

Hake straightens his back, his face pale and sweaty.

He sweeps the room with his gaze and immediately stops on Egill. Hake's eyes widen, and then I see the blood on Egill's shoulder.

"A blade has been drawn," Hake says. "Raise it if you have any honor."

Across the room, a berserker lifts his sword.

Hake motions to him. "Bring it here."

The berserker marches over, kneels, and offers up his weapon. Hake takes it, and for a moment I fear he will execute the berserker with his own sword on the spot. But he doesn't.

"You are no longer of my company," Hake says. "From this moment forward, none of my men will share a fire with you. None shall feed you. None shall defend you. None shall remember you."

The berserker is still kneeling.

"Rise and be no more."

The berserker stands, and as one, every other berserker in the hall turns their back on him. The act takes my breath with its coldness. The only eyes remaining on the lone berserker are mine, Alric's, and Harald's. Even Bera and Raudi look away.

The forgotten one seems to me a man drowning. Weak, sliding beneath the waves, resigned to his death, bereft of the soul that gave him buoyancy. He bows his head and backs away, and a part of me wants to reach out to him.

At the doors, he bumps into Per, who is just coming in from outside. And I see that Asa is with him. The forgotten one doesn't lift his eyes, but slips past them both into the night.

"What is going on?" Per asks.

Asa slinks away from him, as though she is trying not to be noticed.

"Discipline," Hake says. "Your man is injured."

"What?"

Several berserkers and Gunnarr are already addressing the wound. From what I can see, it appears serious, but not fatal if treated with care.

"What happened?" Per demands.

"Your man started a brawl. One of my men lifted his sword, so I banished him."

"Banished him where?" Per asks. "There's nowhere for him to go."

"There is the forest," Hake says.

"That's a death sentence," Per says.

Hake says nothing.

Per turns to his warriors. "What started this?"

Egill winces and speaks. "I was late for my watch. The berserker accused me of being a traitor for leaving the gate unguarded."

"That's all?" Per asks. "So it has become an act of treason to be late?"

"No more an act of treason than seducing the daughter of the king," Hake says.

I gasp.

Per appears stunned at first, mouth open. Then he snaps it shut. "Do you have an accusation to bring before the steading, Hake?"

The berserker captain chuckles. "No. No, I don't. Your own eyes accuse you."

Ole clears his throat. "And would it be treason for a berserker to blindly kill the children of his king?"

Per spins around. "What?"

Ole gestures toward Hake. "The *berserkergang* nearly took him in the brawl."

"He is right," Hake says and then lowers his voice. "The fault is mine. It will not happen again."

"You're an animal," Per says. "You and your kind have no place among us."

Hake nods. "Perhaps not. But the king has made one for us. And we are honest about who and what we are. Can you say the same?"

"Listen to me," Per says. "All of you! There is nothing in my conduct that would compromise the virtue of the king's daughter. Do you understand? I love her only as I love her father."

"Of course you do," Hake says.

Per is trembling with anger, but he turns away from the

berserkers to help his wounded warrior. I know Per is lying about his feelings, but I feel sorry for him. He does love my sister, but it seems cruel to mock that love so openly. And apparently the entire steading knew about it before I did.

If so, then Per and Asa are crossing a treacherous ice floe, one where the snow could swallow them into a chasm without warning. It would take only the whisper of an accusation for my father to execute Per. For his sake and Asa's, I hope that Per was being truthful about his honorable conduct. But at the very least, he has brought suspicion down on my sister, and I am angry at him for so selfishly jeopardizing her reputation.

I watch him now as I would a stranger. He is not the man I thought he was. I've imagined trolls coming down from the mountains for my sister, but perhaps the troll has been in our steading all along.

Asa and I lie awake together, without talking. I worry for the berserker wandering out in the woods. Where will he go? Perhaps he is trying to climb out of the fjord, but that would be impossible. During winter, the mountain pass is closed, sealed shut, rendering our steading accessible only from the sea. Has he already frozen to death? We have not seen or heard the wolves for some time, but perhaps he has met one of them. And Hake took his sword.

When I think of the berserker captain now, he frightens me more than he ever did before. I have caught a glimpse of the animal inside him, waiting just on the other side of its den-shadow. The others in the steading seem to have forgotten quickly about the incident. To them, it is just a part of being a berserker, and the risk my father took when he brought them into his hall.

"Did you know?" Asa asks, scattering my thoughts.

"What?"

"Did you know about Per and me?"

"I did." But I feel guilty for not saying something to her before now, so I add, "But not for very long."

Asa sighs. "Father will banish me just like that berserker."

"Not if he doesn't find out."

"How could he not? Everyone knows."

"But you haven't really done anything wrong." I drop my voice to a whisper. "Have you?"

"No, I haven't."

"Then you'll be all right."

"All right?" Her voice is so loud and angry, I worry she'll wake those sleeping out in the hall. "How could you possibly think I'll be all right? Per and I . . . I don't know what to do."

I think of the two of them walking into the hall together and feel a stab of betrayal. "Well, you could start by not going off alone with Per anymore. That way —"

"Oh, shut up, Solveig. You don't know anything."

Tears spring to my eyes. "I'm sorry."

A moment later, she reaches out for me and takes my arm. "No, I'm sorry. It's not your fault."

I rub my eyes with my sleeve.

She lets me go. "I'm just so confused. Sometimes I want to run away."

"How would you escape the fjord?"

"Not from here. From everything. Away from Father's kingdom."

What is she saying? "But . . . you can't."

There is a very long pause. "No," she says. "I can't."

I wake up late to a meager day meal of cooked oats. I feed some to Muninn and then step out into the yard. The day is dismal, the pallor of death in the sky and on the ground, the world a corpse. I watch a few berserkers heaving snow and I am surprised and relieved to see the banished warrior hard at work alongside the others.

Hake stands nearby with folded arms, watching.

I am wary again of the berserker captain, of the rage he holds within, and keep my distance, but he turns and sees me. I don't want him to think I'm avoiding him, for I know there is kindness in his heart. I force myself to approach him.

"I thought he was banished," I say.

Hake bows his head in greeting. "He was. They found him half-frozen at the gate this morning, begging admittance. He asked to become a thrall to the king and his family. I saw no reason to deny him."

I look back at the man. Yesterday, he was a proud berserker warrior, feared and strong. Now he is a slave, without weapon or property to his name. I cannot decide if it was pity that compelled Hake to let the man back in, or cruelty.

"I must apologize for last night." Hake rubs his knuckles, and I see that they are bruised and split. "I know what you must think of me now, and you are right to. I let down my guard. But you can believe me when I say it will not happen again."

I only nod.

Hake looks up at the troll mountains. "This is a strange place. A steading that can turn warriors into thralls and princesses into skalds."

"I'm not a skald yet."

"No, but you will be. I prefer your voice to Alric's. And I think you are more naturally gifted than he. I believe your father will be proud."

"Truly?"

"Yes. I think so."

His words strike a place in me that has never sounded before, something deep and ignored for a long time. My father proud of me? A rush of joy radiates outward through my body from my chest, a feeling I relish, but have a hard time trusting fully.

My father. Proud of me.

"Don't worry," Hake says. "I won't let that new thrall anywhere near you or your siblings. And he'll soon discover the true nature of servitude."

"But that is still better than death," I say.

"No. It isn't."

▨ ▨ ▨

That evening, I stand in front of the steading telling a story. It is going well, and among the array of faces in the audience looking up at me I imagine my father's. As soon as I've conjured up his image, his eyes like shields, I feel the emptiness of his disregard and all the meager confidence I've gathered slips between my fingers. Were it not for Muninn at my side, I think I should fall to the ground, as though my bird is holding me up by the shoulder.

I barely finish my portion of the tale and find my seat, heart pounding. What if Hake is wrong and my father isn't proud? This storytelling is the one gift that may be mine, and if my father disapproves of it, I don't know what will be left. For the first time since coming to this place, I don't want to leave. At the thought of what I may face at home, a sense of dread pulls back my earlier joy into a knot in my stomach.

Alric finishes, and we go to our beds. I bring Muninn a bit of food and notice a familiar shape in his straw.

"Again?" I pull Bera's key from his cage, and this time he squawks at me in anger. "It isn't yours, you little thief."

Bera laughs this time when I return it, although she can't figure how Muninn stole it from her. "Perhaps he really is Odin's bird," she says. "Got some magic in him."

I regard my magic raven as I return to the bedcloset. Even my bird has secrets. It seems there is no one I can fully trust, no one without a secret concealed inside themselves. And here in this steading, that is the only place left where anything can be hidden.

In fact, if Alric is right, then I'm hiding things there even from myself.

My sleep is restless with tangled thoughts and shapeless nightmares. The stale air in the bedcloset stifles me. The mattress is uncomfortable and the walls feel too small, a cage. I need to stretch, to move and breathe freely. So I climb out, pull on my boots, and tiptoe across the hall. The doors are heavy, and emit a slow groan as I ease them open and slip outside.

The air is deliciously cold, a shock that brings relief. I inhale with my eyes closed, pulling the frost into my chest. Then I look up, and I catch that lonely in-between moment that is neither day nor night, when the boundary loosens between the mountains and the sky. I decide to stay out and watch the sun rise above the ravine, so I walk down the length of the hall. But as I reach the garden patch, I see that someone is already there.

It is Hake. He stands bare-chested in the almost-dawn, his pelt on the ground beside him. His broad back is to me, and he whispers to himself. I turn my ear and listen.

He is praying. He pleads with Odin to grant him strength, to help him stay vigilant and keep his rage under control. "If I ever come so close again," he says, "destroy me, Allfather, before I hurt anyone."

There is pain in his voice, and strain. Hake sounds and looks so vulnerable. And that is something I would never have thought to see in him. I don't want to spy on this moment. I do not want to violate his privacy, so I back away quietly and return to the bedcloset.

But the sight of the berserker remains before my eyes. The sound of his voice in my ears. I have seen Hake's heart, his goodness laid bare. Perhaps he alone has nothing hidden there.

I remember a time when a neighboring chieftain began sending raiding parties onto Father's lands after sheep and cattle. When Father demanded compensation, this chieftain gathered his sons and declared war. You were sent to fight, Hake. You and your berserker men. I was so frightened of you. I must confess now that before coming here, and knowing you, I was always glad when Father sent you and your men away to war.

That is how we all felt, everyone in the kingdom.

You were despised. Before Father, what king had offered you a home? What hall had ever opened its doors to you and your kind? No one trusted you. No one wanted you. The only reason we tolerated you is because Father demanded it.

That is, until Alric.

For you came back from war victorious, as you always do. You recovered what had been stolen and made our people safe in spite of their suspicions of you. And Alric sang of your strength. Your courage. Your cunning. And your loyalty. His tales nudged my thoughts and changed the course of my feelings, so that I gradually came to accept you.

As did we all.

And now, we trust you with our borders and our lives, and you have a place among us.

Though we still give you plenty of room.

FALLEN

The next day, Harald sulks about the hall, eyeing the food that Bera is preparing, complaining loudly. Bera sometimes gives him a taste of whatever is boiling in her pot to silence him, but today she scowls and ignores him. We are all short-tempered.

"But why can't I eat now?" Harald asks.

"Silence, boy," Hake says. "Be patient."

"Ha!" Bera snorts. "Your men complain as loudly as the boy, Captain."

"You take issue with my men, woman?"

Bera points her long spoon at him. "That I do, sir. They become fouler with each passing day. I agree with Per. This steading would be better off if you and your lot had never come."

Hake stands. "Your king felt differently."

"I'm still hungry!" Harald says.

I get up and put my arm around him. "Come, let's go for a walk."

"I don't want to go for a walk," he says.

"But I do, and I don't want to go alone. Will you come to protect me?"

"Take Hake," he says.

"I want you."

Harald sighs as though the weight of manhood has already fallen upon him. "Very well, Solveig. I shall protect you."

I smile, and Bera mouths a thank-you to me as he and I leave the hall. Out in the yard, Harald announces to the berserkers hanging about that he is escorting me on a walk.

"Where would you like to go?" he asks.

"Let's go up to the glacier," I say. I do not want to go into the woods, and Hake would not allow it, anyway. But the ravine is behind our steading walls and feels safer.

"Very well," he says.

Raudi walks up to us. "Where are you going?"

"The glacier," Harald says.

"Can I come?" Raudi asks.

Things between us are still not as they once were. I'm not sure if they ever can be, but I nod, and he smiles, and it's settled. After we've wrapped ourselves in furs and strapped on our snowshoes, we set off across the snow.

It is farther than I remember from that evening I ran up this way. And now I notice the boulders that line the bottom of the ravine are placed at regular intervals, forming a narrow, winding channel, a natural defense against an enemy trying to fight their way up. I realize the rocks must have been arranged that way, rolled into place to protect the cave.

"I've enjoyed your stories, Solveig," Raudi says.

I look at him. "Thank you."

"So have I," Harald says.

"Thank you."

"But I've always liked your stories," Raudi says. "Even before you started telling them like a skald. In fact, I think I liked them better before."

"You did?"

"Yes."

"Me, too," Harald says. "Back when you told them just to me."

I thought I was getting better at telling stories, not worse. "Why were they better to you before?" I ask Raudi.

"I don't know," he says. He crooks one side of his mouth. "I think it's because it felt more real before. It felt like you believed it."

"Alric says it isn't important what I believe. And it doesn't matter if a story is really true."

Raudi shrugs. "Well, he's the skald. But that doesn't make sense to me. How can you make the people believe it if you don't believe it yourself?"

Harald sighs. "I'm tired of you talking about stories."

I laugh. "Then how about I *tell* you one when we reach the glacier? Just for you."

He nods. "If you want to."

A short time later, we stand under the wall of ice. Its weight and depth feel greater for its stillness. The glacier slumbers like something coiled up tight on itself. Wind sails down the ravine, over the lip of the glacier, carrying a bloom of snow into the air above us.

"Why does it groan at the end of summer?" Harald asks Raudi.

"Because some parts of it are freezing faster than other parts," he says.

"You mean like how a hot kettle will crack if you put it in the snow?"

"Just like that," Raudi says. "And at the end of winter, it will groan again."

Harald's forehead wrinkles. "Because parts of it are melting."

"Exactly."

Harald nods to himself. "The groaning makes it sound alive."

"It does," I say. "I even had a dream where it broke free and rushed down on us."

Harald looks into my eyes. "Can that happen?"

"Well, glaciers can break apart and trigger avalanches," Raudi says. "There are stories about floods coming out of them."

Harald takes a step closer to me. "But not this one, right?"

I reach out and smooth his hair. "It was just a dream I had."

Harald turns and looks up the wall of the ravine. "Is that the cave?" He points at the column of steam rising from the mountainside.

"Yes," I say. "But there's more steam than I remember."

"Let's go inside it," Harald says, the glacier already forgotten.

We start up the slope, burrowing and digging through the snow, until we reach the entrance. Heat rises from it, a hot breeze in our faces, with the same stench I smelled last time.

"It smells like a hot spring," Harald says, pinching his nose.

"It's hotter than I remember, too," I say.

"Something is happening under the mountain," Raudi says. "A dragon, maybe."

"I don't want to go inside anymore," Harald says, and starts back down.

Raudi and I linger a moment. I notice a subtle vibration through the soles of my boots. The mountain is humming under its weight. I wonder if the dragon is waking. Is that feeling in the ground the rubbing of its scales against the rock as it climbs out of its den? Is that why its breath feels hotter and closer?

"Solveig, come on," Harald says below me. "Come tell my story."

I follow him down, and Raudi follows me. I look forward to having the audience I am used to. Eager to tell a story without having to think about rhythm and sound, without having to worry about anything beyond the little bit of joy I will bring my brother.

Later in the day, after we've returned to the steading, Harald and I sit in the hall together. I have Muninn out on my shoulder, and even though Harald still teases my bird, I've seen him slip bits of his own food between the bars of Muninn's cage when he thinks I'm not looking.

"When we get back to Father's hall," Harald says, "I want to show my friends your bird, and you can tell them a story, too."

The hall doors open, and two berserkers come in bearing a third between them. The man is barely upright, his ankles bent, feet dragging. Hake is behind them.

"Make way!" he shouts, and sweeps a nearby table clear. A few mugs clatter to the floor.

The berserkers help the unstable man onto the table and lay him down. His face is white and his eyelids flutter.

"What's going on?" Bera asks.

"He just fell," one of the berserkers says.

Bera touches the man's cheek. "Has he been lying in the snow for long?"

"No, ma'am," the berserker says.

"He's cold as ice." She turns to Hake. "Get the children out of here."

Hake nods and crosses to Harald and me. "Get your cloaks," he says. "Come with me." We follow his orders, and he ushers us toward the doors.

I look back at the sick man on my way out. He's started convulsing. The cords of muscle in his neck ripple and his tongue sticks out of his mouth.

"Get me a rag so he don't bite it off!" Bera shouts. "Help me hold him still. And get the fire going!"

Hake pushes me through the doorway into the yard. Then he closes the doors, and Harald and I are left standing outside. We pull our cloaks about us and wait to be let back in.

By nightfall, eight more of the berserkers have fallen, and one of Per's men. After the convulsions, all of them have slipped into a stupor and do not respond to anything. They breathe, moan, and they blink at times. It is sometimes possible to pour water down their throats, though I am not allowed near them. I look at their open mouths, their drying lips, and I cannot help but think of my dream.

With each warrior's fall, Hake has become angrier, but without something to rage against, he can only stand and watch and seethe. I do not think he is accustomed to feeling powerless. He and Per are arguing about what to do with Harald, Asa, and me. They don't know if it is safe to have us in the hall with the sick, but it is too cold for us to remain outside the hall at night.

In the end, we are hurried straight to our bedclosets, and the doors are shut fast. The sounds of the sick keep me awake for some time. Bera calls orders all through the night. But her voice is assured, like she knows what to do, and it comforts me.

By morning, the rest of the steading is taken with the sickness. Gunnarr and the remaining berserkers, as well as the new thrall. There aren't enough tables and benches in the hall to hold them, and some are laid out on the dirt floor. But a few of us remain well. Bera, Raudi, Ole, Per, Harald, Asa, and myself. Hake and Alric, too. None of us have fallen ill.

Hake stares out over the hall, at his decimated troops. He looks so helpless, his hands fisted at his sides. But there is a wildness in him I haven't seen before, even when he was breaking up the fight. He has the desperate, quivering rage of a cornered animal, ready to lash out at anyone.

"Poison," he says, deep in his throat.

"What?" Per asks.

"Three nights ago they all ate the goat." He looks at me. "We did not."

"Could the meat have simply turned?" Per asks.

Bera sniffs deeply, pulling upright at the accusation. I know that she would never have served bad meat.

"No," Hake says. "If the meat had turned, they would have been retching the night they ate it. It wasn't bad meat." He squares his shoulders toward Bera. "It was a slow poison."

Bera folds her arms and stares up at him. "And who do you think did it?"

"You prepared the food," Hake says.

"What?" Raudi says.

"Ridiculous," Ole says, arms crossed.

"A trial at the Thing will decide it. For now, I accuse you, Bera."

Per steps forward. "You can't —"

"I can!" Hake shouts. "I am the highest warrior in this steading, and my king entrusted me with the protection of his children. If you block me from fulfilling my duty" — his eyes look even wilder — "then you are my enemy."

Per pales and backs away. We are all stunned. Hake grabs up a piece of rope, and Bera lets him tie her hands behind her back, confusion crinkling her forehead, as if she can't accept that what's happening is real. Only days ago, we were fine. We were hungry, but we were fine. And now, the hall is filled with dying men, and Bera stands accused of poisoning them. What if others had eaten the goat? Harald? Asa? What if the poison were in some other dish that I would have eaten? Could Bera have done this? I did hear her say she wished the berserkers were gone from here. I sicken at the thought.

Raudi lunges at Hake, fists flying. "Let her go!"

But the berserker captain shoves my friend to the ground and drags Bera across the room. She goes with him, scuffing her feet, looking around at a world I don't think she recognizes.

Raudi gets up. He shouts at Per, "Do something!"

Per only stands there, mouth open, blank. "Hake is right."

"You lie!" Raudi says.

Per turns to him. "Watch yourself, you little bench-ornament."

Raudi falls silent at the insult.

I manage to clear my own head enough to step forward. "You are wrong to do this, Hake."

That stops him enough to at least look at me. "I am not wrong."

"You are," I say. "Bera would never do anything to harm us."

"How can you know what's in her heart? Perhaps she was worried we wouldn't live through the winter, and thought this was the only way to make sure there was enough food." He looks down at her. "Was that it, woman? I could maybe respect it, a little, if you did it to preserve the lives of the king's children." His grip tightens. "But you did it at the expense of my men. Good men who would have died to protect you in spite of your resentment toward them."

"I did not do this thing." Bera finally lifts her head to face Hake. "I did not!"

"You see?" I say.

Hake waves me off and hauls Bera up against one of the wooden pillars. He takes another length of rope and begins to tie her to it.

"Hake," Alric says from behind all of us. He has been so quiet, I'd forgotten he was there. Even Hake blinks at the skald. Alric points at the rope. "Where is it exactly that you expect her to run?"

Hake looks down and fingers the rope in his hands.

"She has done much to heal your men," Alric says. "To ease their suffering. Would you not like her to continue in these duties? It would be quite difficult for her while bound to that pillar."

Hake stares at Alric like the glacier, a wall of ice. Alric manages to smile, the way he does, so mild, and I wonder at his ability to summon it. Moments pass, and gradually Hake melts. I see his shoulders relax, his arms lower. He unties Bera and lets her go.

"You are free for now," he says. "You will make it your sole mission to heal my men. I will be watching you, and if I see any dereliction of these duties, I will tie you in the cowshed to freeze instead of the hall. Is that understood?"

Bera brushes off her hands. "I'll do what I can for your men. But not for you, Captain. I care not what you command.

I do it for them, because I do not want to see a single one of them die." She tries to step past him, but he blocks her with his arm.

"Your larder key," he says and holds out his hand.

She snatches it from her brooch and slaps it into his palm. Then she storms by him and goes to her hearth.

Raudi fixes Hake and Per with a hate-glare and hurries over to her.

"She is still under my arrest," Hake says, and rumbles away.

I turn to Alric. "Thank you, sir."

"She isn't cleared of suspicion," Alric says.

"She will be cleared," I say.

Per leads Asa away into a corner. She appears agitated, whispering and pointing her finger at him. I watch them go, angry at Per for failing us again, angry at my sister for saying nothing to defend Bera.

Alric sighs. "Let us just hope that none of these men die. The captain is not in his right mind. And looking around at this nightmare, I cannot say I entirely blame him."

"You don't really suspect Bera, do you?" I ask.

"I have to. I also must suspect Ole, and Per, and even Hake. And you should suspect me."

I swallow down a skip in my heartbeat. "Why?"

"Because I doubt the venomous traitor ate his or her own poison. The enemy is very likely one of us who did not partake of your goat."

I'm speechless. He is right.

Alric smiles his bland smile and walks away, just as Raudi approaches me.

"Thank you," he says, and his voice catches.

"For what?"

"For defending my mother. But now I don't know what will happen when we leave this place."

"It will be all right," I say. "No one but Hake believes it."

He shakes his head. "But it's Hake. That is enough for the Thing to find her guilty."

"Hake will see the truth on his own before long." I nod toward Bera as she bends over one of the men, adjusting his blankets. "Look at your mother, how she tries to save them."

"You're a true friend, Solveig."

He grabs me into a tight hug that squeezes the air out of me, then he lets me go and walks away without looking back. Surprise renders me silent. I am grateful that Raudi and I have restored some of our old closeness, but I feel guilty that it has come at such a high price.

The hall is very quiet after that, and everyone keeps away from Hake. Now that we know it was poison, no one is afraid of catching this plague. I am allowed to tend to the sick. I wipe their dry lips with a wet rag to keep them from splitting. I change soiled bedding. I whisper encouraging and comforting things to them. And when I am not helping, I sit next to Alric by the fire. Asa has gone to bed, red-eyed from crying about something, and Per sulks in the shadows.

FALLEN

I am unsettled by thoughts of enemy ships, and clouds in the shape of wolves, and falling glaciers.

"What is on your mind?" Alric asks.

"My dream," I say.

He nods. "That has been on my mind as well."

Later that night, one of the berserkers dies.

Asa later wore our mother's dress, the one she had tried on, to a feast. She came out, and Father beamed with pride while those gathered in the hall murmured in appreciation and wonder. She passed the mead-horn, and I think it felt to everyone as if they had a queen again. And you were beautiful, Asa. With Mother's dress, and your hair braided like a woman, and your jewelry. Everyone loved you.

I stood off to the side, next to a pillar, and Per, you came up beside me.

And even as you talked to me, you stared at Asa.

I did not mind. Everyone was staring at Asa.

"That will be you, one day," you said to me.

"Not me," I said.

You then said to me, "Beauty isn't all that matters. Wisdom and kindness, these are important, too. And you have them."

"Do you think so?" I asked.

"I do," you said, looking up at my sister, and even in that moment, you had never looked so handsome to me.

"My father doesn't think so," I said.

That's when your eyes met mine. "Perhaps not yet. And that is why you must show him."

CHAPTER 12

DEATH

The ground is frozen, cemented with ice and snow, so we cannot bury the body. Hake and Per trudge across the yard, carrying the berserker between them, and lay him in the cowshed. No one else goes with them, but I don't think any of us want to treat this as a funeral. The time for burial will come after we have returned home, where we and his kinsmen can honor him properly. For now, I turn my attention back to the suffering of the living.

Bera has assigned me to a group of warriors. One of them is the thrall, the fallen berserker who was banished and taken back in as a slave. I kneel down next to him with a bowl of cold water and a rag. He moans, but it isn't the sound of someone in pain. It is how I would imagine a distant ghost would sound, something lost and wandering in the night. It reaches deep into my chest, and I ache for him. I cry for him as I dab his forehead and squeeze drops of water into his mouth. He is weak, but he swallows.

Then he exhales a raspy breath that carries a single word. "Story."

"You want me to tell you a story?" I ask.

He closes his eyes, and a shiver rattles him. I pull the blanket up to his chin and feel him quivering beneath my hands. How can such a man, once a powerful berserker, feel so weak and frail? And in this moment, how can he want a story from me?

I don't know what story to tell. I try to think of a tale of healing, but I can't remember any. But perhaps it doesn't have to be a true story. Perhaps, as Alric says, it is more important what the story does, and I can tell a new story of my own. I take a moment to gather the words about me, piling them up in my mind, and I begin.

"High up in Asgard, there grows a tree on the Hill of Healing. And surrounding the tree are nine shield-maidens, nine Valkyrie. When our heroes are slain in battle, it is the Valkyrie who escort their spirits up to Odin's hall."

I notice that there are others listening to me now. Those men that can open their eyes watch me, so I stand and continue my tale as I walk among them.

"One of the nine Valkyrie, Eir, who was gifted in the healing arts, grew curious about our mortal world. So she withdrew from the Hill of Healing, passed through the gates of Asgard, and came down to our world, where she spied a frozen fjord. And there in the fjord she found a hall, small and heaped with snow that rose almost to the roofline."

Our fjord. Our little hall.

"She drew near to it," I say. "And she wondered what manner of men would dwell there. She decided to enter, and inside, Eir found Odin's finest warriors. . . ."

Our warriors. My voice threatens to break with grief. I look into the faces of the fallen men around me and tears fill my eyes. But I continue.

"All of them brave, all of them honorable, all of them strong. They had been felled by treachery, struck down by a coward's poison. And the greatness of the men moved Eir in her heart. She leaned and touched the tips of her fingers to their lips, lit upon them snowflake-soft, and left a drop of dew from the leaves of the tree that grows on the Hill of Healing."

I kneel by the nearest berserker and wipe the tears from my cheek. I kiss my fingertips and press them to his lips. Then I do the same for the next. I go to each man in turn as I speak.

"And one by one," I whisper, "the warriors wakened from the poison-sleep. Bodies purified. They strapped on their armor and took up their spears and their swords. They stood tall and proud under the winter sun. Eir smiled upon them, and then she climbed back up the cloud-paths, back to the Hill of Healing. There, she spoke to the other shield-maidens of the healing she had wrought in the finest of Odin's men."

I touch the lips of the last berserker, stand up, and look around the hall. Bera and Asa have tears in their eyes. Per hangs his head as though he cannot look at me, while Alric's wide eyes stare at me almost without blinking. Ole nods from a corner of the room.

I hear heavy footsteps and turn to see Hake rushing toward me. I take a step back as he falls and kneels at my feet.

"My princess," he says. He takes my hand, kisses it, and touches it to his forehead. "You are no skald. You are Eir, herself."

"I am not, Captain," I say. "But I wish that she were here."

"She was here," Alric says. "If only for a moment."

I bow and go back to the thrall I was attending before, the one who asked for the tale. He is smiling instead of moaning, and when I touch him, I find he is no longer shivering. I begin to let myself believe my own story, that my words can summon shield-maidens. That my stories can shape the world. The thought of so much power is exhilarating and terrifying.

I ask Alric about it later.

"I know what you are feeling," he says. "You realize that you now have the power to create gods and goddesses, warriors and dragons."

"Yes," I say. "But if they are not real before, can a story make them so?"

"Real to whom?"

"To everyone."

He sharpens the point of his beard with his fingers. "I can barely decide what is real for myself, let alone what is real to everyone else."

"Alric." I shake my head. "Sometimes I wonder if you're really saying anything at all, or if you just make it sound that way."

"Never trust a storyteller," he says. "We're all of us liars."

The mood in the hall is a little lighter for the rest of the afternoon. The warriors seem to be resting a little easier from the pains of the poison. We attend to them as we have done for the last few days, but my story has stoked the room with optimism. Later that evening, I take some food to Muninn. I have been neglecting him and decide to let him out of his cage. But instead of perching on my shoulder, he flies up into the rafters and glares at me.

"I'm sorry I haven't had you out," I say. "But you can sulk if you want to."

He squawks at me.

For the rest of the evening, as I move about the hall, I notice that he's usually perched on the rafters just over my head. I don't know if he's trying to put more droppings in my hair, or if he's just reminding me that he's not on my shoulder where I want him. But he's there, and it makes me smile.

But then he's not there, and I hear Hake's voice bellowing.

"Who took the key?"

Everyone looks around in confusion, and I search the rafters for Muninn.

"The larder key?" Per asks.

Hake charges right up to Bera and looms over her. "Yes, the larder key. Where is it, woman?"

She puts her hands on her hips. "I have no idea."

And then I see my raven, strutting toward his open cage, eyes glittering, the key in his beak.

"Muninn!" I rush toward him. He flaps away from me, racing for his cage as though he's hoping to hide the key before I reach him. But I grab his tail feathers and snatch it from him. "Bad bird!" I say.

Everyone in the room starts laughing, including Hake.

Muninn caws at me and ruffles his feathers in fury before hopping into a corner of his cage. Then he actually turns his back to me, and I can't believe how like a person he is.

"Your bird thinks he should be running the steading?" Hake says as I hand him the key.

I close the door to Muninn's cage. "I think he just likes the metal for his nest."

"Well, I told you he was a smart one." Hake stands over Muninn with a look of pride. "I'll just have to be more careful around this little thief." He chuckles and walks away.

Muninn jerks his head toward me.

"I'll try to let you out more often," I say.

Not long after that, I climb into the bedcloset with Asa. She lies awake on her side, facing me. I could touch her if I wanted to, without even needing to reach. But I don't want to. I still cannot believe she did not defend Bera, nor can I believe she continues her relationship with Per. I have never felt further away from her than I do right now, our faces inches apart. These months spent trapped together have made my sister a stranger to me, and I feel a loneliness I haven't ever felt before.

"I loved your story," she says.

I want to roll away from her. "Thank you."

"You brought the men comfort."

I nod.

"It was beautiful," she says.

"Why did you keep silent?"

She frowns. "When?"

"When Hake accused Bera. You said nothing in her defense."

"How do you know she didn't do it?"

"What?" I sit up in bed. "How can you say that?"

"You never know what a person is capable of, Solveig. Who knows what's in Bera's heart?"

There is something wrong in her voice. I hear it now that I have learned how to lie. But even though the story I told tonight may not have been true, I didn't tell it to deceive. Not like Asa's words.

"You're right." I lie back down. "You never know what a person is capable of."

"Exactly."

"I would never have thought Per capable of such cowardice."

She is silent. I refuse to look at her.

"Per is no coward." Her voice is hard.

"He did nothing to defend Bera, either. He wanted to, but he was afraid to stand up to Hake."

"He wasn't afraid."

"Yes, he was. And you were angry with him for it. I saw you."

She turns away from me. "That's not what I was angry about."

"Then what were you angry about?"

"Good night, Solveig."

The next day, I go to my thrall. He is sleeping, and I sit beside him to help him eat some oats that Bera has mashed and thinned to a slurry. But when I touch him, he is cold. Rigid. I drop the bowl and scurry backward.

"What is it?" Bera asks from nearby.

I say nothing, simply stare at his face. The corners of his mouth are still smiling.

Bera sweeps over to me. She bends and touches the back of her hand to his cheek. Then she closes her eyes and bows her head. "I'm sorry, child."

"He's dead?" I ask.

"Yes. I'll get Hake and Per to take him out."

She leaves me with him. I stare, wanting to run, but also feel the urge to touch him again, touch his cheek the way Bera did. To feel the absence of whatever it is that once made him alive. Instead, I take a deep breath and cover his face with the blanket, and I cry over him until Hake and Per come to carry him away.

This time, I follow them out of the hall, across the yard, and into the shed. They lay him on the ground, their breath-clouds above him as though his spirit is lingering over his body. There are two in here now. Two dead warriors. How many more will die?

"I'll be right back," Hake says. Per and I wait without speaking.

When the berserker captain returns, he is carrying the sword he took from the thrall three nights ago. Hake kneels and places the weapon on the body. Then he folds the man's arms across his chest, over the hilt.

Hake stands and turns to Per and me. Then he is gone.

Per clears his throat. "I'm sorry."

"About what?" I ask.

He sighs. "Everything. This is not how I . . . I have not ful-filled my duty to protect you."

"Nor my sister."

"Solveig, believe me when I tell you that I have done noth-ing that would dishonor her. But I respect you too much to lie to you. Yes, I love her. I loved her even before we came here. I have done many things out of love for her."

The way he says it needles me with a painful doubt. My throat is dry as I ask, "Have you been my friend out of love for her? Just because I'm her sister?"

"What?" He holds up his hands. "No, no. I am your friend because I admire you. Surely you know that."

I bow my head. I want to believe him. I want to see him as I used to, but it is difficult to forget the ways he has disappointed me.

"Solveig, I —"

Hake walks back through the door. "Come, Per." He frowns. "Another has died."

Per closes his eyes, defeated. "Who?"

"One of your men. The wounded one, Egill."

Per places a hand on my shoulder. "We must finish talking later."

I nod, and he nods, and he and Hake leave. I look around me. In my mind, I see a cowshed full of bodies. Bodies covering the frozen ground, bodies stacked beside and on top of one another. And in that moment, I know that my stories cannot heal, or create, or shape. They are nothing more than words, dead as soon as they're born, lost as soon as I've spoken them. I don't feel powerful anymore. I feel weak.

On my way across the yard, I see Hake and Per coming toward me, death-laden. I step aside and let them pass. They make the trip many times through the evening and night. Five before I go to sleep, and then the hall doors open four times during the night, waking me. By morning, there are only nine berserkers still living, and Gunnarr. But we lose him right after we have served the morning meal.

I sit on a bench with my bowl, the cold contents uneaten, watching them take the body out. Five more soon follow. Later in the day, Ole comes over. He sits next to me and works over the same fishing net he already repaired.

"You're a compassionate person, Solveig."

I don't respond. Not because I don't want to, I just can't think of what to say.

Ole leans back. "I think that's what makes you such a good skald."

"I'm not a skald."

"Do you want to be?"

"I think I do."

"It seems a hard life."

I hadn't really thought about that before. For the first time, I imagine myself walking the cold and lonely roads from one hall to the next, trying to find a patron and lord. If I'm lucky, a chieftain will keep me on, the way my father has done with Alric. Would my father want me as his skald? And what would happen to Alric?

"Would you give up your royal life to tell stories?" Ole asks.

It is a hard question. Telling stories has made me prouder of myself than I have ever been. When I stand up there before the hall with a tale on my lips, I am someone important, and I have something to offer.

But then I think of all the bodies in the shed. In the lowest of times, as we are now, of what value are all these stories? Are they even worth the sacrifice if they do nothing in the end?

"I don't know," I say.

Ole nods. He looks around the room, and I do the same.

Bera and Raudi are sitting on a bench, mother and son. Harald is sleeping, his head in Asa's lap, perhaps a sign that our older sister is returning to us. Hake crouches in a corner, and I think I hear him crying. Can that be?

"It's like the shock after a battle," Ole says. "And it isn't over. I fear the worst has yet to fall upon us."

"How could it get worse?" I ask.

He looks at his netting.

"You were a warrior," I say, "before you became a thrall. Have you been in many battles?"

"Many." His jaw clenches. "But that was another life."

Alric approaches us. "Solveig, come with me a moment." He takes the bowl from my hands and sets it aside. Then he helps me up and leads me off to the edge of the room. "They need a story," he says.

I blink at him. "Now?" A story seems so pointless in this devastation.

"Yes. They need another story from *you*."

"They died."

"What?"

"They died!"

Alric flinches from me.

I point at the hall doors through which the eighteen bodies have been carried. "My story did nothing!"

"I do not think it did nothing."

"But it didn't save them. What good is it?"

"You brought them peace."

"Only for a moment."

"When you are in pain, a moment is an eternity."

"And when that moment is over, what then?" I am crying now.

"You tell another story. You fill the moments with them."

Endless stories for endless suffering. It feels hopeless to me. "I can't."

Alric looks around the room. "Then I will."

When the summer was still new, trailing cold mornings, Per and Raudi began sparring in the yard. Raudi, you held your spear as if it might somehow turn in your hands and stab you, and Per, you were perhaps a little too rough with him, in the beginning. I know that is the way of things. Boys must become men, but I winced each time you knocked my friend to the ground.

But each time you said, "Again," and helped him back up.

Did you both know I watched you? I watched as you hardened, Raudi, and as you, Per, shaped the form he would settle into.

I was watching that day when you began to cry, Raudi. Do you remember that? I do not mean to embarrass you. But I saw you drop your weapon and slump to the ground. I wanted to run to you to find out what was wrong. But by that time you and I weren't speaking much. So I waited, and watched.

I expected you to berate him, Per. I expected you to curse, and yank him to his feet. To beat the tears out of him.

But you didn't.

You knelt down beside him, put your hand on his shoulder, and you spoke to him. I admired you so much for that. I was too far away to hear what was said, and I don't want you to tell me now, Raudi. But whatever it was, it helped you.

You rose to your feet, gripped your spear tighter, and said, "Again."

THAW

Alric strides to the hearth and stands up tall. He lifts his arms before the fire. "Hear me," he says. "Listen." He doesn't say it loudly. But there is weight in his voice, a force that pulls us to him and binds us there. An iron anchor. When all our eyes are on him, he begins.

"It has been foretold by the seers of old that the day will come when brothers will fight and kill each other, when war will reign and all loyalties will be forsaken. An axe age. A sword age when shields are riven. A wind age and a wolf age before the Breaking of the World. The great serpent will writhe, sending the oceans surging beyond their bounds, and the mountains will tremble and fall, releasing the giant wolf, Fenrir."

I wonder why he has picked this story. Our steading is

besieged. We are weak and demoralized, and he speaks to us of the end of the world? I grow angry at him.

"And Fenrir will devour the sun and the moon. The stars will fall, and the earth will burn with a fire to touch the heavens. Odin will die in battle with Fenrir. The serpent will rise to do battle with Thor, and the Thunderer shall fall as the floods cover the land. And after the gods meet their doom, and all have drowned and perished, the earth-sea will remain in darkness for a time."

I want to stand up, to ask Alric what he means by this. Why is he telling us this? But before I can, his voice and demeanor change.

"But from this great darkness," he says, "a brilliant new sun will shine, and the skies will clear. The waves will sparkle and peel away from a rising land. Earth shall emerge from the sea, fertile and renewed, and on this land, the surviving gods will gather to create the world again. Mankind will not be lost. New children shall be born. New fields shall be sown and harvested. Skyr and cheese shall be made, ale shall be drunk, marriages performed, kings crowned, the seasons shall pass as they always have. For even though the world may break, and all shall despair at what they've lost, life will always return."

He bows his head.

And I feel hope. I mourn for what is lost, for those berserkers who have died or may yet die, but I await that which will come. I search the faces of those around me, my siblings,

Raudi and Bera, and Per, and I see that they feel the same. Their tear-washed eyes shine.

When his story is finished, we do not applaud. We sigh. Alric sits down on a nearby bench, sagging like an exhausted farmer come in from a day of threshing in the field. I move over to him.

"Can I get you anything?"

"A drink."

I ladle him some water from a bucket of melting snow. He drinks it down, and some trickles into his beard.

"That was a wonderful story," I say.

He smiles. "Thank you."

"I don't know how you found the strength."

"You have it, too."

I refill his mug, and he gulps it. "Do you know why I told that story?"

I stop to think. What had the story done for me? "Maybe if people can't have an end to their suffering, the next thing they seek for is to know why they suffer. Suffering is a part of life in this world, part of a cycle."

He closes his eyes. "Stories give you a way to see things. A way to understand the events of your life. Even if you don't realize it while you're hearing the tale."

The evening passes, and no one else dies. We all take our hope to our beds with us, and though we are still in danger, we sleep a little better. That hope lingers through the night, like the warm fragrance of woodsmoke, and I begin to believe in the power of stories again. It is a different power than I imagined.

Until now, I thought only of what stories could do in their moment. I was the ploughman, turning the hearts of my audience like soil, thinking I could bend the earth to my will. But stories have a quieter and more subtle power than that. Now I see that I am also the ploughman's wife walking behind him, dropping seeds into the earth, leaving them to grow in meaning. I realize that every story I have ever heard is a part of me, deeply rooted, whispering behind my thoughts.

But suspicion lingers there, as well, and fear that the traitor will soon strike again.

In the morning, we find all of the remaining berserkers alive. I begin to think the poison has worked its way through the men and claimed all the warriors it can, and the rest will be spared. But though they live, they are still not well, and require tending.

Bera sets me to washing their soiled bedding and clothes. I fill a basin with snow and leave it by the fire to melt and warm before scrubbing the filth from the fabric. When the water is brown, and the laundry is as clean as I can get it, I hang the articles from the rafters. Ole helps me to reach the higher beams.

"I have an answer for you," I say.

"An answer to what?"

"You asked if I would give up my life to be a skald."

"And?"

"I would."

He stops what he's doing. "Do you truly mean that?"

"I do."

"Then listen to me, Solveig." His voice changes, hardens. "You must remember what you've just told me. Don't ever forget that you spoke those words, and that you meant them."

"But why?"

"In life, the hardest decisions often have to be made more than once. But each time, it gets easier. Will you remember?"

My mind is reeling. Is he referring to the time when I will have to ask my father? "I will remember," I whisper

He softens. "Good. Now help me with this sheet."

We finish, and I take a moment to rest. While the linens are wet, I can see the glow of the hearthfire through them and the shadows of people passing by. But as the laundry dries, it clouds over. There seemed to be something more behind what Ole said to me. What difficult decisions has he had to make more than once?

The day passes, and Per and Hake never have to make the long journey to the shed. The hope from Alric's tale combined with these signs of recovery eases some of our despair. Though the mood in the hall is still tense, and we are all wary of one another, there is occasional laughter now. And Harald is hanging about Hake again. The berserker captain is letting my brother attempt to lift his war hammer. I think my brother would struggle with the haft by itself, let alone the anvil of a head at the top. Harald strains and Hake chuckles.

I walk over to them. "You almost have it, Harald."

"I don't think so," Harald says through his teeth.

"One day soon," Hake says, "little prince."

Harald gives up with a gasp and stares at the hammer on the ground. "I *am* little."

Hake picks up the weapon with one hand. "But you are fierce."

"And brave," I say.

"Yes," Harald says, out of breath. He nods to himself, and then he walks away.

I turn to Hake. "Thank you for humoring him."

"He's a good boy. Strong-willed. He'll make a fine king."

His statement reminds me of my father, and I worry for his safety. If there is an assassin among us, then might there also be one near him? "I hope things are going well back home."

Hake lets the head of the hammer slide to the ground and leans on the handle as though it's a walking stick. "I wish that I were by your father's side. Not trapped in this frozen place. But do not trouble yourself with these thoughts. Your father is a fearless warrior and a great strategist. He knows how to win wars. You'll see when we return home that everything is well."

"When we return home," I say, both fearing and hoping for that day.

"Yes."

"And what of Bera? When we return home."

Hake runs his hand over his head. "That is something else."

"She didn't do it. I know you know it."

"Yes." He sighs. "I know she didn't do it. I was mad with rage."

"If she didn't, then who did?"

"I don't know." He looks over his shoulder. "It is hard to think that any of them are capable of it. Perhaps the meat had turned after all." But he sounds doubtful.

I, too, would like to think it was bad meat, but there is something telling me that isn't so. A feeling like a beehive in my stomach. I know what I saw in my dream. What I saw was no accident, and neither are the frozen bodies out in the cowshed. Someone has been trying to weaken our steading by robbing us of our food and our warriors. Some enemy who shares our hearthfire. Perhaps even the berserker captain standing before me.

A wolf come ravening.

That evening, I seek out Raudi. His mood has slipped back into a dark place since the night Hake accused Bera of poisoning the men. But I think I can lift his spirits if I reassure him that Hake no longer suspects his mother.

"I'm glad," he says, his voice flat. "Thanks."

"I thought you would be relieved," I say.

"Well, Hake already talked to me about it. He apologized."

"Oh."

"But thank you."

But this raises a new question. "Then what's been bothering you?"

"Nothing. I'm fine, Solveig."

I think back to that night. "Is it what Per called you?"

Raudi's gaze drops.

"Don't listen to what Per says."

"Your father does. Per called me a bench-ornament."

I put my hand on his shoulder. "You are no coward, Raudi."

He takes in a breath as though he's about to speak, but then says nothing. I wait. He takes in another breath, and still says nothing.

"What is it?" I ask.

"I *am* a bench-ornament," he says.

It grieves me that he would think of himself in such a way, but nothing I say afterward changes his mind.

I lie awake that night until everyone else has gone to sleep. Then I rouse Asa, quietly.

"Solveig?" She yawns. "What is it?"

"Shh. Keep your voice down."

"Is something wrong?"

"Yes." I lean into her. "Asa, you have to tell me the truth. And I'll know if you're lying."

"The truth about what?"

"Did Per poison the stew?"

I feel her stiffen and push away from me. "What?"

"Did he do it?"

"No! And Hake accused Bera —"

"Bera didn't do it and you know it. Hake knows it, too. He told me tonight he thinks it was bad meat."

"Maybe it was."

"No. It wasn't."

"How do you know?"

"I know. And that is why I needed to make sure."

"Solveig, listen to me. Per did not do this."

I listen to her voice and I believe her. Or at least, I believe that she believes Per is innocent. That does not mean he is, but it means Asa had nothing to do with it if he isn't. Though I am still angry with her, a meager trust in her begins to grow back.

"Thank you," I say. "You and I and Harald are the only ones we can count on."

"And Per," she says.

I let that pass. "We need to protect each other."

"Oh, Solveig." She pulls me into her arms, and I go reluctantly. "I would never let any harm come to you. No matter what happens, you will be safe. I promise you. We just need to hold out till spring."

I nod and try to relax in her embrace, but I can't. I don't want spring to come. With spring comes the thaw from my dream, the wolf-cloud over the hall, the opening of the ice-fjord, and the terrible enemy ships with their curses on the wind. If I could, I would keep this steading frozen in the heart of winter forever.

We have food enough now, and no more fear that we will run out. But every bite is heavy in my mouth, purchased for a price that I never would have willingly paid. Now we gather silently around the hearth in the morning and evening and eat our guilt.

Over the next few days, the berserkers continue to improve. They regain the color in their faces. They appear alive again. They sleep without fevers. They still occasionally tremble or suffer fits, but they are mostly well. We take up telling stories nightly, as we did before. Alric and I, with Muninn on my shoulder. After several weeks have passed, bringing us closer to the far edge of winter, the berserkers are able to sit up, and one or two of them can even hobble about the hall.

Today, Harald is going to each of the berserkers and challenging them to arm wrestle. They laugh and oblige him, and he wins every time. They tell Harald he is mighty.

"When you beat me," Harald says to them, "you'll know your strength is back."

"Indeed," they say. "Then we'll know for certain."

I call him away to let the berserkers rest.

"Do you want to arm wrestle me?" I ask.

"That wouldn't be fair now, would it?"

"How so?"

"You're a girl."

"Girls can be strong."

"Not as strong as boys."

I tousle his hair. "I dare you to arm wrestle Bera."

He shakes his head vigorously.

"Why, because she's a girl?"

"She's not a girl."

"No? Then what is she?"

He looks at me as though I'm daft. "She's a *mother*."

I laugh. "That makes all the difference, doesn't it?"

He screws up his mouth, and then he blurts out, "Did she poison those men?" The question comes in such a rush that I can tell he's been holding it in his mouth for a while.

"No, she didn't."

"How do you know?"

"I know her, and Bera would never do that. Neither would Raudi."

"What about Alric?"

"I doubt it."

"Per?"

"I don't think so."

"Well, I know it's not Hake," he says. "Ole?"

"He has served Father for so long."

"But that's everyone."

And it is everyone. Perhaps Hake is right, and it was the meat after all. But I still find that hard to believe. The poison came on late and did not work its way through the men in the way of bad food. It persisted too long in their bodies, and those facts hover over me like swords about to fall.

"When they . . ." Harald's lip begins to quiver, and he looks at his feet. "When they poisoned the men, were they trying to kill me? Was it my fault?"

"What? No!" I reach out and pull him into my arms, squeezing him. "Of course not. It isn't your fault, and no one would want to kill you." I'm not just trying to soothe him. My brother is much more valuable alive, for ransom. Which is the only reason I don't worry about him sleeping with Per and Hake and the men. "Have you been worrying about that all this time?"

He nods against my chest.

"Harald, you mustn't think these things. Whoever poisoned the stew knew that you and Asa and I wouldn't eat it. Because it was Hilda."

"Then why did they do it?"

"I think what they really want is to weaken the steading. That's why they got rid of the cows, and why they poisoned the berserkers sent to protect us. If our enemy wanted us dead, they could have poisoned something else that all of us would have eaten, but they didn't."

He slides away, and his forehead wrinkles up. "I see. But now I don't know if I feel better or worse."

"Just be brave for me. All right?"

"All right," he says. "I'm just glad that winter will be over soon."

The weeks are relentless. The days are stretching, lengthening, as though someone is spinning the gray wool of winter-light into golden thread. The others enjoy the sun, and spend more time outside in its warmth, while I hide away from it inside the hall. I have come to dread the sun's rising, and I watch in fear as it drags each day across the sky.

I huddle by the hearth and try not to think of my dream. I pretend that I've locked it in the bedcloset; that it isn't real out in the waking world. It doesn't help that Alric seems to be thinking about it, too. He has started complaining loudly about the cold as though it's still midwinter. He tells stories of terrible snowstorms, and of the icy realm of the frost giants, as though he can keep spring at bay with his words. I have learned that stories do not have such a power. But it helps that I am not alone in my fear. And I have Muninn, on my shoulder even now.

I remember a moment in the sun with him after Hake first gave him to me. I remember looking up and closing my eyes, and the brightness turning the insides of my eyelids red. It felt so warm, and I was content with my raven in his cage beside me.

I wonder if Muninn has bonded to me after these long dark months spent together. Would he leave me if I took him outside? I know that I need to find out sooner or later. I cannot carry his cage with me wherever I go, especially if I am to be a skald and travel from hall to hall.

I turn my head to look at him, and he flaps his wings.

"Will you stay with me now, my memory, bird of Odin?" I stand and move toward the hall doors. "Or will you leave me if I give you the chance?"

I reach the doors and pause, staring at them. I place my palm against the wood and feel the deep grain polished black by smoke and many hands. I whisper, "Please don't go."

Then I pull the doors inward, drawing a sharp draft of cold air over us. I stand under the lintel, one foot forward, a slice of sun across my boot. It is as far as I can bring myself to go. I look at Muninn by my cheek, and he is perfectly still. Transfixed. As though he is trying to remember the sky.

Out in the yard, Harald is throwing snowballs at Ole and Alric, and the two men seem to be fighting back. When my brother sees me, he stops and points. Everyone turns to look at me, but I ignore them. I stand there, waiting to see what Muninn does. It is not too late; I could close the doors.

Muninn bobs his head, cocks it, and turns it, trying to see from all angles. His little talons shift on my shoulder as though he is preparing to leap away. I swallow and wait.

And then I feel it. A cold drop of water on my forehead. I

look up and see the icicle. Dripping. Melting. I look again at the yard and notice that the drifts of snow have begun to sigh and slump in the warmth.

And on the breeze, I can almost hear the sound of voices, low echoes up the fjord. I listen to them and realize they do not come from the sea, but from the ravine. And they are not many, but one. I feel sick and clutch my stomach. I shut fast the hall doors against the sound. The groaning of ice.

Above us, the glacier is waking.

It seems so long ago, now, that Father ordered us to leave. So long since that early dawn when we boarded the ship under cover of darkness. We had so little time to prepare, but we took what we could. And Father chose carefully each man and woman he sent with us.

Per, I think you were chosen because of all of Father's men, he trusts you second only to Hake. And that trust extended to the men you brought with you, Gunnarr and Egill.

Bera, I think you were chosen because you have served so faithfully, for so many years, and proven your love for my family. The same can be said of you, Ole.

Raudi, I think Father chose you because he knows you have as much bravery, if not more, than did your brother, and he knows that you can be counted on when all others fail.

And Hake. It is obvious why Father sent you after us with your men. If there is any warrior or force capable of protecting us, it would be you.

Alric, you sit there silently, but I think you know Father better than anyone here, his mind and his will. In many ways, better than his own children. I think that is why you were chosen.

Aside from me and my siblings, that is everyone.

And knowing that, I ask you, which of you did Father misjudge?

CHAPTER 14

FEAR

The ice over the fjord is thinning. The dark water laps it away from below, rising closer to the surface in faint, shadowy ribbons against the white. So long as the ice holds, we are safe. No ship can enter. But it is thinning, and I do not know how much longer it will resist.

"Father will send someone soon," Harald says. "To tell us that we can come home."

"That is the hope," Hake says. "Come, we must return to the steading."

"Thank you for letting me look again," I say to Hake on the way back.

The berserker captain nods. I think he is irritated with me.

We still do not know who might have left the footprints by the runestone those months ago, who or what might be out in the woods, and even though we have all come to suspect that the enemy is one of us, Hake takes no chances. He insists on accompanying me to the cliff where I go each day to check the ice. Hake thinks, like Harald, that I am excited for the opening of the fjord.

But I am not.

We walk through the gate, now left unguarded most of the time, and Hake closes it. With the surviving berserkers still weakened, there aren't enough men to hold the wall anyway if the steading were attacked. The hall is our only safety.

We go inside for our day meal. Porridge, as it always is. I am afraid to think about what I would trade for just a pat of butter and a drizzle of honey. I am sick of oats.

After everyone has eaten, Alric pulls me aside. "We should think about what story you shall tell your father."

"What do you mean?"

"Well, I'm sure when you tell him you want to be a skald, he'll want you to demonstrate your skill. He'll want to determine your aptitude for himself."

I begin to panic. "I can't. Not for him."

"You must. And you can. You just need to practice, and that's why I suggest we start now."

"No." I've been so consumed by the fear of my dream, that I haven't been thinking about my father or what awaits me back home. "I'm not ready."

"You need to be, Solveig. Winter is ending. You know it is."

I shake my head. "Just give me a few more days."

He sighs.

"Just a few more days," I say. "That's all, I promise."

"All right, then. But this delay won't help you. Practice will." He shakes his head and walks away.

A few days later, we are standing on the cliff, and the wind rushing up to us is warm enough to smell of the sea. And within a moment, Harald is jumping up and down. He points. I see it.

An opening in the ice, a weeping seam.

"We'll go home now, won't we?" Harald says.

Hake lays his millstone hand on Harald's shoulder. "Not until we're sent for. Your father will wait until he is certain of your safety."

"But his messengers will be able to reach us now," Harald says.

"That is true."

Something knots up and sinks in my stomach, like a boiling-stone dropped in a kettle. I turn away from the cliff. "Come, Harald."

Hake raises an eyebrow at me.

"What's wrong?" Harald asks. "Aren't you happy, Solveig?"

No, I am frightened, but I won't tell him that. "I'm tired. It's been a long winter."

"It has," Hake says. "Let's go inside."

Once we've reached the hall, Harald tells everyone that the ice has broken, which prompts cheering and laughter. Everyone except Alric and me. The skald makes eye contact with me from across the room.

Later that night, he asks if I am ready to begin preparing.

Whether I am or not, I made a promise. "Let's begin," I say.

"Good. First, we must select the story. Now, your father prefers the newer tales, nothing too old. He connects better with heroes of recent memory."

I nod.

"He will have also just fought and, I trust, won a war. So something celebratory would probably endear you to him."

It is odd to think of my father in this way. As an audience. I have never paid attention to the particular songs and stories he has chosen. In this regard, he is a stranger to me, and Alric knows him better than I do, his own daughter. At that thought, a deep inadequacy pulls my gaze to the ground.

Alric continues. "We should consider telling a tale *about* your father. To honor him. We need to do what we can to help your case."

"My case? Sir, you make it sound like a trial during the Thing."

"It is a trial, in a manner of speaking. You are making a claim that will require evidence. And witnesses. I will speak for you and recommend your talent, but you must supply the proof that you can do this." He pauses. "You must believe in your own case, Solveig. If you doubt yourself, how can you expect your father to do any different? Do you believe?"

I look up. "I want to believe."

"That will have to suffice for now."

For the next few hours, we discuss potential tales. Some I have never heard before, and Alric tells them quickly, touching on the important details. But then we turn to the events of my father's own life, stories already told of him, again and again, so that I already know them by heart.

"Isn't there something that hasn't been told before?" I ask.

"Perhaps . . ." Alric taps his chin. "Perhaps it is time to . . ."

"Time to what?"

He looks at me with a sly smile. "In fact, it might be the perfect time."

"Perfect time for what?"

"A tale of your father *before* he was king. Do you know how he became the king he is today?"

My father has been king for as long as I or even Asa have lived. I have never known him as anything else, and when I try to think of him as something less, my thoughts fail. But he was once a warrior like Per. I have heard the story of how he fought for another king who died in battle, and even as his fellow warriors fled, my father charged and defeated the enemy chieftain in single combat, claiming both crowns as his own. "Tell me," I say.

"Your father was not of noble birth. He was the son of a fisherman, but he left to become a warrior. It is said that as a young man he was vain and filled with dragon fire. This was in the days before he mastered his temper and became the man you know. There was a time when he would fight any and all at the slightest insult. He left no challenge unmet, and let no injury to his pride pass unpunished. He was wild, and feared."

I think of my father, so silent and immovable. How can a stone be wild?

"And then one day, your father was walking down a road in a fine new cloak he had won in a bet. A rider galloped by him and splattered him with mud. Your father became enraged and shouted a challenge after the man. The rider turned and trotted back.

"'Peace, son,' the rider said. 'Let me buy you a new cloak.'

"But your father would not hear him. He demanded single combat, and the rider obliged. But when the rider dismounted and removed his cloak, your father saw an old man covered in battle scars. He wore no armor —"

"A berserker?" I ask.

"Yes. When your father saw his opponent's age, he smirked, thinking this would be an easy victory. But when they began to fight, with spears and swords and axes, your father realized that this old man still had strength in his bones. Their bodies and boots carved ruts in the road. Their battle lasted a day and a night, until dawn came, and shocked and exhausted, your father fell at last. But the berserker did not kill him.

"'You are a mighty man,' the berserker said. 'But you could be mightier still if you overcome your fear.'

"'I fear nothing!' your father shouted.

"'You fear the beast that is inside you,' the berserker said. 'You are afraid that if you challenge it, you will fail. So you fight with me instead.'

"Your father spat. 'Stop talking and finish this!'

"'I'm not going to kill you,' the berserker said. 'Though that might be the easier road. But no, I am going to train you.'

"'I've no wish to be a berserker,' your father said.

"'Do you wish to be a king?' the berserker asked. 'Because you have it in you to become one, and I can lead you there.' He offered your father his hand, and after a long moment, your father took it. They traveled together for several years, and your father passed through three trials, each a tale in its own right."

I am rapt by Alric's story. The image of my father shifts in my mind like a cloud with each of Alric's wind-words. My feelings for my father have been unseated, and I do not yet know where they will settle.

Alric continues. "First, your father fought the fearsome *haugbui* of a fallen champion that had been tormenting its own village, sending the bloated corpse back into its grave.

"Then, he hunted a great bear, a man-killer, deep into its cave. Their battle shook the mountain by its roots, and the bear's pelt was large enough to cover four benches in the meadhall.

"And finally, your father fell in love with your mother, and served her father for years to prove his worth and earn the right to marry her.

"Along the way, he learned the berserker ways. He learned the prayers that quiet the beast inside. He learned the chants that rouse the beast to a frenzy before going to war. And in those years, your father fought the hardest battle of his life, but mastered himself in the end. The rest of the story, I think you know."

The tale has left me breathless. "And what about the old berserker?"

"Berserkers are not so honored in other kingdoms and chiefdoms. In many places, they are exiles, reviled and feared. But your father gave them a place of honor. He appointed them as his elite guard in tribute to the man he had met, fought, and learned from."

It is a wonderful tale, and I know that Alric has already gilded it with myth-metal. Beneath the firelight reflected in the ornamentation, I can almost see the ordinary truth. I wonder why Alric would go to the effort now for me, his only audience. And then I know. It's about fear. My father has always seemed immune to fear, but now I know that it is something to be mastered, not denied.

"I know what you're doing," I say.

"Whatever do you mean?" he asks, his eyebrows up.

"In my fear, you ask me to tell a tale about overcoming fear."

He laughs. "I didn't think to fool you. Only to surprise you."

I nod. "It is a good tale, and I will tell it."

"It is a good tale."

"And my father will enjoy it?"

Alric nods. "I trust that he will."

So long as he even lets me tell it.

Several days later, I stand at the cliff, staring at the widening gaps in the ice, willing them to narrow and close. A ship could enter now, something Harald reminds us of daily as he shoots about the hall, flying like an ember popped from the hearthfire. He wishes we were leaving this place today.

But we are not.

Though I wish we were as well, even with the dread I feel when I think about returning home. Each day we remain in this place is another opportunity for my dream to emerge from the bedcloset into daylight.

Below me, down by the water, Ole fishes, alone. Hake wanted to go with him, but the old man insisted he could take care of himself, and that no enemy would be interested in an old worthless thrall, anyway. So he casts his lines and his net by himself. I'm too far away to know if he's having any luck, but my mouth waters at the thought of eating fresh fish tonight.

Later that evening, Ole brings in a line of glistening fish. Some of us gasp and others laugh. Bera, Raudi, and I clean them, saving the offal to fertilize the garden plot in back. Then we slap them down on flat cooking rocks among the embers. First, the fish release their briny steam, and then their eyes shrivel above their open mouths, and then their skins begin to crackle and brown, and I don't remember ever getting so much pleasure from watching something cook.

Soon, we are all peeling and eating the crispy skin, and flaking off chunks of moist meat with our hands. I feed some to Muninn, and he snatches the morsels from my fingers as though he is as tired of oats as I am. Harald and I smile at each other, greasy-fingered, and suck on the bones. We add them to the offal for the soil, and Bera plops down on a bench with a sigh.

"Tomorrow," she says, "I think that I shall begin to pack up our things."

Per turns to her. "Pack up?"

"To go home," she says.

"We're not leaving," Per says. "We're staying here."

And with that, joy, our brief guest, leaves us.

"Why would we stay here?" Bera asks.

"Per is right," Hake says. "We have had no news of the war. And even when a messenger arrives, they might not bring welcome tidings."

"This is ridiculous," Bera says. "I see no reason to stay in this place any longer. The fjord is open, the sea is calm. It is the perfect time."

"And what if the king's children are still in danger?" Hake asks. "You would risk their safety for your own sake?"

"Of course not," Bera says. "But do you really think they're safe here? Perhaps you need to go take another look in the cowshed."

Hake explodes, "Don't you dare speak of my men in such a way!"

"Why are you so keen to keep us here?" Ole asks Hake.

The berserker looks at the thrall, and then away. "Stick to fishing, slave."

"It would seem to me," Ole says, "that you must have a reason. Are you leaving some work here unfinished, perhaps?"

Hake laughs. "Such as?"

But Ole does not need to say it. He is accusing Hake of being the traitor. I look at the berserker, and I remember his night-prayer. I know he didn't do it, for I have seen his heart. But the others haven't, and by the wariness on their faces I can see that Ole's words have trailed doubt into the hall after them like a cold breeze.

"I agree with Hake," Per says.

"Of course you do," Ole says, and then he looks at Asa. "Why would you want to go back to your king's hall?"

Per lunges. "You forget yourself!" And he backhands Ole. The old man tumbles over his bench. I cover my mouth, shocked.

Ole struggles up, rubbing the side of his face.

"Ole speaks the truth!" Bera says. "It could have been you, Per."

"Me?" Per looks like he is about to strike her as well. "You accuse me? You're the one who cooked that cursed goat!"

That brings Raudi to his feet. "How dare you!"

Per's hand goes to the hilt of his sword, and Bera gasps.

Harald starts to cry. And the shouting rises to a roar, accusations filling the air like arrows.

It is finally too much. We have fractured under the strain and are undone. It wasn't the hunger that broke us. It wasn't the meat from my Hilda, nor the death that ravaged us. Suspicion is a different kind of poison. A potent toxin of whispers and air. We're all infected, and it will be our end.

In the next moment, I know someone will be hurt. I cannot allow it. I must do something. And so I rise to my feet.

"Listen to me!" I cry. "For I have many stories to tell."

The hall falls silent. Everyone stares.

"All of you! We cannot let this enemy divide us. We cannot let our suspicions and our doubts run wild, or else we will destroy ourselves. Brave and honorable men have died, and it is true that there may yet be a traitor among us. But if there is, we hasten his purpose if we turn on one another."

I look around the room, at the faces of the people I love.

"We cannot forget who we are," I say. "Who we were. If ever you listened to me, hearken to me now. For I would remind you . . ."

Have you listened?

Do you still wonder at the meaning of these stories, and my reasons for telling them?

One of us is a traitor. One of you. I accept that possibility only because the signs all say I must. But it rends my heart.

And that is why I cannot bring myself to accuse any of you. After all that I know of you, after all I have seen and loved in each of you, how can I? Who shall I name murderer among you? Per? Bera or Raudi? Ole? Hake? My own brother or sister? To believe it is possible about any one of you is to believe the stars will die. To accuse any one of you is to slay the stars, myself.

And so I ask you, which of us can you accuse without bringing down the walls of this household? Who can you suspect without poisoning your heart toward the rest? To suspect one is to suspect all. Stop this now.

I know that evil hides here, but I cannot be the one to uncover it. Neither can any of you. Time will do that for us.

And how I fear that day, for I know that when I look into my betrayer's face, I will see someone I thought I knew. And I will still love them.

CHAPTER 15

MESSENGERS

I do not bow my head. I want to look each of them in their eyes, to hold their gaze, till one by one they turn away from me.

At last, Hake clears his throat. "We would be wise to listen to Solveig."

No one responds to him. But I can nevertheless feel the room emptying of anger and hate. I feel the tension in my own body recede before a wave of relief.

"We will have no more of this talk," Hake says. "We stay until the king sends for us. Not because it is what I want. Nor because it is what Per wants. But because that is what the king ordered us to do." The berserker looks around. "Are we agreed?"

Heads hang low around the room, and still no one responds.

"I think we are agreed, Captain," Alric says.

The skald sits away from the rest of us in a corner, and it occurs to me then that he never said a word during the entire outbreak. He sat there and watched, and now he watches me. But the expression on his face is pained.

When he approaches me later, I find out the reason.

"I didn't know what to do," he says. "Nor what to say. But you did. Once more, I see you are a better skald than I."

"But I was not acting as a skald," I say. "In that moment, I was only Solveig."

And I realize that, for once, being myself was enough.

Six days later, Ole comes back to the hall without any fish. He stands in the doorway, a silhouette against the white of the snow and the light of the sun.

"A ship," he says.

We all race from the hall, through the gate, to the cliff. I am already planning ahead, to the attack I dreamt about, and how I will take Harald and Asa and Raudi and lead them up the ravine to the cave. My eyes look for a *drekar*, and my ears strain for battle cries over the sound of my heart beating. But I find neither. Instead, I see a small boat coming quickly up the fjord as though aloft on its white bird wing of a sail.

"Who is it?" Harald asks.

"Messengers," Hake says.

Hake and Per remain by the water to greet the boat. The rest of us return to the hall. I try to sit quietly, feeding Muninn in his cage beside me. Bera frets over the meager food we have to offer our guests. Ole pokes at the fire, and Harald races back and forth between me and the open doors. "I don't see them yet," he reports each time he reaches me, and each time I say, "They'll be here soon."

But eventually, Harald rushes back to the door and stays there. He points out into the yard. "They're here!"

We all stand.

"There's two of them," Harald says.

And then Hake and Per lead the messengers inside.

They are men I recognize but cannot name. Their cheeks are wind-whipped above their beards, and their shoulders sag. One has dark hair, and the other, gray. Their clothes are wet with ocean spray, and they appear exhausted.

"Come to the fire," Bera says. "Eat."

She guides the men to a bench by the hearth. They sit and accept their plates from her with bowed heads.

"Our stores are down to oats, I'm afraid," she says.

They thank her and eat as though it doesn't matter what is on their plates, or where it came from. We all settle in around them.

"How was the voyage?" Bera asks.

While the younger of the messengers replies, I notice Per and Hake talking in whispers at a distance. It seems they have already learned something about why these men are here, and perhaps the message they carry.

When they have finished eating, the older of the two messengers stands.

"Thank you for your hospitality. We made our journey quickly, and have had little food or sleep. We bring a message and a call for you to return to the king's hall."

Bera claps and Harald leaps into the air. I wait for the rest of the message.

The man continues. "The gods have smiled on the king and led him to a victory in battle. Gunnlaug retreated before him, and very few of our warriors fell or were taken. The war is ended, and our lands are safe once more."

My father is victorious. Our hall is safe. Asa is safe. We can go home. And it seems my dream was just a dream after all. Now I sit back as relief and gratitude bathe me, though after a moment, a hint of dread edges in.

"Gunnlaug retreated?" Hake says. "Where is he now?"

"His armies are scattered," the messenger says.

Harald grabs me in a hug, and then he runs to Asa. Bera wipes a tear from her eye with her finger, and Alric pumps his clasped hands before his chest. Hake is the only one of us who doesn't celebrate. The berserker captain frowns and sits by the fire. He leans forward, his chin resting on one of his fists, and stares into the flames.

"Now," Bera says, "I will pack."

"Make haste," the gray-haired messenger says.

I notice that Per is also silent, and Asa is watching him. Knowing that the two most seasoned warriors in our steading are uneasy makes me uneasy as well. Later that evening, I approach Hake where he towers over the hearth.

"How are you?" I ask.

He looks down at me. "Why do you ask?"

"You seem troubled."

"Nothing escapes your notice, does it? I am troubled, but you shouldn't worry."

"Why not, if it worries you?"

"Because I am a restless warrior too accustomed to the battlefield, and you are the daughter of my king."

"It's something about Gunnlaug, isn't it?"

He stares at me, and I see the fire flickering in his eyes. "Yes."

"But he retreated. He gave up."

"Did he?"

I want to say yes, but Hake's question causes a moment of doubt.

The berserker fills that moment with a chuckle. "These thoughts are not for you. Go now and leave them here with me, all right?" He places a paternal hand on my back and gently pushes me toward Alric. "Go and practice with the skald."

"All right," I say, because I'm left without a choice.

We spend the next few days preparing. Bera and Raudi pack up what food we have left, along with some of Ole's fish that they've salted and smoked. Asa and I tie up the blankets and gather all the other gear together, while Hake and Per ready the ship.

During all of this I keep Muninn locked in his cage, and I think he resents it. He flaps around inside, cawing, and I feel guilty. But with all the commotion in and out of the hall, I can't take any chances letting him loose.

The fresh fish have done the surviving berserkers good, and they are able to walk about now and help. Mostly, they just try to keep Harald out of our way, but we did need their backs to get our ship down into the water. We don't have men enough to crew the berserkers' *drekar*, so we're taking the smaller boat in which my siblings and I came here those months ago.

The return voyage will be slow. Without men to row, we'll be traveling entirely by sail. I don't think I will mind that at all, so long as we are moving.

Something must be done about the bodies in the cowshed. We don't have time to dig their graves, but we can't leave them. When summer comes, they will rot and bring scavengers, and we will face the wrath of their unsettled spirits. So we must bring them home with us where they can be honored properly.

When everything else is loaded and stowed, Hake and Per go to the shed and open the doors. The rest of us stand in the yard, solemn as runestones, as the two of them emerge bearing one of the bodies.

They cross the yard and leave through the gates, and we follow them down through the stirring woods. The dry silence of winter is gone, and all around us the trees stretch out of their wet snow-furs. We go down to the water's edge, where the waves are waking up, slapping their cheeks against the rocky shore. Hake and Per carry the body onto the ship and lay it into the tomb-like cargo hold.

They disembark, and without looking at any of us, climb back up through the forest to the steading. And we follow them. They reenter the cowshed and come out again with the body of another fallen warrior. Out of reverence, no one speaks.

We go with them back down to the ship, where they lay the body with the first, and then they climb again, and then again. And each time, we go also. Each of the men deserves his own procession. Each of them deserves our honor and love.

As we make the trip for the fourth time, I begin to breathe more heavily in the brisk air. As we make the trip for the sixth time, the muscles in my legs begin to burn. As we make the trip for the tenth time, my legs begin to tremble, and I do not know if it is because of the strain on my body or my soul.

This grim task, and the grave-ship that waits for us, have made plain what we have lost, what was stolen from us by treachery. These men did not have to die, and I find that as I make the trip for the final time, my grief has turned to anger. Then fury, as we pack in snow and ice around the bodies for the return journey, burying them in the boat. My earlier pain retreats before the storm inside me. But it's a storm without an eye, without an enemy on which to center all my rage. And now the fact that one of us could have caused this is more than I can stand.

When the ordeal is ended, and the shed is empty, we all decide it would be better to wait until tomorrow to leave the fjord. The messengers want to leave this evening, but Bera persuades them to eat another good meal and get another good sleep before they depart in their smaller boat. Our ship waits for us, so heavy with our grief I do not know how it stays afloat.

After we have eaten a slow, silent meal, Alric stands. He and I haven't talked about a tale. I feel unable to gather any words tonight, and I worry that he will call on me. But he begins without looking or nodding toward me, and it seems he intends to tell the story himself. So I am able to relax and listen, a part of his audience once again.

"It seems so long ago now," Alric says, "that Solveig found the runestone down in the forest. I studied it and determined whom it was meant to honor, and then I set about harvesting his story from the lore. Now I will tell you what I have remembered of him." And he begins.

"Many generations have passed since the gods first made kings of men, back when the fjords were still raw from being rent open. At that time, a warrior chose this place, where we have spent this winter, to build his meadhall and make his home. His household grew strong. His sons were mighty in battle, and his daughters delighted the eyes of all who beheld them.

"But then the frost giants came from high above the warrior's hall, through the black forests, and over the mountains. Towering monsters of cunning, with the strength of ten men, the giants looked down on the fjord and spied the warrior's daughters. They decided among themselves to steal the maidens away, to carry them back to their realm of rock and ice as brides."

The story makes me think of Asa, and I glance at her. She sits near me, leaning forward with her hands folded against her stomach, her eyes fixed on Alric as though he is divining her past and her future.

"The giants descended," Alric says. "The ground trembled beneath their feet, and the walls of the steading shook as though to fall. The warrior-king heard their coming and hid his daughters in a cave. Then he and his sons waited with sword and spear. In the shadow of a glacier, in the grip of a ravine, they stood ready to do battle with the giants."

As he tells the story, I can almost feel the walls of our hall shaking.

Alric continues. "The sight of the giants would have caused lesser men to lower their spears, but the warrior-king raised his sword and cried, 'No daughter shall be taken from this land, and death shall fall upon you if you make war with us!'"

As he speaks, I am reassured by the knowledge that my father would do the same for me, and has done for Asa.

"The frost giants roared and laughed," Alric says. "Up the ravine they came, tearing boulders loose and toppling trees.

"The warrior-king looked with pride upon his sons, and spoke. 'We hold them here,' he said. 'None shall break our shield-wall.' And after hours of battle, not one single giant had. Because of the narrowness of the ravine where the warrior-king and his sons had made their stand, no two giants could pass through, and so the warrior-king and his sons fought each giant in turn, and in turn, sent each to the sleep of the sword, filling the ravine with the bodies."

The expression on Alric's face appears more earnest than I have ever seen it. It is almost as if he is finally telling a tale that he, himself, believes.

"After the last of the frost giants had fallen, and the ground was wet with their blood, the warrior-king broke gold rings on the battlefield and rewarded each of his sons for their valor. But there was one son among them, an assassin, who had treasure from the giants in his purse, given in payment for treachery. And as his father offered him his reward, the evil son drew a poisoned dagger and slashed his father's hand."

Around me, the audience gasps and rumbles in anger. The mention of poison falls heavy on us.

"The traitor fled, a coward." Alric says. "And the daughters of the warrior-king came forth from the cave to find their father succumbing to the bane in his blood. They cleaned his wounds with their tears and fed him on their song, until Odin's shield-maidens came to carry his spirit up.

"Then, his sons piled his ship with precious stones, and swords, shields, mead, honey, gold, and spears. They buried him with tribute befitting his final act and lifted a runestone so that his sacrifice would be remembered."

Only the fire is breathing. The rest of us wait. Alric has not bowed his head, and so it seems the tale is not yet finished.

"It is not my custom," he says, "to comment on my own story. But I feel compelled tonight to do so. That runestone down in the woods no longer marks the honor of the warrior-king alone. Many good men died here this winter. A death by treachery is no less honorable, and would our men have been called upon, each would have willingly fallen on the spear instead to protect the children of their king. They were here for their king, and they died for their king.

"Though we sail tomorrow, we do not leave this place emptied. We leave our love and gratitude inscribed on the runestone in the forest, which now marks a new generation of heroes."

He bows his head.

And the room inhales.

Then we applaud him. All of us. Hake actually crosses the room and pulls the skald into an embrace. Again, I find myself in awe of Alric. After a day of mourning, a day spent in the dark wake of senseless death, Alric has given meaning to our pain. Something to help us see our way out of our grief so we can leave this place in peace. My father might be a king, but it seems that Alric also has power to lead us.

I greet the day with a newfound strength. We eat a final meal of oats and fish and throw snow on the fire. Hake gives the larder key back to Bera. Then Raudi comes over to Muninn's cage.

"I will carry him down to the ship for you."

"Thank you," I say.

He lifts the cage, and we all file out of the hall. Harald leaps ahead, rushes back, and skips around us. Bera strides to the larder and locks it. It's empty, but I think there is something in the act of locking it that helps her feel better about leaving.

We make our way down to the water, where we start to board our ships, the messengers in their small boat and the rest of us in our larger vessel. I climb in and find a bench out of the way. Harald is trembling with excitement beside me, barely sitting at all. The boat rolls a little against its anchor. I hear the water gurgling under the planking beneath my feet and smell the brine in the air. Raudi sets Muninn down near my feet and then goes to help the berserkers up the ramp. As one of them boards, leaning on Hake, he looks out across the fjord. He squints. Then he points and shouts.

"Ships!"

Hake looks up. He seats the berserker and thunders up to the prow. The rest of us crowd behind him.

"Who are they?" Per asks.

"Everyone out of the boat," Hake says. Then he shouts across the water for the messengers to do the same.

We disembark in confusion. I look back over my shoulder at Muninn, but decide he's probably safe where he is for now. We gather on the shore, waiting, while Hake and Per scan the water.

"There are two of them," Per says. "I can almost make out their standard."

"Drekars," Hake says. A moment passes. "It is Gunnlaug."

I gasp and Asa pales.

"It can't be," Bera says. "He lost the war."

"He retreated," Hake says, "to bring his war here."

CHAPTER 16

BATTLE

The black ships heave toward us with the beating of their oars, the billowing of their sails. I want to scream. I want to hide. I want to drop to the rocky ground and claw my way under it. My dream has grown flesh. The wolf has come.

The elder messenger rushes up. "We must go. All of you, hurry."

"The fjord is too narrow," Hake says. "Our ship will never make it past them."

"Ours will," the younger messenger says.

"No," Hake says. "It won't. And we need you here."

"Two more swords won't make any difference to you now." The elder messenger backs away from the rest of us, pulling his companion with him toward their boat. "And we must warn the king of what has happened."

Hake shakes his head. "You won't make it through."

"We'll take our chances," the gray-haired messenger says before they both turn and sprint for their tiny craft.

"Cowards!" Per shouts after them, and then he looks to Hake. "Should we stop them?"

Hake turns from the shore. "Why? They would only run at the first opportunity. Let them die on the water." He marches to the trailhead. "Everyone, go up to the steading. Quickly, now."

We all move at the same time, some up the path, while the three berserkers and Per join Hake. Harald and Asa run together, holding hands, and I am about to follow them when I remember that Muninn is still on the ship. I turn back.

"Where are you going?" Alric asks me.

I don't answer and sprint up the ramp onto the deck. I grab Muninn's cage; he flaps inside and caws, shifting his weight. I rush back down to the shore, toward Hake. He motions for me to hurry as he watches the water. I glance toward the messengers' little craft pushing out into the fjord. And the enemy ships looming beyond it. The *drekars* are almost close enough for me to see their snarling dragon prows, almost close enough to hear the men clamoring for our blood. Soon, they will land.

"Go!" Hake says.

I turn away and scurry up the path. But the cage is heavy, and Muninn still thrashes inside it, and after a few steps, my toe catches on something under the snow. I lurch forward. The cage flies away from me, tumbles through the air and lands with a splintering crack against a tree. The cage falls in pieces, and Muninn flutters free.

"No!" I shout.

Muninn flaps up onto the nearest tree branch, and from there he manages to hop and scramble well out of my reach.

"Muninn!" I am nearly hysterical. "Muninn, come back here. Right now!"

Alric rushes up to my side. "Solveig, you must leave him."

"I can't!"

"He survived in the woods before, he'll be all right."

"Muninn, come to me!"

"Solveig, hurry!" Alric tries to push me up the path.

But I fight him. Muninn looks down on me, unconcerned. And he starts to preen.

"You stupid, stupid bird!" I scream as Alric drags me away.

By the time we reach the top of the hill, I am sobbing. And then Asa and Harald are at my sides, trying to put their arms around me. "Muninn," I say to them, but I can barely breathe and get out nothing more. My raven is gone, my friend, and it feels like a part of my own body has been torn away. I take a few deep breaths to calm the convulsions wracking my chest.

Hake and Per come up after me, supporting the three berserkers. Then the two of them charge to the cliff against a headwind, their cloaks flapping, and the rest of us steal up behind them. Below us, on the water, the messengers approach Gunnlaug's ships in their little sailboat. But they are scrabbling against the wind while the *drekars* gallop with it over the waves.

"They're dead," Hake says.

We watch as the first warship reaches the sailboat, close enough, I am sure, for the messengers to see the eyes of the enemy across the water. I wonder if my father's men are pleading for mercy, or if they shout defiant curses, or if they are still trying to escape, their heads bowed, desperate and futile. I am horrified, and do not want to watch them die, but I can't look away.

Arrows like little black needles rain down on them from Gunnlaug's ship, shredding the sail. And then, the sparks of several flames arc through the air, and fire blooms on the sail and the deck. Within moments, the little boat is engulfed, and Gunnlaug's ship prowls ahead. I realize that it never even slowed.

"We'll mourn them later," Hake says. He leads us through the gate into the yard. "For now, we need to get the king's children up to the cave. I will make a stand here." He turns to his fellow berserkers, and something unspoken passes among them. "With my men. Perhaps in the hall, so they think that's where we've holed up the children."

The three berserkers pull upright and nod.

"I'll guide them to the cave," Per says.

"Very well," Hake says. "You are responsible for getting them to safety."

Per bows.

"Ole, Bera, Raudi." Hake points up the ravine. "You, too. Everyone, move."

Raudi stays rooted where he is. "I will stay and fight." He swallows. "I would prefer a spear."

No. I almost reach to grab him in my panic. He is trying to prove he isn't a coward, but now is not the time.

Hake shakes his head, but there is respect in it. "You may yet be called upon to prove yourself, but not now. You must go with the others."

We break into two groups. The warriors march to the gate, while the rest flock toward the hall. I watch them go, divided. Raudi has made me aware of something I'm only now realizing.

"Solveig, move," Hake says.

But I don't want to leave anyone behind. The warriors are going to die if they stay here. And in that moment I realize that Hake has come to mean something more to me. I don't yet know what it is I feel for him, but I know that I don't want to lose him.

"Come with us," I say.

He pulls his war hammer free. "This is what I was sent here to do." He smiles at me. "And I do it willingly. Go, now."

Raudi comes up and tugs me away. I join the others, reluctantly, and we start across the yard. In the commotion, I feel
someone grab my arm. I turn as Ole pulls me in close and
hisses in my ear.

"Remember what you told me," he says. "You are a skald
now, not the daughter of any king." And then he lets me go
and slides away. A moment later, I see him touch Per's shoulder. "There's something I need in the hall," he says.

Per halts, as do Asa, Harald, and I. "What could you
possibly — ?"

"It's my bone knife. Had it since I was a boy."

Alric, Bera, and Raudi don't seem to have noticed that
we've stopped. They race ahead.

"We're not waiting for you," Per says. He leads us away
from Ole without looking back, down the side of the hall, and
then through the garden patch where Raudi and I pulled up
carrots all those months ago. As we reach the far side and
start across the field, Per slows our pace.

"We won't make it up to the cave," he says. "I know of a
better place to hide you."

My skin goes cold beneath my furs. "Hake said to go to
the cave."

"I don't think he thought about how far it was," Per says.
"Gunnlaug's men will overtake us before we make it." He
turns and trots away toward a copse of trees on the north side
of the field. "Hurry, follow me!"

Harald obeys, and then I see that Asa is about to start after them.

"This isn't what Hake told us to do," I say.

"Per knows this place," Asa says. "He's been here before."

"He has?"

"Yes, he was the one who told Father about it. Come on." She runs off.

Something doesn't feel right about this. I see Raudi, Bera, and Alric in the distance. They have nearly reached the base of the ravine, and in a moment of indecision I almost run to join them. But instead, I hurry to catch up with my brother and sister. I find them standing in a small clearing, while Per trudges around in circles, kicking at the snow. Then he bends over and roots around a certain area with his hands.

"There," he says, and heaves upward.

The ground yawns open, and snow pours down into a dark hole. Per holds up a trapdoor. "This was the larder, years ago," he says. "Hurry down inside and hide. They won't find you here."

Harald bites his lip. "It's dark."

"Come," Asa says. "Hold my hand." She takes him and leads him down a set of earthen steps. The two of them look like they are walking into a grave.

"We should go to the cave," I say.

Per stares at me. "Hurry, Solveig. Get inside."

My mind screams at me as my body does what he says. I tremble, and my eyes dart from side to side. I pass under Per's arm and descend the stairs. When I reach the bottom, the smell of mold and clay choke me. I look back up at Per, but his face is all shadow against the white of the snow and the sky.

"Keep quiet," he says. "It will be all right."

The cellar door shuts.

The vein of light framing the trapdoor quickly disappears. Per must be covering it back up with snow. Within moments, the three of us are suspended in a dark and ceaseless void. My eyes focus and refocus, straining in the nothing. I catch glimpses of vague forms that dart and shift before me, black against blacker. It's disconcerting, because I know it's too dark to see anything. The earth is hard beneath my feet. I smell the rot of wood mixed with the sourness of stale mead.

I feel Harald's hand grope for mine. "Tell me a story, Solveig."

"Keep silent," Asa says.

"I'll tell you a story later," I whisper.

I imagine him nodding.

And Asa is right. I hold my breath to hear whatever muffled sounds reach us under the earth. Long empty moments pass. Was that the crack of a sword against a shield? Was that a warrior's cry? I cannot tell if my ears are hearing these things, or if I conjure up the sounds as my eyes conjure shadows.

So we stand here and wait.

And wait.

It seems that minutes pass. Then . . . an hour? I concentrate and realize that I cannot feel the movement of time inside me. Time is something that is seen. It's in the burning of a hearth-log, in the drying of fish in the smokehouse, it's in the lengthening of a stalk of wheat. Cut off from these signs, I wonder if time moves forward. Are Asa and Harald and I now outside of it, and does the world above age without us?

These thoughts consume me. I am surrounded by apparitions; the darkness masses and assails me. The cold and endless hollow pulls on me from all sides, threatening to dissolve me into its emptiness. I need something real, something strong.

"Solveig?" Harald whispers.

"Yes?"

"Shh," Asa says.

And then a loud voice beats upon us from above. "I heard something!" A man's voice. Unfamiliar. "Here!" The sound fractures the darkness, and my senses are so confounded I believe for a moment that I see the shout as a bolt of lightning. But then I realize that someone has lifted the trapdoor.

The endless black around me collapses to a small mud-room. Asa and Harald stand beside me, squinting. I look up.

Three warriors loom over us.

"Come out," one of them says.

Asa and I look at one another. We don't move, and neither does Harald.

"Don't make us drag you out," one of the others says.

I know they will, and I do not want my brother or sister to be terrorized any more than will surely be done to us, so I say, "All right. We're coming."

I take Harald's hand and we trudge up the steps, with Asa behind us, emerging into the white day with our hands shielding our eyes. The faces of the three warriors bear cold expressions. The men are heavily armed and heavily armored. One of them smirks at me and Harald, but his eyes change when he leers at Asa.

"That's her," he says, and points at my sister with his sword.

The other two men nod.

"I'd make war for that."

Asa blushes, and I seethe inside.

"Take the boy and the other one to Gunnlaug," the first one says. "I'll carry the trophy along with me."

He approaches Asa and reaches for her. But I can't bear to see his filthy hands touch her. I strike at him, intending to slap him, but my fingernail catches his nose and leaves a white scratch. He jerks back and looks at me. The scratch turns red.

I try to meet his gaze, to appear defiant.

He lifts his weapon to strike me, not with the blade, but the broad pommel. "Who are you?"

I open my mouth to answer, but I am cut off.

"Solveig!" The voice is Alric's, somewhere close by.

The warrior looks around, and then something huge, a bear, rams into him from the side, lifting him off his feet. It is Hake. I turn as the berserker slams the warrior into a tree. I hear something inside the warrior snap, and then Hake lifts him overhead and throws the body into the trees. That is when I notice the blood covering Hake's pelt. That is when I see his eyes, and I know he isn't seeing me. The *berserkergang* is upon him.

Asa backs away.

"Hake!" Harald shouts, but I cover his mouth.

At the sound of his name, the berserker roars at us. But Gunnlaug's two remaining men charge him, and Hake turns his rage on them. The first one goes down almost instantly with a single swing of Hake's war hammer. The second warrior is stronger and quicker. He dodges Hake's strike and leaps away. The two circle each other for a moment before Hake attacks.

"Solveig!" Alric emerges from the trees behind me. "Harald, Asa, come! Hurry!"

He grabs me with one arm and Harald with the other, pulls us into the trees, and Asa rushes after us.

The branches whip my face and the snow slows my feet as we make our way through the woods. Then we burst from the copse into the field and run a distance out into the open before pausing. Alric pants and looks around, first up the ravine, and then toward the hall, where I see a host of men bearing down on us. Gunnlaug's men.

"Can we make it to the cave?" I ask.

I hear another roar, and then Hake explodes from the trees. His wild gaze sweeps the field, and he sees us.

"This way," Alric says, and leads us straight toward Gunnlaug's men.

"They'll catch us!" Asa shouts.

"But they won't kill you!" Alric says.

I look over my shoulder and see the berserker tearing across the field in our direction. He covers the distance with astonishing speed, and for a moment I am certain he will reach us. But then one of Gunnlaug's men flies by me, knocking me aside. Alric helps me up as a dozen or more men charge past us. In the confusion, I am grabbed from behind, as are Asa and Harald. Two men point their spears at Alric, and he holds up his empty hands in submission. We are captured.

Before us, Hake skids to a halt and braces himself. He snarls, bites his own shield, and swings his war hammer as Gunnlaug's men swarm him. They all clash with him at once, a terrible sound I feel in my stomach. Barely a moment later, four, then five of Gunnlaug's men lie sprawled and bloody on the ground. A few still move.

Hake stomps and smashes through those that remain like a

frost giant, and the sight fills me with awe and terror. Shields split, swords break, and spears shatter. The bodies pile up around him. But before the berserker has laid out the last of them, a new wave of warriors assaults him. Our guards pull us back, away from the battle. I feel the fear in the warrior holding me, and strain against his grip.

A bowstring twangs behind me, and I look up as an arrow flies over us. It thuds in the ground near Hake just as he leaps aside. And then I hear three more twangs. Three more arrows. One of them strikes Hake in the shoulder and throws him back. He bellows in rage.

The archers reach us and pause, grim and determined. They fire another volley and continue past us in their advance on the berserker.

Then I see Gunnlaug coming toward us from the hall. He strides across the field surrounded by his honor guard.

"Take him down!" the chieftain shouts.

Another volley, and an arrow strikes Hake in the thigh. He grabs it and wrenches it free with a spray of blood, just as another arrow pierces his arm. Hake snarls and tries to charge at the archers, but a wall of shields pushes him back. Gunnlaug's men have hedged him in, and he is getting weaker. The archers notch their next arrows.

I turn to Alric. "They're going to kill him!"

Alric shakes his head, mouth open, helpless. And then Gunnlaug is there behind me, his honor guard surrounding us.

"If you know of another way to stop a berserker," the chieftain says, "then speak it." He stands with his hands on his hips, and wears fox furs over his armor. Beneath his helmet, his eyes in their own way are as empty as Hake's.

"I can stop him," I say, though in that moment I don't know how. "Please don't kill him."

Gunnlaug tilts his head. "Hold your fire!" He points at Hake. "A girl like you stop a berserker? This, I have to see."

"Just let me try."

He strokes the pommel of his sword, which is still in its scabbard at his side. "All right. Though I think we're all about to see you die."

I swallow, and the warrior releases me. Gunnlaug's honor guard parts to let me pass.

"What are you doing?" Alric whispers.

I ignore him and march to the ring of shields encircling Hake, and push my way through them. The shields close behind me, trapping me in with the berserker. Arrows jut from his shoulder and arm. He bleeds from his wounds, trembles, and his eyes are frantic with pain and rage. He crouches as if preparing to attack me. I try to hold still, feeling small and powerless.

"Hake?" I say. "Hake, you know me. You took my Hilda, and then you gave me a raven in a cage."

He growls. I see his teeth.

"I named him Muninn. You gave me memory." My throat constricts. "Hake?"

His eyebrows crease. He stops growling.

"I saw you praying in the cold." I take a step toward him. "I heard you ask the Allfather for strength to keep the rage away. To destroy you if it took you again. So you wouldn't hurt anyone. But I don't want you to be destroyed. Can you hear me, Hake?"

His trembling eases and he frowns.

"Come back, Hake. Listen to my voice. You know my voice. I told your men of Eir." I take another step toward him. "Do you remember?"

His wild eyes blink.

I draw nearer. "Eir came down from the Hill of Healing among your fallen ones. When they lay sick and dying, her story brought them comfort." I think he is beginning to see me. I take the last step right up to him, lift my fingers, and kiss the tips. I touch them to his bloody lips.

"Hake," I say.

At the contact, he sighs and squints. I think perhaps he recognizes me. And then he drops to one knee.

"Can it be?" Gunnlaug's booming voice causes me to wince. "The mighty Hake taken alive? Hah!"

The wall of shields presses in on us, now studded with spears. Hake looks up and pulls me close, holding up his hands as if to shield me from the blades. But then he slides down to his other knee. He lets me go, his eyes close, and he collapses to the ground.

"Hake!" I reach for him, but I am yanked away as four men surround Hake's body. The shield-ring disbands, and I am hauled back to stand before Gunnlaug as they drag the berserker from the field toward the hall. "Hake!" I shout again.

"Calm down, girl," the chieftain says. He removes his helmet, exposing his pink, bald head. "You saved him, for now. You with the silver tongue. Though I don't think his honor will thank you for it." He looks around, and his gaze stops on my sister, sliding over her. "Hello, Asa. It is my pleasure to see you again."

Asa looks away.

Gunnlaug laughs. "The steading is ours. Bring them to the hall."

CHAPTER 17

TRAITORS AND LIES

Alric, my siblings, and I are prodded across the field at spearpoint. We march along, surrounded by enemies, and all I can think about is how the snow crunches beneath my boots. Nothing else seems real.

"That was very foolish what you did," Alric whispers to me. He sounds angry.

"I know," I say.

"And Gunnlaug is right. Hake would rather have died than be taken alive."

I look away. I don't care what Alric says, I am glad I did what I did.

But as we draw near the hall, and I see the bodies massed around the steading gate, I want to weep. I think the last three of Hake's men must be among the dead, still weakened as they were by the poison. But they knew that when they chose to stay with Hake and fight.

I wonder what will happen to us. Gunnlaug will likely ask ransom for Harald. It would be foolish to kill my brother, for then my father would reap a bloody revenge on Gunnlaug and burn every field in his kingdom. Asa, I fear, will be forced to marry. But what of me? I have no worth for ransom or as a bride.

I realize I haven't yet seen Per, nor Bera and Raudi. And where is Ole?

I turn back to Alric and whisper, "What about the others?"

"I don't know," Alric says out of the side of his mouth. "I realized you weren't with us halfway up the ravine, and I came back down looking for you. Bera and Raudi continued on."

"But Per and Ole?"

His jaw tightens. "For good or for ill, I think we shall find out about them soon enough."

"What do you mean?"

He shakes his head to quiet me.

Our captors herd us through the hall doors and force us to the ground near the hearth, where a fire has been rekindled. I look around and nothing about this building feels familiar anymore. Except for the benches, all our possessions are gone, stowed in the ship that still waits for us, and the hall is crowded with strange, dirty men. Even the rafters overhead cast sinister shadows against the roof.

Seeing those wooden beams reminds me of Muninn. I hope that he is safe out in the woods.

Gunnlaug enters, flanked by two of his honor guard. "Clear out, all of you," he orders, and except for the two at his side, his men vacate the hall and shut the doors behind them. Gunnlaug removes his gloves on his way toward us, and stands next to the hearth with his palms toward the fire. He looks us over for several long moments, shaking his head.

"I am sad it had to come to this," he says. "The bride-price I offered was more than fair. Your father dishonored me in refusing it. I had no choice."

"How fortunate," Alric says, "that your honor demanded that you take something you wanted." His smile is back, that strange, implacable smile, and I am so comforted by the sight of it that tears form in my eyes. "Honor is seldom so convenient."

Gunnlaug scowls. "I remember you. You're the skald."

"I am."

"And the others," Gunnlaug says. "You are Harald, are you not?"

My brother sticks his chin up in the air.

"I can see why your father is proud of you," Gunnlaug says. "Your bravery is plain."

The hall doors open and Ole walks in, unaccompanied. He strolls down the hall looking grim, and I stare at him, trying to make sense of what he is doing. Gunnlaug glances up at Ole and nods, and I realize that they know each other. Ole knows Gunnlaug.

"Asa, I remember well," the chieftain continues. "And you are more beautiful now than when I first sought you for my wife."

Asa's head droops against her chest. Gunnlaug extends his hand and tries to lift Asa's chin with two of his fingers. She resists him, and Gunnlaug's eyes narrow. For a moment, his smile takes on a wicked air. But the moment passes, and then Ole is there, standing beside him. Ole, our traitor all along.

The chieftain looks at me. "And you? You must be the second daughter."

"No," Ole says.

I look up at him. This thrall who has served us for so many years, this villain in our midst who made me a doll from scraps of rope.

"No?" Gunnlaug asks.

"She is the skald's apprentice," Ole says.

I remember then what Ole told me to remember, and I realize that this is what he meant. He knew this moment would come, and he prepared me for it even as he plotted our downfall. I know I should be angry. I should want to kill him, as

Hake would. But I don't. There is only an immense sadness in my chest that makes it difficult to breathe.

Alric blinks at Ole, and his smile just barely slips.

Gunnlaug pauses. "I took no notice of the second daughter — what was her name?"

"Solveig," Ole says.

"Yes, Solveig. I paid her little mind when I visited her father's hall." He stares at me.

Alric leans toward us. "Siv here has more inborn talent than any of my previous apprentices."

I see the confusion in Asa and Harald, and I worry that they will give us away, but neither of them say anything, and I don't think Gunnlaug notices.

"Siv," the chieftain says. "Then where is the second daughter?"

"Her father chose not to send her," Ole says. "She has little value in his eyes."

His words hurt, and give strength to the part of me that has always believed them to be true.

Gunnlaug looks back and forth between Alric and me, Ole and Alric. I think he suspects something, and I struggle to keep my face calm, my breathing even. "Very well," the chieftain says. "And where are the others of the household?"

"Your men are bringing the cook and her son down from the ravine right now. I do not know where Per is."

So Per is alive. And still free.

"We'll find him," Gunnlaug says. "For now, bring Hake inside and make sure he lives through the night. What of our wounded?"

"No wounded," Ole says. "Only the dead."

"Lay them in the cowshed."

"Yes, sir." Ole begins to walk away.

"You're a traitor!" Harald shouts at Ole's back. The old man turns, and I reach for my brother to silence him, but catch myself partway. A skald's apprentice would never do so familiar a thing with a prince. But Gunnlaug has seen it and raises an eyebrow at me.

"It is true that I am a traitor to your father," Ole says. "But never to *my* king. I served Gunnlaug's father before I was captured, and I serve his son now." Then he looks at me. "You can never trust anyone once you've had to trap them in a cage." He turns again and leaves.

Moments later, several warriors enter bearing Hake. They lay him on a table and begin removing or cutting away clothing. They rinse and wipe away the blood encrusting his wounds, after which they set about pulling the arrows from his body. The berserker appears barely conscious, trembling and muttering incoherently, and I am frightened by the amount of blood still flowing out of him. Gunnlaug watches from a distance, his hands behind his back.

Before long, another group of men drag Bera and Raudi into the hall. Bera claws and kicks, but she gasps at the sight of Hake and pulls free of her guards. "Get away from him!" she shouts and hurries to the berserker's side. She heaves Gunnlaug's men away. "Take your filthy hands off, and let me tend him."

Gunnlaug regards her and then motions for his men to move. "Let her work."

Bera throws off her cloak and inspects Hake's wounds, then gestures to me and Raudi. She tears away some strips from her apron and has us apply them with pressure to the wounds. I feel the warm blood beneath my hands, seeping between my fingers. Bera asks the room for a sword and holds out her hand, waiting. Gunnlaug nods again, and one of his warriors hands Bera his weapon. She sets the tip of the blade in the center of the fire and leaves it there before returning to Raudi and me.

As we're leaning in together, I whisper as quietly and as clearly as I can. "Gunnlaug doesn't know who I am. He thinks I am Siv, Alric's apprentice."

They exchange looks, but nod that they understand.

Gunnlaug comes closer. "Will he live?"

"Where are your medicines?" Bera asks, making it sound like an accusation.

Another of the chieftain's men hands her a satchel, which she rummages through, sniffing the pouches and setting a few of them aside. She blends the contents of these together in the palm of her hand, sprinkling the mixture with water to make a paste, glancing now and again at the sword she left in the fire.

"This wound is too deep," she says, packing the poultice into the hole in Hake's shoulder. "It needs to stay open and weep."

I'm holding my weight on Hake's leg, the fabric in my hand soaked with his blood. I find it hard to control my panic and keep my mind present. I don't know how Bera does it. She takes another rag and uses it to pull the sword from the hearth, the tip of the blade a deep and angry red.

"Step back, all of you." She swings the weapon closer. "Come away now, S — Siv."

I step clear, and as soon as I do, the bleeding goes from a leak to a stream. Bera lays the flat of the sword tip right in the wound and presses down. The skin sizzles and smokes, and I gag on the smell of cooking meat. Bera holds the blade there for a moment longer and then pulls it away. The torn edges of skin are charred, but the bleeding has nearly stopped. She packs some more of the poultice in the wound and then wraps the leg. After this, dressing the arm seems a small thing and goes quickly.

"He might live," Bera says to Gunnlaug, wiping the blood from her hands. "The night will bear it out."

Gunnlaug nods. Then he holds out his hand. "I believe that's the larder key hanging from your brooch."

Bera's glare would cause me to fear sharing a bedcloset with her, but Gunnlaug doesn't flinch. She takes the key from its chain and slaps it in his hand.

"Thank you," he says. "And now, my men are hungry."

"Then I hope you brought some food with you, and someone to cook it."

"We brought food, and you will prepare it."

Bera frowns hard enough to turn her lips white.

"And I will have someone watching you," Gunnlaug says. "We wouldn't want any poison to slip in now, would we?"

For a moment, confusion replaces some of the fierceness in Bera's face. But then it seems she comes to the same realization I do. Gunnlaug knew about the poisoning, and very likely ordered it done.

"My men are bringing up provisions as we speak," Gunnlaug says.

Bera looks down and turns away.

"You, skald." Gunnlaug puts his gloves back on. "You will sing my praises tonight."

Alric bows to Gunnlaug as deeply as he has ever bowed to my father, and the sight of it infuriates me. "Of course," he says.

"And you." Gunnlaug looks at me. "Girl-skald. You will sing as well. I would hear your . . . talent." The edge of menace in his voice tells me that he is not yet convinced of who I am.

I nod without bowing to him.

"Come," Gunnlaug says to his honor guard. "Per is still out there. We go man-hunting." They march from the hall, and my worry for Per follows them. I hope he is safe, wherever he is hiding.

A few warriors remain behind to guard us, so we can't talk freely. Bera returns to Hake's side and feels his forehead. He has begun to shake, and there is so much blood in the straw beneath the table where they laid him. Fear and doubt over whether anyone could survive such a loss force me to look away. "What we need are our blankets from the ship," she says. "Here, give me your cloaks. A wound-fever is setting in. If he lives through the night, I'll be amazed."

"He'll live," Harald says. "He's the strongest man in all of Father's lands."

Bera half smiles and piles our cloaks on Hake. But none are long enough to cover him completely, so she lays them piecemeal, a patchwork over his chest and his heavy legs. We all find benches and settle near him, watching his teeth chatter. Our last berserker. And if Per falls, our last warrior. If Per falls, who will be left to protect us?

I whirl around on Alric. "How could you bow to him?"

"Pardon me?"

My anger rises. "How could you even think of honoring him?"

"Siv," he says. "A story knows no honor. A story knows no allegiance. A story simply is."

I fold my arms. "And what of the storyteller? You can show honor and allegiance in the stories you tell."

"Ah, but whose stories? If the dragon had killed Sigurd, whose legend would we sing? What stories will be told after the breaking of the world? Stories of dead gods? I think not. After a battle, it does not matter who was good and who was evil. As a skald, you will tell the story of the victor, and in the telling you make the victor into the hero."

I glower at him. "Sir, it sounds as if you're saying that my . . . our king, *your* king has already lost."

Alric looks around the room. "Does it not appear that way to you?"

I am so furious with him I can't even think of the words to say. And the guards are still watching us. So the burning stays inside me, in my ears and my eyes.

I lower my voice. "Thank you for this lesson. I have learned more of what it means to be a skald."

Alric sighs. "It is a hard lesson to learn." He touches my arm, and I keep myself from pulling it away. "I have served many kings." He looks at Gunnlaug's warriors. "And I will yet serve many more."

"Are you never tempted to take a side?" I swipe at the tears in my eyes.

"It is a temptation I resist." He looks at me directly. "As must *you*."

I have no intention of resisting it, and no desire to talk to him about it anymore. I leave him and go to Hake's side. The berserker's face is pale, a last smear of dried blood on one of his cheeks. I take a wet rag and dab it against his skin, gently wiping it clean. His eyelids flutter, and I wonder what fever dreams, if any, might be passing through his mind. I hope they are free of pain.

"Oh, Hake," I whisper. "Please come back to us. We are weak without you."

He shows no sign that my words have reached him, wherever he is.

Asa comes up beside me. "I think you are the bravest of us."

"I'm not," I say.

"No one else would have entered that shield-ring with him." She looks askance at Hake, as if she is still afraid of him.

I pluck at the rag in my hands. "Bravery is nothing without strength."

"But you have that, too."

I say nothing.

"You are stronger than me," Asa says. "And in bravery and strength, there is a kind of beauty."

"Not like your beauty."

"No. No, not like mine. Your beauty won't ever fade." And then my sister draws away from me, leaving behind the sweet echo of her words. No one has ever described me as beautiful before.

Several of Gunnlaug's men enter the room carrying barrels

and sacks. Food, and much of it. The enemy came prepared. This was all planned, and I am amazed at how the sight of something I have so wanted can fill me now with such hatred. I decide then not to eat a single bite of it, though my mouth is already watering. The men deposit their load with Bera, and with a sigh, she begins to assess the contents. Raudi is at her side, and she sets about the practiced work of preparing a meal.

"How many of you are there?" Bera asks one of the men.

"We came nearly one hundred strong. There remain sixty-four."

Even though I am amazed at the damage wrought by our berserkers on Gunnlaug's forces, I quail at the number of enemies left. But I remind myself that Per is free, and he will find a way to save us. Though he has disappointed me, and the sting of those failings still lingers, I know he will never allow Gunnlaug to marry Asa.

"This is a small hall," Bera says. "You'll be crowded in here tonight."

"We'll make do."

Bera shrugs, waves him off, and returns to her hearth-business. A reputation to uphold.

I notice Harald sitting by himself. He still watches Hake, and I go to him.

"You are right," I say. "He is strong."

He shakes his head. "It's not that."

"Then what is it?"

He sits up. "If Hake dies. If they kill Per. Then I will be the last warrior."

I want to smooth his hair and kiss his forehead. But I can't. "That is true."

Tears fill his eyes. "I'm not ready. I thought I was, but I'm not."

"You are more ready than you know. Gunnlaug already fears you, because you are your father's son."

He nods and we sit together in silence. In the quiet, I hear the glacier groaning a lament for us. I feel its deep voice swelling under my feet. The sound is pained, as though on the edge of breaking into something terrible.

CHAPTER 18

BIRD OF ODIN

Gunnlaug returns from his manhunt angry. He storms into the hall, stops to survey Hake for a moment, and then goes to brood over the fire. Inwardly, I smile. The chieftain has not yet found Per. I take relief and a small, secret delight at this burr in Gunnlaug's beard.

He throws a log on the fire. "When will the food be ready?"

Bera stirs her cauldron. "Soon."

"How soon?"

She looks up. "Soon."

The cook-smells filling the hall are setting my stomach growling. Bera's cauldron simmers with meat, onions, turnips, and carrots. Flatbreads brown and puff up on a griddle over the fire. There is smoked fish, cheese, dried berries, and honey.

My appetite is already proving stronger than my resolve, my body betraying me.

Ole stands at Gunnlaug's shoulder. "We'll find him. He can't have left the fjord."

"Hmph," Gunnlaug says. "The longer it takes, the harder it will go with him."

"He must have realized that he was lied to," Ole says.

"That matters not to me. His part in this is ended." A log in the hearth collapses. "Though I would see it ended in my own way."

I stand near them, listening, though I don't understand what they're saying. What part did Per play? Did he know of Ole's treachery? The thought that Per might also be a traitor slices into me with the weight of an axe, and is almost beyond my ability to bear right now. Asa also leans toward Ole and Gunnlaug, her face white, and I wonder. If Per had a part, did she?

Before long, the food is ready, and the hall is crowded. But Gunnlaug keeps his men ordered, held firmly by the chain. They line up with their plates before the mealfire, waiting for Gunnlaug to be served first. But before the chieftain takes his seat, he calls to Harald and Asa.

"Come. You will share my table with me."

Harald and Asa slide toward him.

"What I have is yours," Gunnlaug says, gesturing to the bench opposite his as though it has always been his to offer.

Harald and Asa sit. Gunnlaug then goes to Bera and takes the ladle from her. And he begins to dish out the food himself, something I have never seen a king or chieftain do. He carries the first steaming plate and sets it in front of Harald.

"There. A nice big helping for a growing young man. Does that suit you?"

My brother accepts his bowl with a little nod.

"Good." Gunnlaug returns to the cauldron. "And Asa. Let me find a choice cut of meat for you. Something tender and rich."

The chieftain appears to take great care in spooning out her food, and then he sets it before her. Asa forces a smile and accepts her plate.

Gunnlaug sits down and watches them. "Eat, eat," he says.

Harald and Asa look at one another, and both of them take a bite.

"Is it acceptable to you?" Gunnlaug asks.

My siblings both nod.

Gunnlaug leans back, beaming. "Good." He calls to Bera. "Serve me, woman. My men are waiting and they are hungry."

After Gunnlaug, Alric is served next, followed by Ole and the rest of Gunnlaug's warriors. Bera, Raudi, and I are last, though I am still refusing to eat. Bera scoops up three bowls from what remains in the pot, mostly tough little bits of meat and burned vegetables she has to scrape from the bottom of the cauldron. She attempts to force some of it on me.

"You must eat."

"No."

"But nothing is gained by starving," she says.

I push the bowl away.

"You refuse my food?" Gunnlaug asks from across the room, and the hall goes quiet. Somehow, through the crowd, he has noticed me. Or perhaps he never stopped watching me.

I shake my head. "I meant no offense."

"And yet you have given it," Gunnlaug says. "I have been generous, have I not? I do not have to feed you from my meal-fire. I could force you to pick my scraps from the straw on the floor."

I keep my eyes downward, focused on the stains in the table, and the words come out before I can stop them. "I would not eat a thing that has come from your plate."

The room feels frozen around me.

"Well, well," Gunnlaug says. "Such pride from a skald's apprentice."

I notice that Ole and Alric are both staring at me, their eyes desperate, pleading, and I realize that I have made a terrible mistake. I swallow and reach for the bowl to eat.

"Stop!" Gunnlaug shouts. "It's too late for that." The chieftain rises to his feet and stalks across the room. He comes to stand behind me. I do not turn to look at him, but keep my head down, listening to his heavy breath. I hear a sudden movement and I flinch, expecting a blow. But instead, the chieftain reaches over me, grabs the bowl of food, and flips it off the table. It clatters to the floor, and its contents splash on the ground.

"Now," Gunnlaug says. "You may eat it."

I stare at the splattered stew.

"And after you eat it, you will sing for me. And then we shall know the truth of your ability."

I slowly force myself to rise, to step away from the table, to drop to my knees. I look up. Gunnlaug looms over me, his men a snowfield of cold eyes around me. Harald and Asa both appear shocked, helpless. Raudi's face is red with anger, and I notice Bera holding him in his seat. Alric's eyes are closed, he shakes his head. And is that pity on Ole's face? Behind the others, as though forgotten, Hake lies unaware of me.

I reach for the closest bite of turnip, scoop it from the ground, and do not even allow myself to pick away the straw before I put it in my mouth and chew. But the straw and the dirt are not what make it difficult to swallow. Gunnlaug waits until I have eaten another two bites before he nods and moves away.

After he has been gone for several moments, Bera reaches down and pulls me up. "On your feet. I think it's safe for you to come up here now and share with us. He got what he wanted."

I slump next to them, shame turning the food in my stomach sour. "I've ruined everything. I forgot myself."

"No," Bera whispers. "You remembered who you are. And it isn't ruined. You can still save yourself with the story you tell."

I allow myself to eat just enough to satisfy Bera's concern for me, and then I seek out Alric among the warriors. He scowls as I stand before him, and his eyes land everywhere but on my face.

"I'm sorry," I say, but the contempt I still feel toward him robs some of its sincerity.

"So am I." His tone is sharp. "But now, let us decide on a story for you to tell."

My shoulders droop. "I don't know what the point of that would be."

"What do you mean?"

"I don't think it will matter. I'll never convince —"

Alric slaps me. My head whips to the side and my cheek burns. A few of the warriors nearby glance up at us from their food. Is Alric putting on a show for them? The master disciplining his apprentice? I can't tell.

"Enough of that," Alric says. "I want no more doubt. I want no more fear. From this moment forward. Do you understand me?"

I nod, my hand cupping the side of my face.

"Let go of the fetters. You are not some Fenrir, tricked and chained by the gods. You bind yourself. Let loose the strength you have inside." Alric looks over his shoulder. "I will try to get you out of this tonight. But you must be prepared for tomorrow."

"I will be," I say.

He looks at my cheek and frowns. "I'm sorry," he whispers. "I wish that I could say I only did that to give the appearance of an angry master."

"It's all right," I say. After what I did tonight, I deserve to be slapped.

Alric pauses a moment longer. Then a change comes over his face, his usual smile rises, and he saunters off toward Gunnlaug. He approaches the chieftain in a bow and is summoned closer. Alric speaks, Gunnlaug listens, considers, and waves Alric off with a nod. The skald returns.

"We will perform tomorrow."

"What did you say to him?"

"I told him that we are composing a new tale in his honor, and that we need another day to finish it if we are to do it justice."

The delay seems too easily accomplished. I look back at Gunnlaug and find the chieftain staring at me. When he sees that I'm looking back at him, he smiles the same wicked smile he showed to Asa, the confident look of a predator who has trapped his prey and can now take his time with the kill.

After everyone has finished eating, Gunnlaug stands. "Tonight, I honor you, my warriors. It humbles me to lead and fight beside such men. When we return, I will break rings and reward each of you your due in gold and silver. We lost many good and strong warriors this day, but we have captured Hake, whose name is known and feared. And we have righted a grievous wrong done to our people, who will soon have their queen, a queen whose beauty will be sung through the ages."

Gunnlaug's men clap and cheer and begin to chant my sister's name. Asa sits ice-still.

The chieftain continues. "We are honored by the presence of Harald, a noble young man destined for greatness. We will safeguard him until such a time as his father shall claim him with gifts of land and treasure. Lands that once belonged to my father, and which shall be restored to our people."

More cheers and applause.

Gunnlaug lifts his cup. "We drink to those that live and those that have fallen. May all of us find a favorable wind at our backs, a calm sea ahead, and a hearthfire waiting at home."

The warriors all drink and switch their chant from Asa's name to Gunnlaug's. The chieftain sits, and soon his men begin to seek out benches and spots on the floor to bed down for the night. Blankets have been brought up from the ships. Bera and Raudi come over to join Alric and me. I watch to see where Harald and Asa will go, and see that Ole shepherds my brother over toward us.

"Gunnlaug thinks he should sleep with those of his household," says our former thrall.

"What about Asa?" I ask. But then I see Gunnlaug leading her away, back to the bedcloset. I panic. "Where is he taking her?"

"Don't trouble yourself," Ole says. "Asa will have the bedcloset to herself. She is to be his queen, and a queen can't sleep among her husband's men."

"It seems that things have turned out well for you, old man," Alric says.

Ole rubs his wrist. "They can for you as well, skald. And for your apprentice, as long as she stops acting the fool."

"She will," Alric says.

Ole walks away.

"Come," Alric says. "Let us find a quiet corner. We can all sleep near one another."

Everyone but Asa. I don't care what Ole says. I saw the way Gunnlaug looked at her, and I wish I could sleep in the bedcloset with her.

"We need to sleep near Hake," Bera says. "So I can watch him during the night."

Before long, we're all situated on benches and on the floor around our berserker captain. Bera changes out the cloaks over him for blankets. I don't know if I'm imagining it, but Hake seems to be resting more peacefully now. I nestle down next to Harald, wanting to put my arms around him, my nose in his hair, but I don't dare.

"What will happen to us?" Harald asks me.

"I don't know. But try not to worry." I lean in and whisper, "Father will save us."

"Yes. Father," Harald says.

Such a little story to tell him. I close my eyes, wishing I believed it.

But I don't sleep. Not fully. I stand at a crossing on the dreamroads, as sounds barely heard from the waking hall are half-shaped by the darkness. The sleeping men massed around me twist into trolls. Whispered conversations become the low murmurs of the dead and undead. And then I hear a scratching and see black nails carving fell shapes into a runestone.

"What's that scratching?" someone asks.

"It's at the door," comes a reply.

"What's at the door?"

"Open it."

The metal hinges squeal, opening my eyes.

"It's a raven," someone says.

I sit up.

"A raven?" another asks.

"It just came through the door."

Now Alric is up, and Harald. Across the room, a little black shape hops and flaps across the floor, over the men lying all around.

"Muninn!" I call.

My raven caws. He makes his way toward me, and men stir

beneath his little talons. Some bat him away, still dozing. Some sit up, blank-eyed, and watch him pass.

Muninn reaches us, and takes his place on my shoulder. I laugh and I cry. I stroke his head, his back, his bent wing, his night-feathers.

"Hello, bird of Odin," I say. "Hello, my memory. You came back to me."

"What is this?" Gunnlaug shouts, stomping over his men toward me.

The chieftain's voice startles Muninn from my shoulder. The raven leaps and flutters up onto Hake's table. I jump to my feet, and as Gunnlaug reaches me, we both find Muninn perched on the sleeping berserker's chest, where he caws, shifting from foot to foot.

The sight brings Gunnlaug up sharply. He stares, dumbfounded.

Alric glides toward us. "Berserkers are Odin's men, after all. I wonder what the Allfather's messenger brings on its wings?"

Gunnlaug points at me. "You called it Muninn."

"That is his name. Hake gave him to me."

"He sits on her shoulder," Alric says. "And whispers stories to her. Have you ever heard of such a skald?"

A crease of doubt forms in Gunnlaug's brow. I do not think he knows what to do. One of his men offers to remove Muninn from the hall. But Gunnlaug shakes his head.

"The skald is right. Odin's man. Odin's bird. The raven stays as long as it wants to." Gunnlaug turns away. "Back to sleep, all of you."

I stare at the chieftain's back and smile. Gunnlaug, it appears, is a man of superstition. He bends to lore and fears the gods.

Stories have power over him.

CHAPTER 19

PER

I wake feeling more joy than should be possible, given all that has happened. But I have my Muninn. He stands on my knee, and I feed him from my own bowl, just as I did yesterday morning. It seems that he has been gone much longer than a day, that more time has passed since Gunnlaug came wolf-snarling into the fjord.

I help Bera and Raudi clean up after the day meal, which takes up so much time that as soon as we've finished, Bera has to start preparing the night meal.

Bera grinds her teeth and mutters to herself. "All I know is they had better find someone else to wash their clothes."

Raudi leans into me. "I think Alric is wrong. You should be honest, even if that means taking a side. What good is a story if it's a lie?"

"You think I should only tell stories that really happened?"

"Not that kind of lie. A lie about yourself, and what you believe in."

"I think Alric would say that a story isn't about the storyteller."

"I think that sounds like someone trying to make themselves feel better about saving their own skin."

I smile. "Maybe you're right. Alric is the bench-ornament, isn't he? Not you. Especially after you offered to stay and fight with the others."

He looks away.

"I have to tell you, Raudi. I'm glad Hake didn't let you fight. But you were so brave in the face of death."

"But I'm not afraid to die." His voice is sharp.

It takes a moment for the meaning of his words to reach me. "What?"

He sighs, and it sounds like he's been holding it in for a long time. "I'm not a coward because I'm afraid to die. I'm a coward because I'm afraid to kill another man."

I don't know what to say.

"It was so hard when my brother died," he says. "My mother wept for days. I wept. It's never been the same since." He turns to me. "How can I do that to someone else? Every warrior has a family waiting back home. Even the enemy."

After all the years I've known him, I realize how little I understand Raudi. The goodness in him is inspiring. I put my arm around his shoulder. "That's what you were crying about that day in the practice yard?"

He nods. "But for you," he says, "and for my mother, I would have stayed to fight."

"Raudi," I say. "You're the bravest warrior I've ever known."

He blushes, and a moment later I pull my arm away. Then his mother calls him, and I decide to check on Hake. His fever has come down, his breathing is more even, and some color has returned to his face. Bera checks his wounds and changes the poultices and bandages. Hake's leg looks horrible, but Bera says it should heal with time.

"Though I've begun to wonder what I'm healing him for." She removes one of his blankets. "To be a thrall to Gunnlaug, more than likely."

I bite my lip. Perhaps it was wrong of me to save him, after all. What was it Hake said about the berserker he banished? To serve as a thrall to be worse than death? After what happened last night, I am certain Gunnlaug would take great pleasure in bringing Hake low.

"When do you think he'll wake up?" I ask.

"I don't know. Even without injuries and blood loss, the *berserkergang* can leave a warrior unconscious for days after the battle. But it is Hake, and he is not like other men."

"I wish he were awake now."

Bera looks on me kindly. "I do, too, though it's a selfish wish. Asleep, he is unaware."

I touch Hake's cheek and go to find Alric, leaving Muninn among the rafters. With my raven come back to me, and after seeing Gunnlaug's weakness, I feel more confident about telling a story tonight, though I do not know what story I will tell. The thought of singing Gunnlaug's praises knots my chest into a mass of anger and disgust.

The skald is not in the hall, so he must be out in the yard. Gunnlaug has been somewhat lax with us, allowing us the freedom of the steading. The mountain pass is still frozen. He knows we can't leave the fjord except by ship, and the vessels are kept under constant guard. I find Alric talking to some of Gunnlaug's men. He is laughing with them.

When he sees me, he bids them farewell and comes over. "I've been learning a few things about Gunnlaug. For tonight. Let us go where we might have some privacy and compose."

I nod, and we move away from the hall, back to the garden patch and the stacks of chopped wood. I sit on a stump scarred by axe blows, and Alric paces around me. He lists several accomplishments from Gunnlaug's early life: the killing of a great stag, the besting of a rival for Gunnlaug's first wife, his rise to power following the death of his father.

"The chieftain will be pleased to hear you mention these things," he says.

I nod.

"And now" — Alric takes a deep breath — "we must discuss his defeat of your father."

I open my mouth.

But Alric holds up his hand. "I know what is in your heart. This will be a final test of your quality as a skald. Can you put aside your own anger and hatred? Can you praise Gunnlaug's cleverness, his strategy? Can you sing of his love for your sister, and the injustice in your father's refusal of Gunnlaug's bride-price? Because that is what a skald must do, and what *you* must do to prove to Gunnlaug that you are a skald's apprentice."

I clench my jaw. "I can only try."

"True enough. But if you do not succeed, Gunnlaug will kill me for my deception. And possibly Ole as well. Our lives depend on you."

My resolve falters. I had not thought about what it will mean for Alric if I fail, or even Ole, who is a traitor.

"And if I am not mistaken," Alric says, "you were the one who said you wanted to be a skald."

A heaviness greater than the deepest snowfall has settled on me, and I feel like I'm suffocating. I whisper under the weight of it. "I did not think this is what it meant to be a skald." In spite of what I feel, if Alric's life depends on me, I can do nothing but honor Gunnlaug.

Alric sits down on the stump next to me. "This is the shadow-side of what it means to be a skald. A side I had hoped you would never have to see. I had thought you might replace me in your father's hall. Serve him comfortably, and then your brother when he becomes king."

His words stop me. "But . . . what about you?"

"I would find a new king. Or a chieftain. They are easy enough to come by."

I don't know what to say. "Thank you, Alric." In spite of my anger toward him, I am touched by his willingness to sacrifice his position for me. "But I could never truly take your place. You are a better skald than I will ever be."

"I am not." He slaps his thighs and stands. "Let's begin."

We work for several hours. We talk about the words, the language, the high moments of greatest importance, and the quiet moments to pause. I work hard to remember what Alric tells me, what we practice, though the story tastes of decay and corruption. I feel soiled while it remains in my mouth, and anticipate the relief I will feel in spitting it out and ridding myself of its taint.

"I think that is enough for now," Alric says. "Take some time, rehearse it. Prepare yourself. We should go over it again together, before the night meal."

"All right."

"I'll leave you to it." Alric walks away toward the yard.

I sit on the stump for several moments longer and look up at the sky. Clouds tower over the hall, mountain-scraped and ponderous.

Their folds shift before my eyes, kneaded by the wind, changing their shape and drawing me in. After a few moments of gazing, I feel myself falling upward, spinning, dizzy. And then in the white, a long tooth takes shape. Then teeth, a maw, a bristling neck. I recoil from a wolf's head made of cloud, high in the air, as big as the fjord, large enough to swallow our hall. It is what I saw in my dream.

First the longships, and now the wolf. The burning of the hall will come next. And after that, the ice. Our destruction.

I run.

There is no escaping it. The wolf is everywhere over me, watching, overwhelming in its immensity. I must hide from it, but it is the sky. How do you hide from the sky? I fly across the field, wishing I were a tiny mole, able to scurry underground. To my left I see the copse of trees where Per took us, and I scramble there, to the clearing, to the trapdoor over the old larder. Someone has closed it, and I dig and kick through the wet snow until I find it. I heave it open and rush down the stairs without shutting the door behind me, down under the sheltering earth.

My breath is ragged, my thoughts and emotions frayed. I feel as though I have been pushed to the edge of a perilous cliff, and I am close, so close to falling down into the crashing sea.

"Solveig?"

I scream and jump. And then there is a hand over my mouth. I can't breathe. I thrash and kick. I strain against a blackness that suffocates me, but it is too strong.

"Solveig!" a familiar voice says. "Stop, it's me, Per."

I cease fighting. I open my eyes. He takes his hand from my mouth.

"Per?"

He releases me and steps back, but I fall toward him and wrap my arms around him. And then I am sobbing and pounding on him as my whole body shakes. All the grief and fear and rage of the last few days come rushing out of me. Per holds me until I am spent, and I pull away from him, wiping my nose and my eyes. He is changed from when I last saw him. His eyes are red with exhaustion and the wild fear of the hounded. Long strands of his hair have pulled free of their braid and hang in his face. He looks smaller.

"Are you all right?" I ask.

He nods. "Well enough. Hungry. Did Gunnlaug bring food?"

"He did, but I don't have anything with me."

He nods, staring at the floor.

"Is this where you've been hiding?"

"Most of the time."

"Gunnlaug has been hunting for you."

"He doesn't know about this place. Hake killed the three who found it. The ones who found you."

"How did you know that?"

"I watched him do it."

"You were there?"

He nods.

Then why didn't you help us? I want to ask.

"It all happened so fast," he says, as though he heard my question. "I didn't know what to do. And then Alric was there and you all ran off with him." Per begins to pace, ploughing his fingers through his hair. "What could I have done? Fight Hake? He would have killed me, and then he would have killed Asa. And Harald and you. I did the only thing I could do, the best thing to do. I stayed hidden. I knew that Alric would see you to safety." His words have the quality of a well-worn path he's been down many times before.

But I cannot follow him there. "There was nowhere safe for Alric to take us."

He acts as though he hasn't heard me. "How is Asa?"

"Gunnlaug is going to marry her."

He stops pacing. To himself, he says, "I knew it."

"Knew what?" His words remind me of what Gunnlaug and Ole said. About his part. "What did you know?"

He turns away from me and crouches in the darkness, beyond the curtain of light falling through the opening above.

"Per, what did you do?"

"You should go back, Solveig."

"Per, I need you to tell me."

He sighs. "Forget you found me. Just go."

"Not before you tell me —"

"Go!"

I step back, surprised. And then I grow angry. "What about you, Per? How long will you hide down here? What about Asa? What about all of us? You swore you would protect us!"

263

"I'm sorry. There is nothing I can do."

"But my sister. I thought you loved her."

He is silent a long time, and then I hear a halting gasp. "I do love her. Everything I have done has been for her. But I am powerless."

Everything about him, the slack in his voice, the slope of his shoulders, the bend in his neck, all of it speaks of defeat, and the part of me that had placed my hope in him dies. My sadness and disappointment are as raw and torn as the earth around a fresh grave. But I know how it feels to be powerless, and even in this moment I am able to find pity for him.

I turn to leave. "I will try to bring you some food."

He coughs. "I would not have you put yourself in any danger for me."

"Please, don't." I mount the stairs. "The time for such honor has passed." I reach the top, step out into the open, and close the trapdoor. I do my best to cover it with snow and leave Per buried.

I trudge back to the hall utterly vanquished. We are lost. There is no one who can save us. Hake lies wounded. Alric will never turn on his audience. I would not want Bera and Raudi to risk themselves. Harald is a child. And Per — Per hides.

To my relief, the wolf-cloud has broken up and run away in

pieces over the sea. I am reminded of the wolf I saw from the steading wall those months ago. The wolf-king, ember-eyed and covered in frost as he turned and vanished into the trees. So powerful. So right with his world and himself. It makes me wonder how it is that wolves have come to be thought of as evil. There was nothing wicked in the creature I glimpsed, stunning in his mortality, noble in himself.

I stop walking. If there is nothing inherently evil in a wolf, then why have I so feared one? Why have I seen Gunnlaug as the wolf-cloud? There is nothing noble in the chieftain, and in my dream, I realize it was not the wolf that destroyed us, but the fire and ice that came after. Perhaps the wolf is something else. Someone else yet to come.

"Siv!" Alric stands waving by the hall.

I quicken my pace, cross the field, and enter the garden patch.

"What is it?" I ask.

"Hake is awake. I thought you would want to know."

I inhale. "How is he?"

"He was talking with Bera. He said nothing to me."

"Thank you for telling me."

"Where have you been?" Alric looks beyond me, toward the trees.

"Nowhere," I say. "Just wandering, thinking things through."

He nods, but lifts an eyebrow.

I slide past him. "I would like to see Hake."

"Go, go," he says, and shoos me on.

I scamper down the length of the hall and hurry through the doors. Someone has moved Hake to a pallet on the floor. He reclines, propped up on his good arm and shoulder. He sees me, but his face is blank. He doesn't call me over or wave to me. He looks away.

I force myself to approach him. "Hake?"

He grunts.

"Hake, how do you feel?"

"Broken."

That one word confirms what I had begun to fear. That he would rather have died. I keep my eyes down and turn to leave him.

"Wait," he says. "Come back."

Without lifting my eyes, I face him.

"Bera told me what happened. What you did."

I drop down beside him. "Hake, I didn't mean —"

"I am not angry with you."

"You're not?"

"Well, I am angry you took such a risk. And I'm angry that Alric let you do it. But I also honor your bravery. Not one man in one hundred would have dared enter that shield-ring." He reaches out with his wounded arm, wincing, and takes my chin between his thick thumb and first finger. "But I am not angry with you for saving me."

"But do you wish I hadn't?"

"I failed to protect you, your brother and sister." He eases his hand away and looks at his wounded leg. "I fail even now. For this, I deserve to be a thrall to Gunnlaug. I do not deserve to be counted among my men. I do not deserve to have died honorably with them in battle."

I put my hand on his and feel the toughness of his skin. "Your men did not deserve to die. Not one of them. And you do not deserve to be a thrall. Not you. Not you, Hake. You are the only one left who has any honor. You are the only one who has always been honest and true with me."

He turns his hand over and grips mine. "I have spoken with Alric about you." Then he rolls onto his back and shuts his eyes. "You must be honest and true with yourself."

"You think I am not?"

"I think that after all that has happened, you are still afraid. . . ."

"Afraid of what?"

He is falling asleep.

"Hake, what do you think I'm afraid of?"

"Trying." He opens his eyes. "Sometimes, when we want something so badly, we fear failure more than we fear being without that thing." He sighs. "Above all, be right with yourself."

I sit back. I stare at Hake's closed eyes, already sleep-sliding. His words echo my thoughts of the wolf-king and leave me bare and trembling. Alric has said I don't know the strength that is inside of me. That I am afraid of it.

Several moments pass. Hake's chest rises and falls, a slow rhythm.

Perhaps I am afraid of testing that strength for fear I won't be strong enough. Do I hold myself back, fettered? Could I be the very thing that I have feared, the cloud looming over the hall?

No. The wolf cannot be me. I am only Solveig.

I pull the blanket up over Hake. "Rest, now." I stand and notice Bera watching me from the mealfire, and I go to her.

"He is recovering faster than I expected," she says.

"He is Hake."

"Indeed, he is." She crumbles some thyme into the meat she's cooking. "He cares for you. You know that, don't you?"

"He loves my father."

She nods. "True enough. But it's not just that. You've touched him somehow through that thick berserker pelt."

I like to think that maybe Hake does care for me, because I have come to care for him. Not as friend, or a father, but something in between. I watch him sleep for a few moments more.

Gunnlaug has stripped away our berserker's weapons and placed his mighty war hammer near the hearthfire for all to see. A trophy. Hake will never wield it again, and I know what that means to him. He'll be given a hoe instead, his fieldwork no longer in battle, but in the sowing and harvesting of grain. The cowshed and pigsty will be his glory.

I hurt for him.

But I fight back my tears and help Bera finish preparing the night meal. Within hours, I will tell a story for Gunnlaug, praising a man who does deserve to die for what he has done. To our men. To Hake. To my family.

It feels impossible.

CHAPTER 20

FETTERS

The meal begins as it did the night before. Gunnlaug calls Harald and Asa to his table. He again serves their food and places it before them, but before they can eat, he addresses my brother.

"You may take that and go eat with those of your household."

Harald holds his spoon and knife, confused. Asa grabs his arm.

"Leave my table," Gunnlaug says.

Harald stands with his bowl and steps away, Asa's fingers trailing after him. My brother's face turns red as he crosses the hall, passing among Gunnlaug's men. But he keeps his back straight, his eyes up. Pride in the face of an insult.

"This is a calculated slight," Alric whispers. "Harald is noble and should eat at the chieftain's side."

"Gunnlaug is still waging a war," Hake says.

Harald reaches us and sits down beside me, then waits for all of us to be served before he eats. He is silent at first, but before long he is beaming at each bite our berserker captain takes, telling everyone that he knew Hake would live. I think it embarrasses Hake to have Harald watching him while he chews his food, but I am glad to have my brother close to me. I wish that Asa were here as well, but she is still up there, poking at her food while Gunnlaug drinks, and laughs, and slides up against her.

It pushes me to an edge I didn't know was there. And peering over it, a desperation begins to seize me.

"Why did he send Harald away and not my sister?" I ask.

"He's cutting her off from her reinforcements," Hake says. "He wants her to think she's all alone. Outnumbered. So she'll surrender."

"She won't," I say.

But I see the doubt on Hake's face. And Bera's. And Alric's. They think the war is already lost.

I can only manage to eat a little. Muninn enjoys my food, but the nervous rattling in my stomach and chest has left me without appetite. My time is approaching, and I cannot fail.

But it is hard to think about telling a story when I look at Gunnlaug next to my sister. Words evade me, like trying to catch dust in the air. The fear, the anger, and the apprehension scatter my mind, and my thoughts crumble even as I try to build them. I feel as I did when I first began to stand before the hall, unable to remember the story I had planned to tell. The story I rehearsed with Alric. Tonight, the story praising Gunnlaug.

Gunnlaug. Across the room, he lifts his arm and drapes it around Asa's neck.

Everyone sees it. Some, like Alric, pretend not to. Hake balls his fists and stares at his leg. Bera and Raudi shake their heads. None of them can stop the chieftain. No one will save my sister. No one will save us.

"Siv!" Gunnlaug bellows. "Stand up."

I rise to my feet.

"Come forward."

I drift toward him, Muninn on my shoulder, until I stand before his table.

Gunnlaug points at me. "I have given you more time than I should have to prepare. The time has come. Speak your tale."

Next to him, Asa is crying. She tries not to show it, but tears leak from her eyes when she blinks. Gunnlaug's arm is a flesh-chain around her neck, binding her. She doesn't even pull away. She accepts the fetter, staring at me, not helpless, but hopeless. She has surrendered, just as Hake said.

I must save her. But how?

A story is not a weapon. If it were, I would thrust my spear-words straight into Gunnlaug's heart. I would slice his throat with the blade of my voice and let the river of his blood pour freely on the ground.

"I am waiting," Gunnlaug says. "Or has your voice already failed you?"

The men around me snicker.

"It has not failed me," I whisper.

"What's that?"

"It has not failed me."

"I think it has." Without taking his eyes from me, he slowly strokes my sister's cheek with the back of his finger. At his touch, she looks up to the ceiling, or to someplace beyond it. "I see your anger," Gunnlaug whispers to me. "Come. We both know who you are, Solveig."

No.

At his words, the fog rolls away from my mind. This man may know my name, but he does not know who I am. He does not know what is inside me. I feel a swelling there, a rising strength and power. A howling in the wind that strains against the doubt and fear that bind me.

The chieftain leans forward. "Shall we end this now?"

I let go of the fetters. Muninn stretches his wings at my side.

"We shall end it," I say. "But not how you would see it finished."

"Is that so?"

"It is. You come here as a thief."

Angry murmurs begin to stew around me.

But Gunnlaug waves his men to silence. "A thief, you say?"

"Yes. But others have come to this place before. Like you, they sought to satisfy their greed and lust. My raven whispers to me of their fate, a fate that you will share."

There is a moment of silence in which I realize that everyone is watching me, and I am surprised that it does not bother me now, for I know it means they are all listening to me. A weapon-tale is forming in my mind. A sword-story. The truest tale I have ever told. The earlier doubt I glimpsed in Gunnlaug has returned to his brow. He pulls away from Asa and leans back, arms folded across his chest.

The inspiration for one of Alric's stories rises in my mind. "There is a runestone down among the trees near the shore. Its rock-voice tells of a warrior felled by the treachery of one who sought his lands and his wife. Have you seen this stone?"

Gunnlaug shakes his head.

"It is but a short distance from where you sit now. A restless place. Would you have me tell you what is inscribed upon it?"

It takes a very long moment for Gunnlaug to nod.

I raise my voice. "Many generations have passed since the glacier first sounded its cry of retreat and crawled back up the mountains to brook and moan. When the fields were rich and ripe, a warrior brought his wife here and built a hall. Her beauty surpassed the sea's, and even the mountains and the sky waged war to prove which could better please her."

I look directly at Asa. And as I do, so does Gunnlaug, as though he is seeing her for the first time. I continue.

"The world all knew of her as they knew of the sun, by her warmth and the light with which she shone. But there was an enemy who harbored a secret hatred in his heart-fjord, a man who desired the woman for his own."

I stare at Gunnlaug.

"He came with treachery to the warrior's hall, with an army to swear a false allegiance, and once inside the steading walls, the enemy let loose their swords and raised their spears. They murdered the warrior and all of his men, spreading the yard with slaughter-dew."

I wonder if Gunnlaug is aware of what I am doing. But it does not matter if he is. Men are often aware of the axe-blow in the moment before it lands. I continue.

"The enemy buried the warrior down by the waterside, in the ground, without a barrow for his bones or a stone to speak the story of his life. And then he went up to the hall to claim the woman as his wife. He ate and drank the spoils of the warrior's death late into the night, as wolf-howls sounded in the silent wood."

Here, I look directly into Gunnlaug's eyes. He tips his head to one side and stares back at me, perhaps not aware after all. He shall be soon.

"And then a distant roar broke upon the hall, a sound of rage and hunger, and a groan filled every ear with ice, and every warrior shook with growing fear. The wailing drew nearer, up from the waterside, advancing as a storm-rise out at sea. The enemy ordered every man to arms, and marched out with them into the moonlit night. They shivered as the shrieking voice, now closer, called the woman's name."

I pause and look around.

"And then over the hill he came, a *haugbui*. The corpse-giant of the fallen warrior, risen from its grave death-corrupted, rot-blackened, hate-swollen, and mountain-strong."

I pause to let the hall sit in its silence and the haunted groaning of the glacier. Gunnlaug's eyes are open wide, his face pale. There is now a space between him and my sister. I have frightened him. *Me.*

"The sight," I say, "drove the enemy soldiers mad. Some cowards tried to flee before the beast, but the dead warrior snatched them up and snapped their necks like twigs. Those few with any honor fought to hold their ground, but no axe, nor spear, nor sword could kill what was already dead, and all were felled until their leader stood alone to face the dead warrior."

Gunnlaug leans toward me, following my flashing lure-words like a fish.

"They clashed, and though the enemy was strong, the *haugbui* was stronger. It broke and sundered the enemy's body, then stood amidst the wreckage of its wrath. In pain it called the woman's name again, and hearing him, she came out from her hiding in the hall. She took his bloody, trembling hand and towed the black ship of his body back down to the shore, down to the earth-sea from which he had arisen. She guided him back into his grave, and having given her love and loyalty, she lay down by his side, with her arms around him, to sleep the last sleep."

Asa is crying. I wish I could tell her that her warrior is also under the ground. But I can't, for I know she would, too, go to him.

I continue. "And her handmaidens came forth to cover them, to bury them, and mourn their love, both winter-deep and legend-strong."

The tale is finished, but I do not bow my head. Muninn caws beside me. Gunnlaug is silent, as still as the runestone I have just spoken of.

"The warrior is still here," I say. "He sleeps under the hall. Can you not feel him watching you?"

Around me, Gunnlaug's men shift on their benches, a *haug-bui* over each of their shoulders.

I reach up and stroke Muninn. "He still protects the women of his fjord."

Gunnlaug says nothing. I remain poised, waiting. And still he says nothing. He says nothing until my confidence begins to weaken, like a creaking in the ice beneath my feet, and I swallow. In that moment the chieftain stands and sidles, very subtly, away from Asa. Perhaps no one else notices it, but I do, and I know what I have done.

At least, for now, I have saved my sister.

"I am convinced," Gunnlaug says. "You are a skald."

I am windblown by disbelief, and a rush of relief lowers my tense shoulders.

Gunnlaug bends over the table into the hall, propped up on his fists. "I perceive the truth of your tale. But it is a tale no skald would have dared tell. Not to me. Unless that skald was also of noble blood."

It takes a moment to know that I have heard him. And then I become frantic.

"You *are* Solveig," he says.

"Sir, I —"

"Silence!" Gunnlaug pounds the table, knocking a goblet off its foot. "I will not be lied to! You will only make it worse for *them*." He points in the direction of Hake, Bera, Raudi, and Alric. "Do you understand me?"

I nod. My vision is collapsing, my thoughts are thinning.

Gunnlaug tosses something to one of his men. "Take this and lock those deceivers out in the larder."

"No," I say.

Men marshal around me, all leather clothes and scuffing boots. They take hold of Bera, Alric, and Raudi. They force Hake to his feet. Bera argues with them about the cold, pleading for her son, while Raudi shouts to defend his mother. Alric calls to me, while Hake sways next to him. I watch Gunnlaug's men drag them all from the hall, and I feel as able to stop it as I do the waves and the tides. What power I felt inside me, whatever I thought I was, is gone. I am not the wolf.

I round on Gunnlaug. "Please don't do this."

He frowns at me. "Solveig the Skald. You and your sister will share the bedcloset tonight." Then he turns his back on both of us and goes to the middle of the room. "Where is that traitor, Ole?"

I look for him, but do not see him in the hall.

"He is gone," says one of Gunnlaug's men.

"No, he isn't." The chieftain looks through the open door. "He is out there. And tomorrow, we'll find him and that coward, Per. Their bodies shall join this *haugbui* in the ground."

This is not what I thought would happen. But then what did I think? How could I have thought to save us with a story? How could I have ever believed in myself? The others are in greater peril now than before.

And it is my fault.

The bedcloset is as cold and hollow as an iron cauldron left outside in the snow. I wanted to bring Harald in with us, but Gunnlaug insisted my brother sleep among his men. Muninn seemed reluctant to enter, so I left him among the rafters, praying that superstition keeps him safe.

Asa and I lie apart from each other. She is crying, and her sniffing and heaving infuriate me. Why did she submit to him? How could she surrender to Gunnlaug? If she had been stronger, I might not have been so reckless with my tale. I might have instead recited what Alric and I had planned, and the others would still be in the hall instead of freezing out in the larder.

"Solveig?"

I snap inside. "What?"

She inches closer to me. "Thank you."

I ignore her.

"You saved me."

I roll away, but she reaches out and takes my arm.

"You were so brave," she says. "You stood up to him —"

"Why didn't you?"

"What?"

"Why didn't *you* stand up to him?"

She lets me go, and in disgust I move to the edge of the closet, as far from her as I can.

"I'm not strong like you," she says.

I mumble into the wall. "You could be."

"No, I couldn't. And besides. Gunnlaug is only what I deserve."

That pulls me back some of the distance toward her, mostly out of pity. But I don't want her to know it. I want her to come the rest of the way and be honest with me.

"This is all my fault," she says.

I wait.

"We never meant for any of this to happen. Solveig, I'm so sorry."

It isn't far enough. "What did you do?"

She exhales. "I love him. I do. But Father would never have allowed it."

"And?"

"We only did it so we could be together. That was all."

"Asa, what did you do?"

"When Gunnlaug first came to Father's hall, Per knew he wanted land more than he wanted me. So he met with Gunnlaug in secret and made him an offer."

I do not want to hear it, but I have to know. "What offer?"

"If Gunnlaug agreed to let Per have me, then Per would deliver Gunnlaug the lands that he wanted."

So Asa is a traitor, too. My sister. I should have known it from the beginning, and maybe I did, but couldn't admit it. The enemy has been in my own bedcloset all along. I feel sick.

"Gunnlaug and Per arranged everything," she says. "The declaration of war, Father sending us here, all of it. Per suggested this fjord as a hiding place. It was supposed to make it easier. Gunnlaug would come here and take us all prisoner. Father would ransom his lands and me to have Harald safely returned, and Gunnlaug would then give me to Per. So easy. But the plan failed when Father sent the berserkers."

"You poisoned them," I whisper in horror.

"No! Of course not," she says. "I would never — no one was supposed to be hurt."

Before I can ask my next question, she says, "And it wasn't Per, either. I know it."

"Then it was Ole?"

"Believe me, Solveig, we didn't even know Ole was loyal to Gunnlaug until Per confronted him for spying on you down by the runestone. Per wanted to find other ways to weaken the berserkers."

"Like killing the cows?"

"Yes. But Ole didn't think it was enough. Gunnlaug was coming, and he didn't expect to find Hake and a force of Father's best warriors waiting for him."

All these answers rain down on me like boulders.

"And then," she says, "when Gunnlaug finally came, Per wanted to make sure he kept his end of the bargain. That was why he tried to hide us in the old larder."

I cover my ears. "Stop."

"I never meant for anyone to be hurt."

"Just stop."

She begins to cry again. "I'm so sorry. Forgive me, Solveig. Forgive me."

Forgive her? I can't, and my anger robs me of any desire to try. Forgive her? How many are dead because of her? Her selfishness. Her cowardice. Her weakness. There is nothing in her worth honoring, aside from her beauty, and even that has been darkened by the emptiness behind it.

So I don't answer her.

"Even if you can't forgive me," she says, "I wanted you to at least understand."

"I'll never understand you," I say. "Do you realize that I told that story tonight to save you? What about Raudi? What about Hake and Alric and Bera? They are out in the larder, freezing, because I was trying to save you! You deserve worse than to be with Gunnlaug."

Her sobbing intensifies.

And because I am angry, and I don't think she has hurt enough, I say, "Per is alive."

Her crying stops.

I continue. "He is alive, and he knows that Gunnlaug is going to marry you, and he is too much of a coward to do anything to stop it."

The silence that follows is wide enough for a little guilt to slide in.

"How do you know this?" she whispers.

I hesitate now. "He told me."

"You've seen him?"

"Yes."

"Where is he?"

"It doesn't matter."

"Solveig." She grasps my hand, her fingers soft and cold. "I know what you think of me, and you are right. But I beg of you, you must tell me where he is."

She is still only thinking of herself. I begin to cry then; I can't hold it back. I am so tired of crying.

No one is who they say they are, not even my sister. I was such a fool. Only a few months ago, I thought so much of Per. He was so kind, so handsome, so strong, but I see through it all now. So much has changed since then, and only now am I aware of it. *I* have changed. I am stronger. I am braver. And I have not surrendered.

"Please," Asa says.

"No."

"Why?"

"Because I can't trust you. If I tell you where he is, you'll go to him, and Gunnlaug will find out, and he'll punish all of us."

"I won't."

I roll away from her.

"Solveig, I won't."

"Sleep, Asa."

She says nothing more. I close my eyes and try not to think about her, or Per, or poisoned berserkers, or Hake's leg, or how cold it is tonight, but for what seems a very long time, I can't think of anything else. Guilt and anger consume me until nothing is left but exhaustion. There is a wind grasping at the hall, and not even the groaning of the glacier can drown it out.

CHAPTER 21

FIRE

Shouts awaken me in the middle of the night, a man out in the hall calling cries of alarm.

I sit up. "Asa?"

No reply.

I sweep my hand through an empty bed beside me, and I am not surprised to find her gone. I open the bedcloset door and peer out into the hall. One of Gunnlaug's men charges up and down the ranks of his sleeping comrades, kicking and pulling them awake.

"Fire! The cowshed burns!"

Men rush to pull on clothes and boots. They race outside through opened doors, into an orange light that forces its way into the hall. I smell smoke.

Gunnlaug storms among them, dragging Harald behind him. "Outside, all of you!"

"It was Per, sir!" the watchman shouts. "I saw him running into the woods as the fire started."

Per started it? I remember the last words I said to him, my accusations and contempt, and I wonder if I somehow stirred him to action.

Gunnlaug nods. "Gather as many men as can be spared from the blaze. Double the guard on the ships. Tell the rest to come to me. We're going after him."

"Yes, sir."

As his warrior races outside, Gunnlaug turns toward the bedcloset. He sees me.

"You and your sister get out of here. The fire could spread to the hall."

"My sister is gone," I say.

He laughs. "Of course she is. Well, come out and see to your brother." He heaves Harald toward me. "Keep him safe and out of the way."

I nod and climb out of the bedcloset. Gunnlaug marches outside, and I am left alone with my brother. He watches as I pull on my boots and lace them up.

"Asa is gone?" Harald says.

"Yes."

"Where?"

"I don't know. I think she went to find Per." I look up and call to Muninn. A moment later, he comes flapping down from the rafters to my shoulder. "Stay with me now," I say to him.

"What are we going to do?" Harald asks.

"For now, what Gunnlaug said to do. I'm going to keep you safe."

"What's that?"

"What?"

Harald points at Muninn. "He's got something in his mouth."

I turn to look closely and see that my raven is holding a black key in his beak. The larder key.

I take it from him and kiss his head right between his blinking eyes. "You mischievous, magical bird."

"Can we use that to help Hake and the others escape?" Harald asks.

"Yes." In the chaos of the fire, and with Gunnlaug hunting Per through the woods, this might be the only chance we'll have. But where will we go? We could hide in the cave, but there is no way of knowing what Per or Ole have told Gunnlaug of the fjord. The cave could defend us, but it could trap us, too, and become our tomb. Then there are the ships, but with the guards doubled, we'd never succeed in taking one, and with all the men Gunnlaug has at oar, we'd never outrun him anyway. The mountain pass is the only remaining escape from the fjord, and it may still be frozen shut. But what choice do we have?

"Let's go," I say.

I lead him across the hall, but as we pass the hearth, I see

Hake's war hammer still resting there. I reach for it to bring it with us, unsure of whether I have the strength to carry it, but Harald stops me.

"Let me," he says. He takes it with both hands, grunts, and heaves it up over his shoulder, wincing a little under the weight.

"Are you sure?" I ask.

He tightens his lips and gives a quick nod.

"All right, then."

We reach the doors and pass through them into a red and angry world. The cowshed is lost, engulfed in a column of flame that rises high into the sky. Waves of heat roll away from it, beating my face. Gunnlaug's men race back and forth extinguishing the bits of burning debris and ash carried away by the wind, trying to prevent the fire from spreading to the other buildings or the trees. Harald stares.

"Hurry," I whisper and tug him on.

I keep a constant glance over my shoulder as we approach the larder door. No one has noticed us yet. I insert the key and twist the lock. The door opens, and Raudi stands before me, his arms outstretched, shielding his mother. Alric kneels on the ground.

Raudi lowers his arms. "Solveig?"

"Everyone, come with me," I say. "There isn't much time."

But then Alric gets up, and I see Hake lying there. My heart lurches. I haven't given a thought to how we'll move him. Alric and Raudi help him as he struggles to his feet.

"Go on," he says. "I'm fine."

"You can't walk on that leg," Bera says.

Hake gently pushes her away. "Yes, I can." He limps to the door. "Let's go."

"Where?" Alric asks.

"The mountain pass," I say. But that was before I had thought about Hake.

The berserker's eyes fall for a moment, but then he rolls his shoulders back and points at the war hammer Harald carries. "I believe that's mine."

My brother frowns at Hake's leg. "I can carry it for you."

Hake hesitates a moment before nodding. "Meet behind the hall at the woodpile. We'll take turns so we don't draw attention. Raudi, you go first, then you, Bera."

Mother and son nod, and one at a time, they duck across the yard. Alric follows after them, then Harald.

As soon as my brother has disappeared around the corner, Hake turns to me. "Now, you go. And when you reach the woodpile, start up the ravine and don't stop. I'll be right behind you."

I am about to leave him, but something in the tone of his voice stops me. I turn back. "I want you to go first."

He ignores me. "Hurry, that fire won't keep them occupied much longer."

"I'm not leaving you behind."

The berserker touches my arm. "You know there's no way

I'll make it up there. If I go with you, I'll only slow you down. If I stay here, in the larder, I can buy you some time. Now, leave me."

I shake my head.

"Go," he hisses, and tries to push me out the door.

But I fight back. "No. You serve my father, and so you serve me. And I am ordering you, as the captain of my father's ber-serker guard, to escort me to the woodpile behind the hall. And from there, you will see me safely up to the mountain pass. Is that understood?"

He stares at me with more surprise than I have ever seen on his face.

"I'm waiting, Captain."

He lifts one of his eyebrows, and then the corners of his lips. "Let's go," he says.

Muninn flutters to the ground as we lean on each other and stumble forward, emerging into the open just as the cowshed finally collapses in an explosion of sparks that sends burning wood flying. Falling embers sizzle all around us as they hit the snow. I worry about Muninn hopping along beside us, but he appears to be keeping up.

Hake's body is heavy against me, heavier than I thought it would be. I don't know how long I can support him. I'm exhausted by the time we reach the corner of the hall and find our household gathered, waiting at the edge of the field.

"Go," I call, panting, and wave them on. This next part of

our escape is the most dangerous. Even at night, we'll be easy to spot against the open snow.

Bera and Raudi take Harald by his hands and jog on toward the ravine, but Alric comes back to Hake and me.

"Let me help," he says, and shores up the berserker's other, wounded side. I try not to show Hake how relieved I am, and the three of us move forward.

"Do me a favor, skald," Hake says a few steps later. "When you tell a story about this, leave this part out."

Alric chuckles. "How about I have you carrying Solveig and me out of the burning hall, one under each arm?"

Hake sounds like he wants to laugh, but it comes out more of a groan. "I'd enjoy that tale."

We move a little faster with Alric helping, but we are still barely halfway across the field when Bera and Raudi reach the far side with Harald. I think Hake and Alric see it, too, because both men furrow their brows in determination.

"This isn't working," Hake says. "You should leave me."

I reaffirm my hold on him. "We already settled this."

Behind us, the hall squats in silhouette before the roaring fire. The blaze seems to have grown, and dread seeps through me as I realize the flames have reached the larder. Gunnlaug's men will try to get the prisoners out, if they haven't already, and then they'll discover the escape. We must hurry.

But Hake suddenly misses a step, and we stumble to a stop. "Where is your sister?"

I try to pull him forward. "I don't know."

"We need to find her," he says.

"No." I cannot think about her right now. She made her choice. "They betrayed us, Hake. Asa and Per and Ole. The three of them brought Gunnlaug here."

Hake frowns.

"We'll talk about it later. For now, come. Please."

Hake reluctantly moves, and the three of us resume our awkward gait. We are almost to the woods when I hear a distant cry behind us. I do not need to turn to know that we have been spotted. But we still have some time before Gunnlaug will be able to gather all his men.

We reach the trees, and though we are no longer easily visible, our progress slows. The branches, roots, and snow-laden underbrush hamper us, moving side by side as the three of us are. Muninn has an easier time of it, flapping from tree to tree in his awkward way. I am watching him when Hake trips, and his heavy arm takes me down with him. My face hits the snow, filling my mouth and my nose. I come up sputtering, cold and wet.

"Solveig . . ." Hake lies on his back, breathing hard.

I grit my teeth. "Don't you say it."

Alric helps me up, and together we get Hake back on his feet. Eventually, we break out of the trees and come to the base of the ravine. Bera and Raudi are waiting there with Harald. When they see us, they rush up and surround us. Harald still carries Hake's war hammer, proudly, though he is sweating.

"They spotted us," Alric says.

"Then we'd best get moving," Bera says.

"Here." Raudi slides between Hake and me, splitting me away. "Let me take him for a spell."

I do not protest, and a moment later, Muninn is back on my shoulder. But with my exhaustion, he feels heavier than he ever has before.

The narrow path winding up the ravine forces us into a column. Bera leads us, followed by Harald. Next, Alric and Raudi help Hake, and then I bring up the rear. We trace the course through the boulders and pathways that lead up to the glacier and the mountain pass, the same course taken by the spring runoff on its way to the sea. But where there should be a robust stream this time of year, a thin runnel trickles past our feet.

"Where is the water?" Bera asks.

Her question goes unanswered.

The uneven footing makes the going even slower for our berserker, and he grimaces every time his leg slips. I notice a spreading stain of red on his leg bandages. He must be in tremendous pain, but he doesn't once complain.

As we pick our way upward, I notice it is getting lighter, and the mountains wear the cold crown of dawn. The glacier's lament swells as we ascend, sounding both pained and alarmed, heralding a doom-rise. Before long we are able to look back out over the field, toward the distant hall and burning buildings, where there is now more smoke than flame.

"There," Alric says, pointing. "Gunnlaug comes."

And then I see the black wedge of his forces driving through the snow, almost to the trees below.

None of us says another word. We simply turn and continue on.

But a short while later, as we finally near the top, I begin to question why. What is the point of our flight? We have no hope. Hake looks pale, and his eyes have begun to drift toward listlessness. Alric and Raudi sag under him and need someone else to take a turn, but I feel no more able now than when Raudi relieved me. Even if the mountain pass is open, how can we hope to cross it before Gunnlaug overtakes us?

We are not escaping, I realize. We are simply choosing not to die as prisoners.

I reconsider the cave. Per kept the old abandoned larder a secret from Gunnlaug. Perhaps he kept the existence of the cave from the chieftain as well. Ole might have told Gunnlaug of it, but there may still be a chance we could hide there. And if not hide, then at least make one last stand inside it. This new plan of mine is perhaps only a little less foolish than taking the mountain pass in the first place, but at least it holds some hope.

"When we reach the glacier, climb to the cave," I say. Everyone simply nods and plods along.

But then we crest the final rise, and the order of the world is overturned.

CHAPTER 22

THE BREAKING OF THE WORLD

The ground trembles. Whether from fear or anticipation, I cannot tell. But through my boots I feel it quiver with the flex and slide of muscle under skin. The cave billows a pungent steam into the ravine, filling it with a fog that obscures the glacier above us. The boulders and slopes of shale to either side are coated in rime, a pale frost-skin gathered from the air. I move forward in awe and fear, as though crossing the boundary into Niflheim, the mist-world of ice and death.

The others appear to be as overwhelmed as I am, for no one speaks, and it seems that for each of us, a single step is an act of will. Even if there were words I could summon, I am certain the fog and cold would freeze them to my lips as I spoke them.

Up around the mouth of the cave, the rocks are bare and wet. They glisten in the heat that churns from the mountain, from the dragon breathing in its lair. I remember the warmth I felt in that cave before, and fear that to hide there will be impossible now.

"Keep moving," Hake says, some life restored to his voice.

We pick our way forward, and soon the glacier looms out of the fog. At first I suspect my vision of betrayal, for the ice appears alive. Through the haze, the glacier's face writhes. I blink and peer up at it as we draw closer, and before long we stand at its feet.

"By the gods," Hake whispers. "There's a whole lake trapped in there."

Bera's question coming up the ravine is now answered. The glacier, it seems, has been hoarding itself, refusing to let go of its melted, watery flesh. It has somehow bound itself with the twin chains of warmth from the mountain and the cold from the air, and now it thunders and cracks and moans under the strain.

"A story must be told of this," Alric says.

Glacial water moves behind a transparent layer of ice in great ropes and coils, twisting on itself like the great serpent holding the floods at bay. I feel so small standing at the feet of this uprighted fjord, so insignificant. On my shoulder, even Muninn has stilled.

"Gunnlaug will be upon us soon," Bera says. "We should decide what to do."

No one responds.

"Please," Bera says.

Hake looks at her, then up at the cave. "The mountain burns inside. You must try for the pass."

Not this again. "*We* must try for the pass," I say.

Hake limps over to Harald and holds out his hand. My brother looks up at him and then gives the berserker his war hammer.

"Thank you for carrying my weapon," Hake says. "You are already a fine warrior. Little in body, but not in heart."

My brother bows.

"Harald," I say. "What are you doing? He still needs you to carry that."

Hake turns to me. "No, I don't." He twists his hands on the haft of his weapon. "I will hold the enemy here. And as I die, so will Gunnlaug." He smiles at the war hammer as he says it.

I roll my eyes and walk right up to the berserker. I take hold of his war hammer, and as I do it, I realize how unthinkable it would have been for me to do such a thing only months ago. "Give it to me, Hake. We already decided we go together."

Hake lifts his weapon out of my reach with his good hand and nods to Alric. The skald comes up and takes my shoulders in a firm but gentle grip, sending Muninn fluttering to the ground.

"Come, Solveig," the skald says.

I twist him off. "Hake, I command you to give me your weapon."

The berserker shakes his head. "Forgive me. But I cannot obey you." He points up the mountain, up the path that skirts the glacier's edge to the pass. "Bera, take your son and Harald. Your only chance now lies that way."

Bera takes Harald by the hand. "Thank you, Hake. Thank you."

Hake nods. "Alric, take Solveig —"

"No!" I shout. He cannot abandon me. He cannot leave me. I can't bear to lose anyone else, especially not Hake. Not Hake. I'm shaking. I grab his free hand. I tug on him, toward the direction of the path. "You're coming with us!" I'm sobbing. But he doesn't move, and I yank harder, but it's like pulling on a tree. He says nothing, but he winces, and I realize I'm holding his wounded arm. I let him go.

And in tears, I beg. "Please, don't do this. Don't do this. I need you."

The firmness and determination remain on his face, but his eyes soften. "Twice now you have refused to leave me behind, but now you must." He sets his war hammer on the ground. Then he lifts his massive hands and lays them against each side of my face. He closes his eyes, and then he bends at the waist until his forehead touches mine. He holds it there for a moment and sighs. "I would be honored to have a daughter such as you."

Then he pulls away and wipes a thumb under one of his eyes. He picks up his war hammer and turns his back on me.

"Hake," I whisper.

He doesn't turn around. Alric rests a hand on my shoulder.

I step out of the skald's reach. "Hake," I say, but now Raudi is here, helping Alric lead me away.

"Come, Solveig," Raudi says. They force me toward the path.

"Hake!"

The berserker never looks back.

My feet slide on the rocks as Alric and Raudi haul me up the side of the mountain toward the pass. Harald is with us, glancing over his shoulder. Muninn follows, too, but he appears reluctant, hanging back and then catching up in bursts of flapping. He knows we're leaving someone behind. Does he remember that it was Hake who caught him and gave him to me?

I fight to tear free of them. "How can you do this?"

"He is Hake," Bera says. "And he is not only doing this for you."

That stops my thrashing. She is willing to let Hake die for her and her son. I fall silent, but look back, hoping to see my berserker loping up the trail after us. Instead, he stands alone before the glacier, war hammer hanging at his side, waiting in the mist. And then he moves. In spite of his injury, he stomps, leaps, and spins.

"Wait," I say. "Look."

They pause with me and watch as Hake begins to dance. At least that is what it seems to be, but it is nothing I have seen before. It is ferocious. It is wild. It is power and rage and bravery in motion. Even from where we are, we can hear his prayer-roar, his call to Odin. The raw beauty of it frightens me, and we cannot help but linger to watch him.

"He is trying to bring on the battle rage," Alric says.

"Can he stop all of Gunnlaug's men?" Harald asks.

None of us gives him the answer. No, he can't. Not even with the *berserkergang* upon him could Hake kill them all. Some will get by him, and they will come after us. And I think the others must know it, too.

"He can't save us this way," I say. "We're going to be caught, and his sacrifice will have been in vain."

Alric stares at me. Hake chants below us, and Alric swallows.

"Hake wants to die with honor," Bera says. "Would you take that from him?"

I narrow my eyes at her. "Do not pretend you leave him for his sake."

"Be quiet," Raudi says. "Listen."

Then I hear them through the fog, an extra chill in the air. Gunnlaug's men are almost here. They climb, shouting and cursing, vile voices from my dream. But instead of terrifying me as they have before, they enrage me, even more than when I told the tale to Gunnlaug.

I *want* to be the wolf. I want to be Fenrir, let loose from my chain so that I might swallow Gunnlaug whole. I want the serpent to release its tail, for the floods to rise and drown our enemies. I would break the world to save us. But those are just stories.

Or are they? I look at the glacier, ready to shatter. I look at Hake, at the war hammer in his hand. Though a story may begin as a lie, perhaps it can be made true. Perhaps their ultimate power is found in how they inspire us to action. I tear free of the others and race down the hill.

"Solveig!" I hear Raudi call.

But I ignore him.

I come up on Hake fast enough to surprise him. He looks down at me, wide-eyed and panting. He is about to speak, but before he can, I snatch the war hammer from him and sprint to the glacier's face. The weapon is heavy in my hands, but I will wield it. I adjust my footing on the rocks and look up at the ice, but before I can swing the hammer, Alric and Raudi reach me. Hake limps up behind them.

"Stay back!" I scream. "All of you."

Raudi reaches toward me. "Solveig —"

"No, Raudi," I say, and pull away from him.

"What are you doing?" Alric asks.

"I am *making* your story true!"

The sounds of Gunnlaug's force are closer now. Alric cocks his head toward them. He listens a moment, looks at me, and something flashes in his eyes.

He extends a hand toward me. "Solveig, listen to me now. Everything I have told you. Everything I have taught you. You must forget it all."

"What?"

"Last night, as I watched you tell your tale, I realized I was in the presence of legend itself, and I have been a fool."

The war hammer slips a little in my hand.

Alric takes a step closer to me. "You have the strength to break every dusty rule and tradition I have hidden myself behind. You have in your voice the power to shape the world. You are more than a skald, and you will shake the earth by its foundations. Not even your father can stop you. I only wish that I could see what you will become."

"Alric, I —"

He lunges at me and easily wrestles the hammer from my hands. I stagger away from him, and Raudi gathers me into a hold that is more of a hug. The skald looks up at the ice and pauses for one brief moment.

"Raudi," he says. "Get her up the mountain. You, too, Captain."

"What are you doing?" I ask.

Alric lifts the war hammer over his head. "Choosing a side." Then he swings the weapon, bashing it against the ice. The sound of the impact echoes through the ravine.

"Now, Raudi!" Alric says, and swings again.

Movement in the fog catches my eye, dark man-shapes

advancing. An army of trolls and frost giants. Over the top of their voices, I hear Gunnlaug driving them on.

"Kill everyone but the boy!"

Alric swings again. And this time, the ice shudders, a rumble that disrupts the roiling of the trapped water, as though the great serpent inside has become aware of us.

"Go!" Alric shouts.

Gunnlaug and his men emerge from the mist. Hake leaps toward me. He pushes me and Raudi up the path, though I keep looking back at Alric. The skald swings again and again, leaving a gaping white crater in the ice. The ravine is filled with the sound of his striking, a god-anvil ringing through the mountains. Alric sweats. He laughs as Gunnlaug barrels down on him. And then I hear a cracking. A shifting in the ground as though the serpent's grip has slipped, its strength giving out.

Hake, Raudi, and I pause a distance up the mountain. Gunnlaug has almost reached Alric, his blade drawn. The skald looks up at us. At me. He is smiling, but it is not the lie-smile he has always worn. It is a truth-smile. A torch-smile. His deep-self burning through all his layers.

Alric swings again. The war hammer lodges in the ice, and the world breaks apart

The force from the exploding glacier knocks me to the ground, and Hake falls with me. A surging white ocean erupts from the ice. It scours the ravine, deep enough to claw at the path just a few feet below us. Millstones of ice tumble through the water, grinding and cracking. The water leaps over itself, stampeding down the mountain, annihilating everything in its path.

Alric is gone.

Gunnlaug and his men are gone. All of them.

And still the water flows. But it slows as the glacier sheds its burden, the source of its being and also its death. Hake and I rise to our feet, and he puts his arm around me as though afraid to let me go. I hold him up and embrace him. Within moments, Bera and Harald come down the path.

"Oh, mercy, you're alive," Bera says, barely holding on to Muninn. "We thought the water took you."

My raven caws and flaps and bursts from her arms. He flutters right over to me, and I lift him to my shoulder. "Alric saved us."

"Where is Alric?" Harald asks.

My eyes take in the devastated ravine, the walls, and the water running down every crack and fold. My throat feels tight. I clear it, and swallow. None of this seems real. Alric's death cannot be real. Right now, it feels as though we could all just be inside one of his tales, and he will soon tell us out of it, and we will be sitting with him by the fire in the hall.

"Alric is dead, Harald," Hake says, but the berserker is looking at me.

Everyone is looking at me.

"His story isn't finished," I say, but I don't know how it is supposed to end. It cannot end like this.

The sun is fully up, and the fog has been swept away. The water flowing out of the glacier weakens from a flood to a river. We wait until the ice has sloughed off all it can, until the strength of the falling stream is right with the season. Then we descend, slowly, until we stand before the glacier's empty belly.

Where once stood a monumental face now yawns a crystal cave to which there seems to be no end. Water-sounds fill the vaulted space, sigh-drips and gurgle-whispers. Spears and columns of ice the size of trees jut in all directions, while openings in the ceiling let in rays of sunlight.

"What a hall this would make," Raudi says. "Fit for giants and gods."

"We must see if the boats have survived," Hake says.

I nod. "And our own hall." And we must try to find Per and Asa. I hope they were out of the water's path as it fell.

We turn away from the ice cave to the ravine. The way down is even more difficult than the way up. The water has left the rocks wet and scraped bare. Hake slips more often, but we all help support him. Before long, we come to where we can look down on the field and the hall.

But there is no field. Only a shallow, black lake scattered with islands of ice. And beyond it, we see the path of the serpent, the long, wide swath of snow-stripped ground stretching to the ocean.

"Let's keep moving," Hake says.

We reach the base of the ravine, the edge of the lake-field, where ragged stumps are all that is left of the trees. But the woods up against the mountains to either side have been spared. It seems that as the water spread out over the open ground, it lost some of its strength.

Harald takes my hand. I look down at him and find him staring at the water. I follow his gaze.

There ahead of us, amidst the branches, mud, and ice, floats the ruined body of a man. And then I see another. And another. They are everywhere, tangled and broken, eyes open. This is where the torrent left some of its cargo of flesh. I turn Harald into me, and I avert my eyes. I do not want to see the faces.

We decide without speaking to avoid the field, the bodies, and the water. Instead we choose the long way around and head toward the standing woods, our procession hushed with reverence as we traverse a drowned world.

In the forest we find higher, dry ground, and before long we come to the clearing with the old larder. I cannot help leaving the others to go lift the trapdoor and call down for Asa. Or Per. But there is no answer.

"We'll find them," Bera says. "I'm sure they are alive."

They might be alive, but that does not mean we will find them. I do not think they would want to be found, even by us.

We reach the hall, which still stands, though sodden and damaged. The whole structure leans to one side as though favoring an injured leg. It might be livable, if necessary. For now, we continue over the corpse-strewn, puddled yard, past the charred remains of the other buildings, and through the broken steading gate. We follow the path down through the woods. The water-swept grass and underbrush lie flat, pointing toward the sea. I try to ignore the few bodies tucked and snagged in the tree roots. And then we reach the shore.

The ships are in decent condition, though sitting a little low in the water. They will need to be bailed out. But there are only two. The boat that first brought me and my siblings here, the smallest of the vessels, is gone. I wonder if perhaps the water ripped it free of its anchor, but if that was the case, I think we would see it floating out in the fjord. Unless someone sailed away with it before the flood.

"Could it . . . could it have sunk?" I ask.

Hake shakes his head.

"Could the three of them have sailed it alone?" Bera asks.

"No," the berserker says. "Ole and Per must have persuaded or bribed some of Gunnlaug's men."

Raudi grits his teeth. "The bodies were on that boat. Our men."

Hake closes his eyes. His arms drop to his sides, and his head hangs. His warrior-brothers, our fallen ones, have died a second death, for now we cannot bury them. Asa and Per have robbed us even of our chance to mourn. It is unthinkable, and yet the boat is gone. I listen to the waves lapping the rocks, the wind through the trees.

"What will they do with them?" Raudi asks.

Bera whispers, a catch in her voice, "Probably throw them overboard."

Hake lifts his head. "We must see to the hall. Bera, take stock of our provisions. We cannot sail these war vessels by ourselves, and we do not know how long until the king comes for us. Hopefully, it shall be soon. Go, now."

"Let us help you back up the path," Raudi says.

Hake looks up into the trees. "I'll be along on my own. I just need to rest a moment."

Bera and Raudi look doubtful, but they nod and lead Harald back up the path. I wonder if I should go with them or stay here. Hake lingers at the water's edge, his back to me. I don't know whether he wants to be left alone, or if he would let me try to comfort him, but a moment later he starts to wobble on his leg. I rush to his side before he falls. He tries to smile as I lead him over to a large rock, and he sits down with a grunt. I take the spot next to him. Together, we stare down the length of the fjord.

A moment later, he clears his throat. "I hope they at least said a prayer before they gave their bodies to the sea."

"I'm so sorry, Hake."

"As am I."

I slide my arm through his, and then I straighten up and lay my head on his shoulder. We sit that way for a long time, without saying anything more, and then we slowly make our way back up to the steading.

CHAPTER 23

A NEW WORLD

Everything in the hall is wet. We leave the doors open to let in the breeze and the sunlight until the hearth is dry enough to hold a fire. We hang out our blankets over the tables and rafters. The stores in the larder burned up, but the food Gunnlaug had brought into the hall survived. There isn't much, but with just the five of us to feed, it should last us a short time.

And we can fish. Ole left his net piled in the corner of the room where he used to sit and mend it.

Hake limps around inspecting the hall, every post and beam. In spite of its slant, he proclaims the building safe. So we go about the business of settling in. The blankets and floor dry throughout the day, and by the time the sun sets, we are gathered around a small fire in the hearth. I sit in shock, unable to hold all of what has happened in my mind. We eat together, but none of us speaks. What is there to say when nothing beyond the food and the fire makes sense?

I look at our little household and consider telling a tale. But I decide against it. I can't begin my story yet.

Alric's isn't finished, even though I know he is gone. And yet he isn't. How can he be gone when his voice is still in my ears, and his stories still hang in the air? Even if he were standing right next to me, it would feel no different than it does now, for he is still here with me. How can the others not feel it?

The next few days bring a lashing of winter back to the fjord, a chill in the air though the ground is warming beneath our feet. We're crossing that unstable battlefield of seasons where neither side holds its position for long. Hake's leg is back to mending, in spite of what we put it through climbing up the ravine and down again.

The hall seems so empty with just the five of us, and none of us ventures much outside. The ravens and other scavengers have begun to bring in their harvest, and death is everywhere. The hall has become a place for me to hide from it. When we speak now, it is in whispers. But I think the others are just wary around me. Sometimes I hear them in hushed conversation, Bera, Raudi, and Hake. And sometimes I catch Alric's name. But when they realize I'm listening, they go stiff and fall silent.

They think I haven't accepted Alric's death. But they don't understand, and I can't explain it to them. I am only starting to understand myself.

So I pretend not to hear them.

I wake the next morning, and Hake is gone. Harald and I sit at the table with Raudi, watching Bera serve up our day meal of porridge.

"Where is he?" I ask.

Bera sets a bowl before me. "Eat your food, now."

"Where is Hake?"

She doesn't answer.

Raudi hands me a spoon. "He said he needed to stretch his leg."

"Then why didn't you just tell me that?"

Bera points her ladle at me. "Eat."

So I force myself to finish the food she has served me. And then I wait. And I pace the hall. Harald stays close to me, his hand never far from mine.

At least once a day he asks about Per and Asa. Where do I think they are? Do I think they are safe? When will Asa come back? Why did they leave? The weak answers I mutter do not appease him. There are no answers, and even if there were, they would not change a thing.

It is afternoon before Hake returns. He staggers through the door, and we all rush to help him. But he waves us off and takes a seat, his leg outstretched, breathing hard. His clothes are soaked to the waist.

I fold my arms. "Where have you been?"

He tips his head back. "I need to keep my strength up."

"You need to heal."

"I can't wait for this leg to heal before I use it."

I shake my head. "You're as stubborn as Hilda was." And I walk away in exasperation.

The berserker is gone again the next morning.

I march toward the door. "I'm going out there to get him and bring him back."

"Leave him be," Bera says.

"He needs to rest."

"He knows best what he needs. He knows what we all need."

"Well, I need him, and he doesn't seem to know that."

Bera rubs her eyes. "He knows that better than you think. Just be patient, Solveig. He'll return soon."

And she is right. A short while later, Hake enters the hall, and once again his legs are wet. But they are also black with mud, as are his sleeves, and dirt outlines his fingernails.

"Everyone please come with me," he says. Then he pivots and leaves the hall.

We all file through the doors after him.

I squint in the sunlight and hold my hand to my brow to shield my eyes. The world is so sharp and vibrant, the blue of the sky, the deep green of the pine trees, the gray stone mountains. The sight of it is almost painful.

It takes a moment to notice that the bodies are gone from the yard. Is that what Hake has been doing? He leads us through the steading gate and down the forest path. The corpses have been removed from the trees as well. We reach the shore, and from there, the berserker leads us into the wood, toward the runestone.

I'm not sure why he would want us all to go there, but as we reach the clearing, and I see the monument rising from the ground, I understand.

There at the foot of the stone, next to a freshly dug hole in the earth, lies Alric's body. I look away.

Somehow, Hake found him in the wreckage left behind by the flood. He brought him here and dug him a grave. I don't know what to do. I don't know what to say. Hake stands near the body, his hands behind his back, his head bowed. But his eyes are watching me, and I see the worry in his face.

"Solveig." His voice sounds so gentle. "We must honor him. His story is ended."

When I hear those words, it feels as though my insides are wrenched sideways. How can it be ended? I start to tremble.

Hake holds out his hand. "Come here."

I step away from him.

"Solveig, he must be laid to rest."

"Only Alric can end his story," I say. "Only him. Not me."

Hake touches his chin to his chest, frowning. A moment later, he looks up. "Did he not finish your tales for you?"

"What?"

"When you were first learning, did he not finish the tales you started?"

"He did."

"Well, now it is your turn to repay him. He cannot finish his story, so you must do it for him."

"I can't." And I am afraid that if I do, his voice will fade.

"If not you, then who?"

My throat feels as though it is collapsing. He is right. There is no one else. I hug myself and cross the few steps between Hake and me. I take a deep breath and I look down at Alric's body. I force myself to notice all the signs of death. I make myself aware of his shrunken eyes. I acquaint myself with the paleness of his skin. I memorize the features of his empty expression. And then I begin to weep.

I fall to my knees, and cover my face. He is gone. He, of all of us, seemed able to pass through any storm, to find purchase and thrive wherever the wind and waves carried him. But this time, he did not allow himself to be carried. This time, he fought against the current. And so I kneel before his lifeless body.

Alric. Skald. My teacher, whom I only really knew by the act that took him from me. And yet he knew me, somehow.

He saw what I was, and who I was, though I was too afraid. But he found me and led me to myself. He showed me what a story is and can be.

Hake and the others let me weep and mourn undisturbed for some time.

But eventually, the grief retreats to a place where I can contain it, at least temporarily. I lift my face and take a surface-breaking breath. Then I rise and watch as Hake lays Alric's body into its grave. I bend and help cover him with icy half-winter soil. This hole must have been very difficult for Hake to dig.

Bera was right. He knew what I needed.

Nearly a week later, a mighty longship enters the fjord. And even from the cliff, I know it is my father.

We gather at the waterline to greet him. And as his vessel plows toward us, it seems that even the waves bow down before him. Harald bounces next to me, and I try to hold my head high, though my heart is beating fast. The longship touches land, and the men on deck extend a gangplank to the shore.

My father appears then, broad and tall, and makes his way down toward us. He wears a cape of fur over his gilded armor, and a golden helmet that shines like a captive sun. When he reaches us, he removes the helmet and reveals his mane of thick black hair. If he is surprised by what he sees, our ragged little group of survivors, he does not show it.

All of us bow.

Then Harald rushes to him "Father!"

"My son," our father says, and places a hand on my brother's head. He looks down at me. "My daughter."

I cannot help but drop my eyes. "Father, it is wonderful to see you. I thank the gods that you are well."

"And I thank them for your safety. Where is your sister?"

I look up. Of course he would ask about her, before he has even embraced me. He waits for my answer, his face a guarded battlement, and I don't know what to say to him. I do not want to be the one to tell him.

"Solveig," he says. "Where is Asa?"

Hake clears his throat. "My king, there is much you and I must speak of."

Bera is busy cooking the night meal for our father and the boatload of warriors he brought with him. When the messengers he had sent failed to return, he assumed the worst and set sail immediately, expecting to find Gunnlaug waiting for him. But instead he finds a drowned fjord, a broken steading, and only a handful of us remaining.

He and Hake speak at one end of the hearth, where they have been for much of the day. My father listens without showing any emotion, and I wonder if Hake has mentioned my desire to become a skald. I hope not. That I want to tell him, myself.

I think I may have an opportunity when my father approaches me later in the day.

"Solveig, I would speak with you."

"Gladly, Father."

He leads me out of the hall, out into the yard. Muninn is on my shoulder, and my father stares at him as we walk.

"Are you not worried your raven will fly away?" he asks.

"No, sir."

"Why not?"

"Because he did leave me once. And then he came back."

My father nods. "I see."

We walk around to the back of the hall, to the woodpile, and he gestures for me to sit on the stump there.

"I am troubled," he says. "Hake has told me much. Per's treachery weighs heavy on my mind, as do the deaths of so many good men. But Asa's betrayal is a dagger to my heart."

"She disappointed us all."

"She did. But for now, I do not wish to speak of her any further. I want to talk about you."

I wait.

"Hake has told me a great deal about what transpired in this place. I realize now that I am not as wise as I believed myself to be, and that is a hard thing."

I brace myself.

"I misjudged the people closest to me." He kneels down next to me. "And I have overlooked you, my daughter. Hake tells me that you are the reason he, the servants, and your brother are still alive. You have made me proud."

I repeat his words in my head, turn them over and over to make sure they are what they seem to be. I have waited so long to hear them. For a single, beautiful moment, I relish his approval. But then I start to wonder why I have wanted it so desperately.

My father rubs his dark beard. "He also tells me that you have something you wish to ask me, and that I should listen to you."

"I do have something to ask you," I say. And he *should* listen to me. Before coming here, I didn't think I had anything worth listening to, and maybe that is what has changed. Now that I know some of the strength I have inside me, perhaps I no longer need my father to tell me that I have it.

He smiles, and it lifts the shields from his eyes for a moment. "Ask me."

I take a deep breath of spring air, the cleanest I have ever tasted. All winter long, I dreaded this moment, but now that it is here, I feel only joy and pride. "I would like to be a skald."

He raises an eyebrow. "That I did not anticipate."

"I trained all through the winter with Alric."

"I would hear of him. Hake tells me he showed great courage in the end, but that you are the one who should tell me about that, also."

For a moment, I wonder why Hake would leave Alric's

bravery for me to speak of, but then I realize why. Hake has thought of a way for me to show my father my abilities, while paying honor to Alric.

"Let me tell you a story, Father. Let me be your skald tonight, and then you will see."

"You want to tell me a story? You and your raven?"

I look at Muninn. "Yes."

"Very well. Tonight, then." He stands, and I feel some of his soul-armor returning. "I must speak with Harald and then survey the steading. Go see if you can be of help anywhere. And I believe Hake wants to speak with you."

"Yes, Father."

He leaves, and I am at peace.

I find my berserker standing at the cliff. I join him, Muninn preening on my shoulder, and side by side, we face the ocean. The air, though not yet warm, smells of sea and pine. The sky is clean, new like the buds of green sprouting from the tree branches, and the fjord is open wide.

"I must thank you," I say.

"For what?"

"For helping me see what I could be."

"You would have seen it without me."

"I don't know if I would have. I don't know who I would be if not for you. Or for Alric."

"You would be who you have always been," he says.

319

I pull my braid around in front of me and untie the leather ribbon holding it. Perhaps there is some truth in what he says. There is still much I have to learn. I finger out the braid, and then I vigorously rub my scalp and let the wind run through my loose hair.

"Father said you wanted to speak with me about something."

"I do. Will you perform tonight?"

"Yes."

"A story about Alric?"

I smile. "Yes, Hake."

He nods. "Your father will be proud of you."

"Perhaps he will."

He looks at me out of the corner of his eye.

"I don't think it matters to me as it used to," I say. "I will be a skald, with or without my father's approval."

"For what it's worth," Hake says, "I am proud of you. But you are still young, and the world is dangerous. But I could . . . that is, your father might be more agreeable to your plan if he knew you would be safe. Perhaps . . . perhaps if I offer to come with you, wherever you choose to go. To guard you. Perhaps then he might agree." Hake swallows. "If you would have me."

My joy blossoms into a smile. "I wouldn't have anyone else."

He inhales deeply and returns his gaze to the sea. "I enjoy this time of year. Everything is so new."

He is right. We have risen from the flood to a new world. One upon which we can write our own stories. Craft our own legends. I do not know what Alric meant about me shaking the earth or shaping it. But I know that I feel as if I am just waking up. I do not have Asa's beauty, but I know that my stories do. I do not have Harald's strength, but inside I feel a power of my own.

I know who I am.

I am Solveig.

ACKNOWLEDGMENTS

Icefall was a challenging book, and I would like to express my gratitude to those who supported, encouraged, and assisted in the writing of it. When I first presented the idea to my agent, Stephen Fraser, his advice and enthusiasm were what gave me the reassurance I needed to approach something new and different. The individual members of my critique group each offered their valued and unique perspectives. Danielle Jones provided additional insights, as did fellow writers DaNae Leu and Carrie Brown-Wolf. I owe a special debt to author Rebecca Barnhouse, for it was while reading the manuscript for her novel, *The Coming of the Dragon*, that the inspiration for Solveig's story came to me. My editor, Lisa A. Sandell, guided me through the revision process with great patience and care, and her insights helped bring Solveig more fully to life. My coworkers in the Davis School District continue to provide me with friendship, especially Laurel and Don, who have each found special ways to show their support. As always, my family has been a source of love and encouragement, as well as much-needed first readers.

And finally, though there are no words to adequately express it, I am grateful to Azure, whose grace, intelligence, and understanding are what make my books possible.

ABOUT THE AUTHOR

Matthew J. Kirby has been making up stories since he was quite small. He was less small when he decided that he wanted to be a writer, and quite a bit larger when he finally became one. His father was a doctor in the Navy, so his family moved frequently. Matthew went to three different elementary schools and three different high schools, and he has lived in Utah, Rhode Island, Maryland, California, and Hawaii, which means that while growing up he met many people and had many wonderful experiences.

In college, Matthew studied history and psychology, and he decided that he wanted to work with children and write stories for them. So he became a school psychologist, a job he truly enjoys. He then went on to write novels, including his debut, *The Clockwork Three*, and now *Icefall*.

Matthew currently lives in Utah with his wife, where he still works with children and continues to write stories for them. You can visit him at his website: www.matthewjkirby.com.

Their stories come together like the turning gears of a clock....

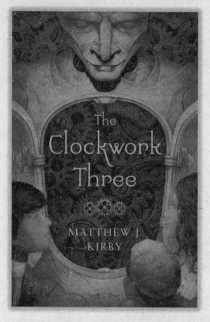

Giuseppe is an orphaned street musician who sees no way to escape his ruthless master, until he finds an enchanted green violin.

Frederick is an apprentice clockmaker with a past he cannot remember, who secretly works to build the world's most magnificent clockwork man.

Hannah is a maid in a grand hotel, whose life is one of endless drudgery, until she learns of a hidden treasure.

As mysterious circumstances bring them together, the lives of these three children interlock, and they realize that each one holds the key to the others' puzzles.

Uncover the secrets of Matthew J. Kirby's *The Clockwork Three*.